W9-COH-674

## ANNETTE BROADRICK

believes in romance and the magic of life. Since 1984, Annette has shared her view of life and love with readers. In addition to being nominated by *Romantic Times* magazine as one of the Best New Authors of that year, she has also won the *Romantic Times* Reviewers' Choice Award for Best in its Series, the *Romantic Times* WISH Award and the *Romantic Times* magazine Lifetime Achievement Awards for Series Romance and Series Romantic Fantasy.

## STELLA BAGWELL

sold her first book to Silhouette in November 1985. More than fifty novels later, she still loves her job and says she isn't completely content unless she's writing. Recently, she and her husband of thirty years moved from the hills of Oklahoma to Seadrift, Texas, a sleepy little fishing town located on the coastal bend. Stella says the water, the tropical climate and the seabirds make it a lovely place to let her imagination soar and to put the stories in her head down on paper.

She and her husband have one sone, Jason, who lives and teaches high school math in nearby Port Lavaca.

## KATHIE DeNOSKY

lives in her native Southern Illinois with her husband and one very spoiled Jack Russell terrier. She writes sensual stories with a generous amount of humor. Kathie's books have appeared on the Waldenbooks bestseller list and received the Write Touch Readers' Award and the National Reader's Choice Award. She enjoys going to rodeos, traveling to research settings for her books and listening to country music. Readers may contact Kathie at: P.O. Box 2064, Herrin, Illinois 62948-5264 or e-mail her at Kathie@kathiedenosky.com.

# Annette Broadrick
# Stella Bagwell
# Kathie DeNosky

# *Getaway*

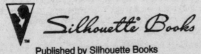

Published by Silhouette Books
America's Publisher of Contemporary Romance

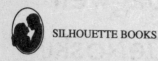

SILHOUETTE BOOKS

GETAWAY
Copyright © 2004 by Harlequin Books S.A.

ISBN 0-373-21818-4

The publisher acknowledges the copyright holders of the individual works as follows:

TWO'S COMPANY
Copyright © 2004 by Annette Broadrick

HOME ON LEAVE
Copyright © 2004 by Stella Bagwell

SMOKY MOUNTAIN CHRISTMAS
Copyright © 2004 by Kathie DeNosky

Printed in U.S.A.

# CONTENTS

TWO'S COMPANY 9
Annette Broadrick

HOME ON LEAVE 135
Stella Bagwell

SMOKY MOUNTAIN CHRISTMAS 261
Kathie DeNosky

# TWO'S COMPANY
## Annette Broadrick

# Prologue

"Your attention, please. All flights leaving from O'Hare International Airport have been cancelled due to the winter storm that has worsened in the past hour. We will keep you informed when the runways will be opened again."

A collective groan rose along the American Airlines concourse at the Chicago airport. It was three days before Christmas and the terminals were packed with people traveling for the holiday.

Stranded passengers began to mill around the area while three young women who sat near each other— one with a small child—continued to stare at the snow blowing past the large plate glass windows.

Finally, one of them turned to the others and said, "Nothing like starting off our holidays right, is there?"

The other two turned to look at her.

The speaker said, "Hi, I'm Megan Bennett. I live in Springfield, Illinois, and I'm trying to get to Knoxville, Tennessee. I have a cabin in the Smoky Mountains and I figured that would be as good a place as any to be during the holidays." She looked at the woman seated on her left. "What about you?"

The dark-haired woman said, "I'm Kayla Parker and I live in Salem, Oregon. A longtime friend and I plan to meet at St. Croix in the Virgin Islands for a few days." She glanced at her watch. "I have reservations at a hotel for tonight in Miami. The flight to the islands leaves early in the morning. That's the flight I don't want to miss."

The woman seated on Megan's other side, the one holding the young girl said, "I'm Greta Barstow and this is my daughter, Lilly," she said, smiling at the child. "We live in Kennebunk, Maine, and we're flying into Houston to visit Lilly's grandparents."

Lilly spoke up. "Uh-huh, 'cause we haven't been there in a long, long time. Not since Daddy died."

Megan and Kayla both gave Greta sympathetic looks. Kayla said, "I'm sure this is a sad time for you. Has he been gone long?"

"Three years. It was very sudden. He was only

thirty-eight. We both miss him so much. It's been tough seeing his parents, although they made it a point to come visit us a few months after his death. I feel guilty for waiting so long to bring Lilly to see them." She glanced out the window. "Even the weather isn't cooperating."

Kayla glanced at her watch. "I don't know about you, but I'd like to find some place where I could sit down to eat something. I saw several restaurants as I passed by. I'm sure we'd find someplace more comfortable than sitting here at the gate. Would you like to join me?" she asked, smiling at them.

Megan stood. "Sounds like a good idea to me. Let's all go. At least we can get something to drink. It's better than sitting here watching the storm."

Several hours later, the three women were seated in the Admiral's Lounge the airline had opened for some of the stranded passengers.

By this time, they were comfortable enough with one another to share more information about themselves.

Kayla asked Megan, "Will you have family waiting for you in Knoxville?"

Megan sipped on a cup of coffee before she replied. "Actually, no. My grandfather built the cabin and when he died, he left it to me, so I'll be there alone." She sighed. "I just want to get away from Springfield for a while. My life seems to have fallen apart these past few months. I got laid off as a travel agent a few weeks ago and let me tell you, this is not the best time of year to be looking for work." She glanced at the other two and said, "And I've recently ended a two-year relationship with the guy I've been seeing. I can't say I'm brokenhearted about it, but I'll admit I have a bit of a bruised ego at the moment."

She looked at Kayla. "So, is this old school friend a long-lost love?"

Kayla laughed. "Hardly. Karyn and I have known each other since the third grade. When we graduated from high school, she and her family moved back east but we stayed in touch by phone and e-mail. Plus I've visited her a few times since then. Karyn found a wonderful job in Manhattan, which she loves. Although we've continued to stay in touch I haven't seen her in almost two years."

Greta smiled. "You're fortunate to have longtime friends. I became so wrapped up in my marriage and being a mother that I lost track of most of my college friends."

"So you've finished college, as well?" Megan asked Kayla.

"Yes, but I'm still in school. I just completed my first semester of law school. I sometimes feel like I've turned into a professional student."

By the time the three women heard the announcement that some of the runways had been cleared, they felt like friends. Each of them had found a certain amount of relief by sharing some of their lives, their disappointments and their fears with people they'd never see again.

Until Kayla said, "You know, we mentioned earlier that our return flights come through Chicago. Why don't we plan to get together and share how our holidays went on our way back home? I think it would be fun."

Megan looked at her skeptically. "Well, I can tell you what mine's going to be like. I'm going to hibernate the whole time I'm in the mountains. In fact, I may not come out 'til spring!"

Kayla looked at Greta. "How about you? Would you and Lilly be willing to meet me on our return trips?"

"I'd like that," Greta said with a smile. "I'd love to hear what it's like in St. Croix."

"So would I, actually," Megan said. "So count me in on that meeting. I'd like to know that at least somebody enjoyed the holidays."

When they returned to the end of the concourse, where several gates formed a circle around the passenger seating, they all hugged and wished each other well, then boarded their respective planes.

# Chapter 1

By the time Kayla Parker's flight reached Miami, there was not enough time for her to go to the hotel. As it turned out, she was lucky to make her connection to St. Croix. She'd been up for over twenty-four hours and she was completely exhausted. Although she'd attempted to sleep during the flight, the drone and vibrations of the engines kept her from doing more than dozing.

What did it matter? At least she'd made her connections despite the long delay in Chicago. So what if she'd lost a few hours sleep? The delays and sleep deprivation were a small price to pay for the opportunity to visit an exotic island and to see Karyn again.

Kayla had never been to the tropics before and to be going during the cold, wet Oregon winter made the idea of sunny skies even more alluring. She was so pale compared to the crowds she saw at the Miami airport. A good tan would be a great souvenir from her midwinter vacation.

She and Karyn Stevenson had been best friends since they were children. They'd grown up in Salem and lived a couple of blocks from each other. Kayla's parents taught at Willamette University, which is where Kayla had completed her undergraduate program and where she was now attending her first year of law school.

Although Kayla had gone to visit Karyn in Manhattan a couple of times, Karyn's busy schedule in advertising had kept her from doing much traveling. As a result, Karyn hadn't been back to Oregon since high school.

As Karyn had said in their last phone conversation a week ago, the two of them deserved some downtime to kick back and relax, soak in some rays and enjoy each other's company.

Memories of her childhood played in Kayla's head as the plane winged its way south over the vastness of the Atlantic Ocean...

"Mom, I want you to meet my new friend," eight-year-old Karyn said to Janice Stevenson.

"This is Kayla Parker. Her mom and dad teach at the university."

Janice smiled at Kayla and said, "It's good to meet you, Kayla. Karyn speaks of you often. I'm pleased that your parents gave their permission for you to come visit us after school today."

That was the day Kayla discovered how different her home life was from Karyn's—her mom and dad showed great interest in Karyn's and her brother Mark's activities and made an effort to attend their children's programs and ball games. Mr. and Mrs. Stevenson actually seemed to enjoy listening to their children as they shared the events of their day.

Kayla knew her parents loved her, but the last thing either one of them expected by the time they reached their late-forties was a child. Her mother laughingly referred to her as "our little surprise."

Both of them were involved in their work and the many university activities. Neither of them could find much time nor patience for a little girl who was curious about everything and asked a million questions.

After Kayla met the rest of Karyn's family, she asked, "How old is your brother?"

"Twelve."

"Wow. I wish I had a brother," Kayla said wistfully. "I hate being an only child."

"Mark's okay, I guess," Karyn admitted, "for a boy. He can be your brother, too, if you'd like."

"Really? But then, you'd have to share him with me."

Karyn stared at her in disbelief and then they both burst into laughter.

The Stevensons' house became Kayla's other home. After learning that Kayla returned from school each afternoon to an empty house, Janice suggested that Kayla stay with Karyn at the Stevensons' until the Parkers came home.

Kayla's parents were fine with the arrangement, so Kayla was invited into what she considered the magic inner circle that was family life in the Stevenson household.

Sometimes the girls played catch in the backyard with Mark and his father or shot hoops with them in the driveway. Other times Mrs. Stevenson taught them how to bake cookies and other goodies. Both parents made themselves available if either of the girls had trouble with their homework.

When Karyn had told Mark that Kayla wanted a brother and he was nominated, he'd laughed at their silliness and said that he'd do his best.

Mark seemed to be good at everything he did... whether he was playing football or basketball, baseball or running track. He was enthusiastic about life in general, a trait Kayla admired and sometimes envied.

There were times when Kayla wished she looked

more like the Stevenson family. They were all good-looking people, comfortable with themselves and others. Kayla felt a little self-conscious when she went anywhere with them, but they didn't seem to care what she looked like, which was a relief, since her mother always found something wrong with her appearance.

Karyn was an attractive child who became a vivacious teenager without ever going through the gawky adolescent stage. In high school, Karyn was very popular and was homecoming queen their senior year.

Kayla, on the other hand, was anything but beautiful. She'd been a skinny child with flyaway hair, a condition that her mother found most irritating. Her mother harped on getting her to eat more as well as complaining about her messy hair. Because her hair was thick and fine Kayla soon discovered that any attempt at neatness on her part was generally foiled when her barrettes immediately slid from her hair as soon as they were in place.

As if that wasn't enough, she'd worn glasses for what seemed like forever—thick, unattractive glasses that made her eyes look weird. By the time Kayla became a teenager, she was still skinny as a stick and seemed to be all arms, elbows, long legs and knobby knees. When her parents insisted she wear braces on her teeth for almost two years,

Kayla had resigned herself to being ignored by most of her peers.

Mark had been the only male who wasn't put off by her appearance. He treated her the same way he treated Karyn—he loved to tease and torment them and in general played big brother in a casual, offhand way.

It was no surprise to Kayla that she developed a serious case of hero worship where Mark was concerned. By the time she was twelve, she'd fallen for him in a big way, a secret she would have died before revealing to anyone, even Karyn.

Mark, like Karyn, was popular with his schoolmates. He'd been captain of the football team his senior year, student body president and a member of the National Honor Society.

He dated the most popular girls in school and had something of a reputation for refusing to go steady with anyone. He enjoyed playing the field and the ones he dated were all beautiful and bright.

Kayla managed the bright part but knew that Mark Stevenson would never see her as anything other than his sister's friend. He spent time with her, listening to her with respect and as an equal. Mark seemed to enjoy getting into all kinds of discussions with her on any given subject, whether it was history, literature or philosophy.

She treasured those times with him because she knew that he saw her as a person, not a nonentity to be ignored like the rest of the boys did in school. He liked to challenge her to back up her opinions and would vigorously argue against them.

Mark made her think and process what she was learning in school and how that knowledge related to daily life. One of her favorite subjects was current events, a subject she'd always found fascinating, and they would debate for hours about what they saw happening in the world.

No wonder the two of them had chosen to become lawyers.

By the time she and Karyn entered high school, Mark had graduated, so she didn't see much of him after that. He'd gone east to attend Harvard and only came home for the holidays.

She and Karyn remained close in high school, despite their different interests and activities.

Maybe their differences drew them closer in some way. Karyn enjoyed people. She was outgoing and upbeat. Kayla, on the other hand, was never comfortable in a group of people and was hopeless at parties. She felt awkward attempting casual conversations with people she didn't know very well.

Tom and Janice Stevenson were justifiably proud of their children. What touched Kayla's heart was the fact that they were proud of her and her accomplishments, as well.

A miracle happened to Kayla during the spring of her senior year, something so great that it made her classmates view her in a different light and gave her some much-needed self-confidence.

Mark called her one evening. He would soon finish his classes at Harvard and had already been accepted into the law school there.

As soon as she answered the phone, he said, "Hey, Kayla. How's it going? I haven't talked to you in a while."

She clutched the phone in shock. "Mark? Oh my goodness. I can't believe you're calling me!" This was the first time he'd ever called her.

He laughed at her, but she didn't care. "You'll be impressed to know that my dexterity has improved to such an extent I can actually punch numbers on the telephone. So how've you been?"

Her heart raced, she trembled and could scarcely catch her breath. Of course she couldn't tell *him* that! "Fine," she finally managed to get out.

"Looking forward to graduation?"

"I guess. How about you?"

"Oh, yeah. I'm counting the days."

A silence fell and she felt horribly embarrassed. She wasn't used to making conversation with someone on the phone—except Karyn, of course. She kept reminding herself that this was Mark and she had always been able to talk to him.

She wondered if he'd be interested in discussing current events?

Finally, Mark said, "So, who's the lucky fellow taking you to your senior prom?"

Her stomach clenched. "Oh," she said, hoping to sound casual and relaxed. "I don't go to things like that. There's no reason to punish a date by stepping on his feet all evening."

"I'm crushed."

Puzzled, she asked, "What are you talking about?"

"Well, here I am hoping against hope that you don't already have a date to the prom so that you'll ask me to be your escort. Here you go shooting me down before giving me a chance."

Her face flamed. Mark wanted to take her to her senior prom? Not likely.

She faked a laugh, hoping he couldn't hear her unsteady breathing. "Who put you up to calling, your mom or Karyn?" she asked.

"I'm wounded that you would think such a thing," he replied.

She could hear the laughter in his voice, which made her smile a little. "Well, how did you know the prom was coming up?"

"Because they have one every year, that's why. It's a hallowed tradition and one you shouldn't ignore. So, what do you say? May I escort you to the big senior bash?"

She swallowed, butterflies invading her middle. "That's really nice of you to offer, Mark, and I'm touched," she said, "but I'd make a lousy date." The truth was that she'd never been out on a date. She'd gone to study sessions with several students where they might end up going out for pizza, but she'd never gone out alone with a boy.

"That's not true, and you know it, Kayla. What do I have to say to convince you I really want to go with you?"

To be able to attend the prom with Mark would be so great. Mark Stevenson, a good-looking college man—a popular college man—escorting her on her first date—the senior prom, no less!—was a fantasy she had trouble grasping.

Tears slid down her cheeks. "You're the best big brother a girl could have," she managed to say.

"Of course I am and don't you forget it. I'll come home that weekend. When is it, a couple of weeks from now?"

"Yes," she said faintly. "Thank you, Mark. You have no idea how much I appreciate your gesture."

The teasing note dropped from his voice. "Look, Kayla, you're one of the brightest and most likeable persons I know and I consider it a privilege to escort you."

"So, I'll see you then," she said, softly.

"Okay. See you then."

She hung up, her exhilaration battling for supremacy with her fear and anxiety. What would she wear? She didn't have a formal dress. She didn't even know how to go shopping for a formal dress. What was she going to do?

She finally did what she always did when she needed advice. She phoned Karyn.

Shopping with Karyn and her mom was always fun and looking for a dress for the prom was no exception. Her parents had been surprised to hear she'd been asked to go to the dance and gave her a huge allowance to buy whatever she needed.

Karyn had bought her dress two months before, right after she'd accepted an invitation to go with one of the most popular guys in their class. She knew which shops to go to and between her and her mother, the three of them found the perfect dress for Kayla to wear.

She was thankful the braces were gone, but there was nothing she could do about her glasses. She'd been toying with the idea of getting contact lenses for some time, but there hadn't been any urgency to do so until now. Unfortunately, she didn't have enough time to get used to them before prom night.

Besides, what difference did it make? There was little she could do about her tall, skinny frame. And Mark already knew what she looked like, which was a big relief.

The night of the prom Mark arrived at her home with an orchid corsage for her. He wore a black suit that set off his dark good looks to perfection. After he greeted her parents, he said, "Wow, Kayla. You look great!"

Her mother said, "It was a poor color choice. She has so little color in her face, I would have chosen something more vibrant for her."

The gown was a muted gold that fit her perfectly. She'd gone to a hair salon where they'd pulled her hair into a topknot near the crown of her head, allowing curled strands to fall at her ears and nape. They'd used so much hair spray that she doubted she could put a dent in it, but at least the style would stay in place.

"I do wish those bits weren't falling down like that...her hair has been the bane of my existence," her mother continued.

Mark took Kayla's hand and said to her, "I think you look absolutely perfect. Here, let me pin this corsage on you."

She would never forget that night. Mark had been so complimentary about her appearance that she soon lost her awkwardness in the unfamiliar situation. He rarely left her side, unless it was to get them more punch, and he danced almost every dance with her. Either they danced, or they watched the others while they caught their breath.

Mark had made her feel like a fairy princess...or Cinderella, all decked out for the ball.

He was most definitely her prince that night.

He'd made her laugh and forget about her lack of dancing skills. She'd ended up thoroughly enjoying herself and had been the envy of every girl there. She'd even caught a few admiring gazes from her male classmates.

Mark had no idea what a precious gift he'd given her that night. She'd floated on a cloud for weeks afterward until Tom Stevenson announced that he'd accepted a job offer from a company back east and the family would be moving that summer.

Kayla had been devastated. Her safe little world was destroyed by circumstances she couldn't control. She and Karyn wouldn't be attending Williamette University together, and what was equally painful, she was losing the daily support of the family.

It took her a long time to adjust to the loss.

Kayla opened her eyes and gazed out the window at the blue expanse of water below her.

Thank goodness for e-mail. Although she and Karyn stayed in touch, Kayla had never asked her about Mark, for fear Karyn might suspect she had deeper feelings for him than she wanted her to know. Karyn talked about him once in a while and Kayla would drink in any news about him.

She'd learned that Mark had accepted a lucrative position with a high-powered law firm in Washington, D.C., once he'd passed the bar exam. Karyn visited him whenever she could get away, but when she returned, she'd complain to Kayla about the women he dated.

"He goes for looks, not substance," she once complained. "They're either ambitious, using him to meet potential business associates, or complete airheads, which really gets me. I can't imagine what he sees in them."

Kayla chuckled. "Maybe you have to be male to understand."

Karyn laughed. "Undoubtedly. I know I shouldn't worry about him, but I do. He lives and works in the fast lane—works too hard, plays too hard and burns the candle at both ends."

"Ow, that must smart."

"Oh, all right. I'm overreacting, I know. He's the only brother I have and I can't help worrying about him."

Kayla listened and commiserated with her friend. She would always hold a special place in her heart for Mark, but he was part of her past. She'd let go of her dreams of Mark along with the rest of her souvenirs from childhood.

She dated when she had time, but hadn't met anyone with whom she wanted to give up her study hours to be with. Flirting was beyond her and she discovered that the men who invited her out were, generally speaking, self-absorbed, wanting to impress her with their accomplishments and plans for the future.

They were also impatient to get her into bed. Once they found out she wasn't interested—in either knowing or sleeping with them—they never called back.

Which was just as well. With another two and a half years of school to complete, her social life wasn't near the top of her list of priorities.

She'd made some changes in the past few years. She wasn't as shy with people. In fact, she was rather outspoken and impatient with lazy thinkers.

Her appearance had changed, as well. As her mother put it, Kayla was a late bloomer.

She'd gotten contact lenses and learned how to control her hair, and since Karyn had last seen her, she'd gained some weight.

With the weight gain, she'd actually developed some curves so that she no longer looked like the model for the stick figures used in illustrations. There was nothing she could do about her height and she was still slim, but the tropical clothes she'd brought with her would definitely show off her new shape.

Life was good. The chance to see Karyn again was exciting. Kayla had a hunch they'd be talking until they grew hoarse. It would be like a weeklong slumber party.

Kayla glanced at her watch for the third time in fifteen minutes. They were on their landing approach to St. Croix and she was more than ready to get away from airplanes for a while.

She was so tired that she yearned for a bed where she could sleep for a couple of hours. Karyn had been smart. She'd flown down the night before for a good night's sleep. Plus, she hadn't had to cross four time zones to get there, either.

Once on the ground, Kayla found transportation to the resort. During the drive she tried to see everything at once. The cab had no air conditioning and didn't need any. The breeze off the water felt wonderful. The view was even more beautiful than the photos she'd seen on the Internet.

When the driver turned into the road leading to the hotel, Kayla was astounded that Karyn had chosen a luxury resort for their stay there. Karyn had made this trip her Christmas gift to Kayla. With Kayla's limited budget and school expenses, she would never have been able to afford the airfare, much less such a sumptuous place.

The only thing she'd brought Karyn for Christmas was a hand-carved ballerina figurine made out of myrtle wood, a rare wood found in Oregon. She hoped Karyn still collected them.

Registration at the resort was in the main building, along with a snack bar, a café and a fine-dining restaurant. Something for everyone's taste. She giggled at the pun, knowing she'd gone past exhaustion into silliness.

The desk clerk gave her a map and showed her where her thatched-roof cottage was located. One of the employees of the hotel, a gorgeous young man with dark skin that glistened in the sunlight, picked up her bag and offered to show her the way.

The soft, warm breeze wafted around her and she could feel the warmth of the sun through her woolen dress. She could hardly wait to get out of it. For the next week she intended to wear as little as possible.

Their cottage was practically on the beach. It was built on stilts, which made sense. The steps were wide and well made and the porch held chairs, which would be a wonderful place to sit and watch the waves roll onto the shore.

Kayla half expected to find Karyn waiting at the cottage when she arrived, but the door was locked. She unlocked it and stepped inside, while her escort placed her luggage near the front door. After she thanked and tipped him, Kayla closed the door and looked around.

The front room was large and open, furnished with white wicker furniture and decorated in a tropical theme, with shell-framed mirrors, tropical photographs on the walls and colorful cushions on the furniture.

A kitchenette with a breakfast bar was at the far end of the room. There were two doors leading off opposite sides of the main room. She looked into one of them and saw that it was a bedroom. The bed was unmade.

Kayla carried her bag to the other bedroom. Once inside, she sighed with pleasure. Slatted windows allowed the breeze to drift inside. Mosquito netting draped over the bed from the ceiling. At the moment the netting was tied back at each corner.

She glanced into the private bathroom, delighted with its roominess.

Karyn was probably somewhere on the beach and not paying attention to time. She couldn't blame her. If she weren't so tired, she'd go look for her. Since she'd waited this long, Kayla figured she could stand to wait another hour or so.

The bed was sending out sleep vibrations that she couldn't resist.

She didn't bother to open her luggage. Instead, she showered, washed her hair and, once she was dry, wrapped herself in one of the mammoth fluffy towels provided by the resort. Back in the bedroom, she slipped into bed and stretched out with a relieved sigh. Her bed felt wonderful.

She'd hear Karyn when she came back. Until then, she'd get some much needed rest.

"Who the hell are you and what do you think you're doing here!"

A loud, angry male voice interrupted her dream

of a tropical island with a full moon gilding everything it touched. She forced her eyes opened and discovered the room was now in shadows. She must have slept for hours!

Where was Karyn? And who was this rude man whose voice had jerked her out of a sound sleep? The only thing she could see without her contacts was a shadowy shape standing in her bedroom doorway.

What was he doing here yelling at her, when she knew she was in the right cottage?

And how had he gotten inside? Had she forgotten to lock the door?

She responded to his presence by sitting up before she remembered she had nothing on. She grabbed the sheet and pulled it up to her chin.

It wouldn't do to sound as alarmed as she felt. "It's none of your business who I am," she said in an icy voice. "All you need to know is that my friend and I have rented this cottage for the week. I don't know how you managed to get in here, but if you don't leave immediately, I'm calling security."

"Go right ahead," the man snapped back.

"I will as soon as you get out of my room, you creep, so that I can get dressed."

He didn't move right away and she fought down the knowledge that she was alone in the cottage without anything to use for protection. She glared at him, hoping he couldn't tell how vulnerable she felt.

Finally, he shrugged and turned away. "Don't waste time. I want you out of here. Now."

He walked away without closing the door. What a jerk. She searched the sheets for her towel, found it, wrapped it around her and got out of bed. Despite her inclination to do otherwise, Kayla quietly closed the door behind him, locked it and went into the bathroom.

The first thing she did was put in her contacts. Then she went to her bag and opened it, quickly looking for something to put on. She grabbed the first thing she saw, a sundress that bared her shoulders with a full skirt that swirled around her knees.

Once dressed, she returned to the bathroom and looked into the mirror with a groan. She'd gone to sleep with her hair toweled dry. The result had her looking like she'd stuck her finger in a live socket. Well, he could just wait while she made up her face, wet her hair and combed it away from her face.

After she was through, Kayla announced to her image that she was ready to take on the marines—or at least one lone male—for the privilege of being here. She fully intended to call security and report him.

She stalked out of her room.

Where in the world was Karyn, anyway?

She found the stranger pacing in the shadows between the front door and the kitchenette in long, agitated strides. The only light on in the room was the one over the kitchen sink.

As soon as the bedroom door opened, he spun around to face her.

In an obvious attempt to keep a tight hold on his temper, the man said, "Look, if you'll just gather your things and get out of here now, we can forget this ever happened. If I were interested in having a woman with me, I would have brought one."

Kayla stiffened. "Are you implying—?" She stared at him incredulously, shocked by the implication of his words. Incensed, she said, "All right. That's it! Get out of here. Now." She looked around for the phone.

He folded his arms and leaned back against the kitchen bar where the light gave her a clear view of his face for the first time.

Her heart began to pound. No. It couldn't be. Not after all these years. Her heart had already recognized him while her mind worked to convince herself otherwise.

"Mark Stevenson?" she asked in amazement.

He straightened and his frown intensified. "How do you know my name? Oh, I get it. You got a look at the registration list. Sorry, but if you're part of the resort's amenities, you're wasting your time here because I'm not interested."

She did her best to ignore his words in the shock of realizing that Mark Stevenson was actually standing there in the room with her. She could be forgiven for not recognizing him at first, not only because he was being obnoxious, but because this was the last place she'd have expected to see him.

"Has something happened to Karyn?" she asked, going to the crux of the situation. Had Mark come here to break some unpleasant news to her?

He started toward her. "All right. Enough games. Just who the hell are you that you know my sister?"

"I'm Kayla Parker and you're being exceedingly rude, Mark. Or don't you remember me?"

Her words caught him in midstep and he almost stumbled before he stopped in front of her. "Kayla Parker?" he repeated incredulously, staring at her in disbelief. "It can't be!"

He didn't have to look so shocked, for heaven's sake. "Well," she said crisply. "It is. Deal with it."

He circled her before he said, "I don't believe this. What's happened to the girl I used to know?"

"I grew up, which appears to be more than you have!" She crossed her arms, feeling more than a little self-conscious while he continued to inspect the changes in her.

"I'm sorry, okay?" he finally said. "But the last thing I expected to find here was a woman I didn't know asleep in one of the beds."

"Call me Goldilocks." She looked around and started to ask where Karyn was when Mark said, "I can't get over how different you look since I last saw you." He touched her shoulder. "By the way, it's really great to see you again." He stepped back, grinning appreciatively. "So…what are you doing here?"

That grin of his still made her knees wobble. The changes in him during these past few years had only made him more attractive.

"Karyn and I are here to spend a few days together." She looked around the room. "Which brings up the question of where is she? Did you decide to come down with her? If so, I'm sorry I claimed your bedroom as mine. Of course I'll bunk in with Karyn and we can—"

"Karyn isn't here."

She'd been nervously chattering until his words penetrated her brain.

"Oh." She took a deep breath. "Well, I can see she's not here in the cottage, but where did she go?"

Mark's eyes narrowed. "I meant that she isn't in St. Croix."

Kayla stared at him in bewilderment. "I'm afraid I don't understand. We planned this trip months ago. In fact, the plane ticket and accommodations are her Christmas gift to me."

He lifted a brow. "Really? How interesting," he said, crossing his arms. "I wonder what this is all about?" He turned and walked over to the large window facing the beach, his hands resting on his hips.

When he said nothing more, she asked, "Are you saying she isn't coming at all?"

He didn't answer right away, which unnerved her. What was going on here? Finally, Mark turned to face her. "That's exactly what I'm saying, Kayla. Karyn isn't coming." He glanced at his watch and said, "I returned to the cottage just now to shower and dress for dinner. I don't know about you, but I'm starving. Why don't we sort this out over dinner?"

Thoughts, which she couldn't pin down, whirled around in her head. She remembered snippets of e-mails exchanged, of phone conversations, of their plans to meet here.

Finally, she nodded. "All right," she said. "I'd like to find out what's going on."

Mark went into his room, saying, "That makes two of us."

# Chapter 2

Mark sat across from Kayla in the dimly lit restaurant and wished he could stop staring at her, since he could see that it made her nervous. However, he was still stunned that this beautiful young woman was the same skinny, awkward little girl he'd first met when he was a kid.

He'd never noticed that her eyes were a smoky blue-gray. Had her skin always looked so soft and creamy? Had her smile always been so inviting? And her hair. It framed her face in soft waves and he wanted to reach over and slide his fingers through its silkiness.

She cleared her throat and looked around the restaurant.

He was doing it again!

"I'm sorry to keep staring at you," he said. "I'm having trouble adjusting my image of the girl I once knew to you now. I wouldn't have recognized you. Come to think of it, I *didn't* recognize you. How long has it been since we've seen each other?"

She shrugged. "Since Karyn and I graduated from high school, which will be five years this May."

"That long. It's hard to believe," he murmured.

The fat candle inside the hurricane lamp at the center of their table cast a flickering glow on her face. She turned her head and looked out the plate glass window to the shadowy beach, her blush a silent reminder that he hadn't stopped staring.

After a lengthy silence, Kayla glanced back at him. "Why isn't Karyn here, Mark?"

"What she told me was that she'd made these reservations several weeks ago before she found out that she wouldn't be able to get away—something about an ad campaign she was working on. She called me to see if I could go in her place since everything was paid for and she'd be unable to get her sizable deposit back. She never mentioned that you would be here and, I'll admit, I find her behavior a little strange."

Kayla folded her hands on the table and asked, "When did she make that offer to you?"

He thought back. "A couple of weeks ago. Why?"

"Because I spoke to her Saturday and she talked as though nothing in our plans had changed. Her parting words were, 'I'll see you next week.'"

He frowned. "I don't know what to tell you. I guess you'd have to ask her why she didn't mention to you that she wouldn't be here."

She rubbed her forehead, pressing the frown lines that had formed between her brows. It was obvious that Kayla was upset and he didn't have a clue how to deal with this situation.

Mark felt relieved when the waiter appeared with their meal. He couldn't imagine what Karyn had been thinking not telling Kayla she wouldn't be here. Had she been afraid Kayla wouldn't come?

For that matter, why hadn't she mentioned Kayla to him? They'd talked for a long while about all sorts of things and yet it never once had occurred to her to tell him that he wouldn't be alone down here?

"Well, whatever her reason, I'm here now," Kayla said, sounding weary. "As soon as we finish eating, I'll talk to the manager about getting another room."

"No! I mean, why would you want to do that? There's plenty of room at the cottage and Karyn obviously meant for you to stay there. After all, there are two bedrooms and plenty of privacy."

She shook her head. "As you so loudly pointed out earlier, you came here to be alone. I understand and respect that. I, on the other hand, came to see and visit with Karyn, which I'm obviously not going to do. There's no reason for me to stay at the cottage."

"I'm sorry about what I said to you earlier. I over-reacted, okay? I'd really like for you to stay, Kayla. I'd enjoy your company."

Kayla sighed. She was too tired to think clearly.

Had Karyn somehow guessed how hung up on Mark she'd been all these years? She'd been so careful never to give her feelings away. On the other hand, Karyn knew her better than anyone and may have known her secret.

"Are you afraid I'll take advantage of the situation?" he asked when she didn't respond, which caused her to blush.

"Of course not," she stammered. "I suppose that we could make the situation work. After all, we don't have to plan our time around each other. You can have your solitude and I can catch up on some rest."

"And we can also use the time to visit." He handed the waiter a credit card and said, "It's early yet. Why don't we walk on the beach for a while? It's really beautiful at night."

"Thank you, but I think I'll go back to the cottage for more sleep. I just finished finals after weeks of studying and I'm sleep deprived."

He casually took her hand, lacing his fingers between hers, as they left the restaurant. His hand felt warm, solid and reassuring.

"You mentioned finals. How do you like law school, so far?" he asked, once they were outside.

"So far, so good. You know what it's like. Some of the professors are excellent teachers and it's easy to grasp the subject. Others manage to make a person feel like an imbecile with their convoluted explanations." Her hand tingled where his palm rested against hers.

"I bet your folks are pleased that you decided to continue your education, aren't they?"

"Who knows?" She had to work to keep her mind on the conversation. She was so aware of him—the warmth of his hand, the hint of aftershave mingled with Mark's own masculine scent. "They talk as though they expect me to teach at Willamette University someday."

"I take it you want to set up practice once you're out of school."

"I want to practice law, yes. I don't particularly want to be out on my own, though. A midsize firm would be nice. But I still have a long way to go before I can make those kinds of plans."

They reached the cottage and walked up the stairs. Mark opened the door for her. "I'll see you later, then. Sleep well."

Kayla watched him take the steps two at a time and disappear into the night before she walked into her bedroom. Talk about sensory overload. Her plans for a fun and relaxing vacation with Karyn had taken a sharp turn. Somehow, she had trouble picturing Mark nattering away and reliving their old times together in a slumber-party-type situation.

Karyn's deception really hurt. Why had she told Mark one thing and Kayla something else?

Was this her way of playing matchmaker? Oh, she sincerely hoped not because Mark had always been, and would always be, out of her league. How embarrassing could a situation be?

All she knew at the moment was that she was too tired to think. Her nap had only made her groggy. Maybe after a good night's rest, she'd be better able to cope with all of this.

Mark walked the beach with his hands in his pockets. The tropical darkness enclosed him with his own thoughts. There was only a sliver of a moon and the stars filled the sky with their brilliance.

What was Karyn up to? He knew his sister well and this had all the markings of a carefully planned campaign. But what did she hope to accomplish?

He recalled a conversation they'd had over Labor Day weekend when they'd been in Connecticut to visit their parents. The two of them had been seated beside the pool at a table with an umbrella shading them. He'd slept in that morning and had felt more rested than he had in a long while.

He supposed that was why Karyn's comment surprised him.

"You know, Mark, you're looking tired. What's going on with you these days?"

He ran his hand through his hair and shrugged. "Work is going on with me. Long hours are part of an associate's job description. It's what we do."

"Do you like the firm you're with?"

"I suppose."

"You don't sound too enthusiastic, which I find a little surprising. I remember when you passed the bar and called to say they'd offered you a job. You were so excited and I thought you were following your dream. What changed?"

"I guess I really haven't given the matter much thought. But you're right. I've certainly lost my enthusiasm for what I'm doing."

"Why?"

He sighed. "I don't know. I mean, I want to practice law and I don't mind the long hours. I suppose I was caught off guard a little when I witnessed other associates jockeying for position and realized that their behavior was normal in a large firm. The fawning and the eagerness to make a favorable impression on the powers that be just aren't my style. In fact, I find it irritating. I wanted the work I do to speak for me, not how well I get along with the senior partners.

"I guess I'm not what they call a team player. I

want to do my job and at the end of the day go home without spending every evening after work schmoozing at a nearby bar."

"Have you ever thought about going solo?"

"As a matter of fact, the thought has crossed my mind, but it's much too soon to think about making a change. There's so much I have to learn. I need some trial experience before I attempt to go out on my own."

"Have you gotten to try any cases, yet?"

"I've worked on several—done research, prepared pleadings, that sort of thing. I was second chair on a couple of them, but I've never questioned or cross-examined a witness."

"That will come."

"Yeah, I know it will. Eventually."

"What about your love life?"

He narrowed his eyes. "What about it?"

"Still going the uncommitted route? Dating only the women who don't want to plan a future with you? Or have a family?"

He frowned at her. "And what if I am? I'm comfortable with the type of women I date. They're bright, intelligent women with ambition. I can relate."

"I think you'd be much happier if you had a wife and family to help balance out your life. Someone like Kayla, for example. Did you know she's going to law school now? The two of you have a great deal in common. You always liked her, as I recall. Would it hurt for you to get to know her as an adult?"

He looked at her as if he were certain she'd lost her mind. "Are you talking about our Kayla? Good grief, Karyn. She was part of the family. I don't think of her that way. Even if I did, I'd have a tough time dating someone clear across the country, now, wouldn't I? Now that you've poked your nose into my personal life, does this mean you're going to tell me all about the men you've been dating so that I can critique them?"

She grinned. "You really want to hear about my love life?"

"Not only no, but uh-uh. At least I have the decency not to pry into your life. The last thing I need from you is your unsolicited advice."

Karyn reached over and patted his hand. "I want to see you happy, that's all. I've watched you change since you finished school. You're more cynical now and more suspicious of other people's motives. I find that sad."

"What you're saying is, I've grown up. The clients our firm represents, the people we've sued and the general atmosphere and attitudes around D.C. all helped to remove my rose-colored glasses, that's all. People, by and large, are always out to get something, preferably for free."

"Well, I'm glad you took the time to come up this

weekend. I've missed seeing you. I think it's good to be with family, don't you? It grounds me in a way I can't describe. I suppose that's why I've been thinking about Kayla so much lately. She's a part of the family and I really miss her."

"For all you know, she's in a serious relationship and thinking about getting married. Remember how she used to talk about wanting a large family some day?"

"She's not. In fact, she shows little interest in the men she dates. She's always finding something about them that turns her off. She's so careful not to bring up your name when we talk that it's almost funny. She had the biggest crush on you when we were kids. Of course I wasn't supposed to notice her looks of adoration, so I never let on. I think she hasn't gotten serious with anyone because she's still carrying a torch for you."

"That's complete nonsense, Karyn, and you know it as well as I do. We were good friends when we were growing up and I think I would have noticed if she had a thing for me." He smiled. "What I remember are some of the rather heated debates we'd get into. She didn't show any signs of interest in me when she questioned my logic and knowledge about something. No, it's my guess that Kayla Parker hasn't thought of me in years."

Mark paused and looked out over the surf. He hadn't given their conversation much thought at the time, but he now realized that it hadn't been an accident that Kayla's name had come up in the same conversation as the suggestion that he needed to find a wife and start a family.

So, Karyn had decided to play matchmaker. He certainly had a few things he wanted to say to her as soon as he returned to the States. She'd been sneaky and underhanded and neither he nor Kayla appreciated her meddling, if Kayla's attitude was any indication.

Karyn had been right about one thing, though. He'd needed some time away from work and his busy schedule. He'd thoroughly enjoyed today, being on his own with no one to answer to, no schedule to keep and no staff meetings to sit through.

If he had to share his time with someone, at least it was with someone he liked and enjoyed being with.

Kayla had shown no signs of being interested in pursuing a romantic relationship with him, which suited him just fine. He wished that Karyn hadn't planted that seed in his mind. He was determined to put the conversation out of his head. He intended to enjoy his time with Kayla without any messy complications.

He wondered if Karyn would have been so eager to send her friend to keep him company if she'd known that he would have such an immediate and strong attraction to her? Or did that play into her hands?

Just the thought of actively giving in to his attraction to her and convincing her to hop into bed with him made him wince. She was Kayla, and that meant she was off-limits, no matter how much she turned him on.

On his way back to the cottage he was honest enough to admit to himself that she was going to be a temptation that he would find difficult to resist.

But resist, he would.

The scent of coffee woke Kayla from a sound sleep the next morning. She stretched and looked at her watch. It was after eight o'clock, which meant it was four o'clock in Oregon. Her extended sleep since she'd arrived had gone a long way to help her adjust to the time change.

She didn't hear anything from the other side of her bedroom door. Was Mark there or had he gone off for the day? She had mixed feelings about whether or not she wanted to see him first thing this morning. She needed to prepare herself for his being there.

She'd briefly considered calling Karyn before she went to bed last night but decided against it. Whatever Karyn's plans, Kayla knew it was no accident that she and Mark were here together. She just didn't know why. And she was disappointed that Karyn would pull such a trick on her without giving her some warning.

Once she finished dressing, Kayla unpacked her bag and put her clothes away. She wasn't sure what she wanted to do today. Should she spend the day on the beach or should she explore the island?

Today was Christmas Eve. Maybe she'd go shopping for souvenirs for her parents and some of her friends. She could pick up something for Lilly and her mom, as well as something for Megan to give them when they met in Chicago again.

With her decision made, Kayla left her bedroom.

Mark sat in one of the chairs reading a book, a cup of coffee at his elbow.

His slow smile went straight to her heart. "Good morning, sleepyhead. Coffee's made, if you want some."

He wore a sleeveless T-shirt and a pair of cargo shorts that showed off his muscled thighs and calves. She'd been so rattled last night, she hadn't really noticed much about him other than he'd filled out since she'd last seen him.

She walked over to the coffeemaker and poured herself a cup. She felt so awkward, wondering how she was going to get through the next few days without making a complete fool of herself.

"Did you sleep all right?" he asked, when she sat on the love seat opposite his chair.

"Fine, thank you." She sipped on her coffee. "I didn't expect to find you here this late. I thought you'd be on the beach."

"I went for a swim earlier, then decided to wait for

you so we could go to breakfast together. There's a great buffet set out for guests."

"Oh." She took a swallow of coffee. "There was no need for you to wait. I know you have things you want to do today. You needn't worry about me. I'll be fine."

"Well, that certainly relieves my mind," he said with a grin. "You make it sound like I'm here to baby-sit you and that isn't the case. I would enjoy your company for breakfast."

She flushed. "Oh. I didn't mean to sound rude."

"Have you made any plans today?"

"I thought I'd look around at the various shops to see if I can find a few items to take back with me. Plus, I'd like to learn a little of the history of the island, maybe visit a museum or two. I noticed there were brochures near the front desk that looked interesting."

"Sounds good. May I go with you?"

She froze. "You want to go shopping?" She must be hearing things. She'd never known a man who enjoyed browsing.

"Sure. It'll be fun to play tourist. We could rent a car and do a tour of the island. I'd enjoy that."

Spend an entire day with Mark? She'd be a nervous wreck! Then again, she'd always enjoyed his company in the past. If she could gain some control over her emotions and think of him as her brother, she might be able to pull off their unexpected vacation together.

She could only hope.

"If you're sure, then of course you're invited to go with me."

"Great." He stood. "Do you have a hat? You'll need some protection from the sun. And sunglasses. You might want to put on some sunscreen, as well. I wouldn't want to see your luscious—uh, lovely—skin fried."

His ears turned red and she realized he was embarrassed. Her luscious skin? Oh, my.

"I don't have a hat, so that will be the first thing on my shopping list." She went into her bedroom, and took a couple of deep breaths. Why was it she tended to hold her breath around Mark? She was being ridiculous. She was a grown woman who happened to be with an attractive man. She could do this.

He'd called her skin luscious. She glanced at herself in the mirror. More like deathly pale.

She gathered up her purse, glasses and sunscreen and left the room. "I'm ready," she said, wishing she didn't sound so nervous.

"Good. Let's go." He held out his hand to her and it was the most natural thing in the world for her to take it.

The shops fascinated Kayla. She found a large straw hat. Mark insisted on buying her a shell necklace to get into the island mood. He seemed to be enjoying himself and slowly Kayla found herself relaxing with him.

He treated her like a sister, teasing her and making her laugh. If she didn't know better, she might think he'd set out this morning to entertain her.

Once she'd bought something for everyone she could think of, they went to the car rental agency, where they were given a brochure with a detailed map for a self-guided driving tour of the island's historic sites and natural areas.

She'd forgotten how much fun Mark was to be with. His enthusiasm was contagious. They visited a rum distillery, a couple of plantation museums, a botanical garden and several plantation ruins as they drove around the island, following the map.

They returned the car a few minutes before the rental agency closed that evening.

"I imagine many of the shops and restaurants will be closed tonight, don't you think?" she asked Mark. "After all, it's Christmas Eve."

"Warm sand and soft breezes aren't much of a reminder of Christmas, are they? What would you like to do tonight?"

She didn't answer right away. She and Karyn had talked about things they could do to celebrate, none of which would work with Mark.

"Maybe we could have dinner at the resort and take that walk on the beach you suggested last night."

"Sounds like a plan. I was just thinking…were your parents upset that you chose to be away over the holidays?" he asked.

She smiled. "Obviously you've forgotten that my folks live in a world of their own. They'd already planned some kind of trip during Christmas break. I'm not sure what this one was about. They're either saving the whales, guarding the redwoods or fighting to preserve dolphin freedom."

They strolled back to the resort. They weren't the only ones ready to eat and the dining room was quickly filling up. "We'd better get something now, don't you think?"

She nodded. Mark had been attentive to her today. He'd made certain that she drank enough water, stayed out of the worst of the sun and in general had been a perfect date.

Only they weren't dating.

Once they'd been ushered to a table and were seated, Mark said, "I remember when we were kids. You used to come over Christmas Day and have dinner with us. It became a family tradition."

She smiled. "I was so grateful to be invited each year. Being at your house made the holiday more real to me. Your mom had Karyn and I help hang decorations in the weeks beforehand and had us help her with the baking—even today, the scent of pumpkin pie immediately takes me back to those days.

"She'd let us wrap some of the presents and made us promise not to give you and your dad any hints."

"I guess I never thought about this before, but I bet it was tough for you when we moved away, wasn't it? As Karyn is fond of reminding me, you were part of our family."

She didn't know how to answer his comment. Finally, she said, "I survived." She picked up the menu. "What are you going to have tonight? Everything sounds so good."

After they ordered, Mark returned to the subject of Christmas. "Once you're married, you'll probably start your own traditions around the holiday, won't you?"

She turned her head away and he studied her profile. Her beauty was understated—there was nothing flashy about her—and yet he responded to her on a deeper level than he had with any other woman. He felt connected to her in some primal way that unnerved him.

Too bad she was a family friend. He would have liked to explore this chemistry that had been obvious today. If it were anyone other than Kayla, he'd suggest they have an intimate relationship while they were there.

He'd already forgotten his question when she finally answered. "I suppose it depends."

Oh. Right. Her marriage and Christmas traditions. "On what?"

She lifted her shoulders slightly. "On who I marry and how he wants to spend our holidays."

"Oh."

"How about you?"

He took a deep breath. He'd asked for that one. The problem was he'd never given the matter thought before. Usually, Christmas was a series of parties to attend, speeches to listen to and other festivities with friends.

"I guess if and when I marry—which won't be for a few years—I'll probably leave all of that up to my wife."

She looked amused and he felt like squirming. "What about you? Planning to get married any time soon?"

She shook her head. "I want to finish law school and find a suitable place to practice first. That's going to take a few years."

"Do you plan to stay in Oregon?" Now why had he asked that? Of course she'd stay in Oregon. It was her home. And what difference did it make to him, anyway?

"I'll have to see who offers me a job. I don't want to go through the headache of studying and passing the bar in one state and then having to take it again in another. I have a few years to make that decision, too."

They ate their dinner without much conversation. He had no idea what she was thinking, but his mind was racing, questioning his reactions to her. Was it some kind of power of suggestion, thinking of Kayla and marriage at the same time, all thanks to Karyn's comments the last time he'd seen her?

Or would he have felt this same strong physical reaction toward her, no matter what?

He didn't know. All he knew was he felt uncomfortable with some of his thoughts. He reminded himself that this was Kayla Parker, a good friend, and he had no intention of coming on to her.

After they ate, they returned to the cottage. By common consent, they left their shoes when they walked out where the waves were rolling in. Kayla wrapped her sweater around her shoulders when they started down the beach.

"Are you going to be warm enough?" he asked after the silence between them had gone on for several minutes.

"I just needed something to cover my shoulders. I'm fine." She looked up at the sky. "You were right. It's beautiful here at night. I'm so glad I came."

"I'm glad you came, too." He'd enjoyed being with Kayla today. Her amazement and awe at all they had seen were like a child's. He caught glimpses of the little girl he'd once known, her eyes widened with wonder. He wanted her to be happy. What worried him a little was his unexpected desire to be the one to make her happy.

What was wrong with him, anyway? He never gave this much thought to any woman he was around. Maybe it was because he knew Kayla so well—the kind of childhood she'd had and the loneliness she'd once mentioned to him in a rare moment during which she shared her feelings with him.

"Are you involved with anyone?" he asked, surprising both of them.

"Do you mean, am I dating?"

"Yeah, I mean, seeing someone exclusively, that kind of thing."

"Why do you ask?"

Good question. What did it matter to him? "I don't know. I suppose I'm trying to get to know the adult you a little better."

"I date once in a while. Nothing serious. How about you?"

"Me?" He laughed. "You know me. I never date anyone exclusively. The women I see are generally ones I've met through my profession."

She stopped and faced the water, staring out as though mesmerized by the rhythmic sound of water rolling onto the shore. He didn't want to disturb her.

What he wanted to do was to kiss her, a thought that almost panicked him.

Eventually, she turned back to him and said, "I think I'm ready to go back to the cottage. This has been a busy day."

"Tomorrow, we'll do nothing more strenuous than lie on the beach and soak up the rays. Sound interesting?"

She grinned. "At the moment, I'd like nothing better than to stretch out somewhere. I'd be asleep in two minutes."

The closer they got to the cottage, the antsier he became. He was uncomfortably aroused and she'd done nothing—absolutely nothing—to cause this kind of reaction.

As soon as they walked inside, he said, "I guess I'll see you in the morning, then," and started toward his bedroom before he embarrassed himself.

"Mark?"

Mark stopped abruptly. "Yes," he said, sounding wary.

"Merry Christmas."

Aw, to hell with it. He walked back to where she stood. He hugged her to him and said, "Merry Christmas, Kayla."

When she looked up at him, it was the most natural thing in the world to kiss her.

It was supposed to be a friendly, brotherly, innocuous kiss, but once he touched her lips, he was a goner. He forgot that he wasn't supposed to touch her, much less kiss her. He forgot everything but the joy of having Kayla in his arms.

Her soft mouth opened to his in silent invitation.

He almost groaned out loud. There was a raging inferno inside of him that could only be put out by this one woman.

Her arms were around his waist and she could be in no doubt that he wanted her. Instead of being shocked, she moved closer to him until there was no space at all between them.

When they finally broke apart, they were both breathing hard.

Mark took her hands, which were shaking, into his and said, "Kayla, I'm so sorry that happened. I don't know what I was thinking. I want you to feel safe with me instead of waiting for me to pounce on you again."

She blushed a fiery red. "That's all right. I understand." She turned and went into her bedroom, closing the door behind her.

Damn. He retreated to his bedroom frustrated and irritated at himself. She been there a little over twenty-four hours and here he was, making moves on her.

He could still taste her on his lips. Angry with himself, Mark went into the bathroom to take a long, and very cold, shower.

Kayla leaned against her door, unable to wipe the silly grin off her face.

Mark Stevenson had kissed her.

Wow.

He'd been aroused, mute evidence that he wanted to do more than just kiss her. The problem was, she'd wanted to make love to him, too.

For most of the day, she'd been imagining what it would be like to come here for a honeymoon. Everything was so romantic. She'd fantasized a little, picturing herself with Mark. Not the friendly Mark who'd accompanied her today, but a Mark in love with her, a Mark who was eager to get her into bed.

Part of her fantasy had come true tonight…until he dumped icy water on her by apologizing.

Only then was she embarrassed by her wholehearted response.

How in the world was she going to be able to face him again?

Just being around Mark gave her a heightened awareness of her body she'd never felt before. Her breasts tingled where they'd touched his chest and there was a deep ache within her that yearned for release.

Once she was in bed and had turned out the light, she imagined Mark lying beside her, Mark kissing her, caressing her, making love to her.

Kayla closed her eyes and willed herself to sleep.

# Chapter 3

Kayla woke up early the next morning and when she noticed that the sky was beginning to lighten she decided to give up her efforts to get some more sleep. She'd tossed and turned for most of the night.

When she did manage to fall asleep, she'd dreamed of Mark. He'd made love to her with a passion that made her tingle just remembering it.

She put on her two-piece swimsuit and studied herself in the mirror. The suit revealed all her curves and the fact that she'd finally developed breasts. Eyeing herself as objectively as possible, she thought she looked good.

Would Mark notice?

After that kiss last night, she was encouraged to think he might.

The hours of sleeplessness had given her plenty of time to think—about her being here, about Karyn sending Mark in her place, about her feelings for Mark that had never really gone away.

Her most startling thought came when she wondered if sending Mark down here to meet her was Karyn's real Christmas present to her—the opportunity to have a red-hot fling with Mark.

Karyn had already told her that Mark showed no interest in long-term relationships. All of his were strictly the no-strings-attached kind. Kayla could live with that. The more she considered the idea, the more excited she became.

He might be a little hard to convince, though, since he'd shown reservations last night about getting involved with her.

However, the steamy kiss they'd shared encouraged her to think he could be persuaded to change his mind. If she were provocative enough. If she sent a few subtle signals to let him know she wanted to make love with him.

She sighed. Did she have the nerve to come on to him? If she didn't, she knew she'd go home furious with herself for not pursuing this intriguing idea.

Kayla hoped that seeing her in this next-to-nothing outfit would turn him on. Or she could forget about being subtle, trip him some evening and fall beneath him.

No, that would never work. He'd be so busy apologizing for his clumsiness that he'd ignore the fact she wanted him to make love to her.

She pulled her hair into a topknot on her head, put on the matching cover-up to the suit, slipped on a pair of shorts and went into the living room.

There was no sound from Mark's bedroom. She wondered if he'd had as tough a time sleeping as she had. If so, the last thing she wanted was to disturb his sleep. She quickly made coffee and, once it was ready, took a steaming cup out to the front porch.

She sat in one of the chairs, propped her feet against the railing and watched as the sky grew lighter and the clouds on the horizon turned pink. How wonderful. She'd never been on the east coast to watch the sun come up over the ocean. She'd seen some spectacular sunsets in Oregon and now she had the opportunity to greet the day with equal splendor.

Eventually, she went inside for more coffee before returning to her perch. Still no sound from Mark's room.

She sat and watched people stroll along the beach. A few intrepid souls were actually swimming. She idly watched as one swimmer turned and swam toward the shore near the cottage, cutting through waves with strong strokes. When he reached the beach and stood, Kayla saw that it was Mark. She grinned. So much for being quiet so she wouldn't disturb his sleep.

He paused to pick up a towel and continued toward their cottage while he dried his hair and body.

His swim trunks clung low on his hips and she sighed in appreciation. The man was quite a hunk. Even if she didn't know him, she had a hunch she'd want to hop in bed with him. Everything about him turned her on—the direct way he had of looking at a person, his gorgeous eyes and strong jawline, his well-defined shoulders and broad chest, his six-pack abs and long, muscular legs.

The tan he'd already acquired didn't hurt his looks, either.

Mark reached the bottom of the steps before he spotted her watching him. She hoped he hadn't seen her heated look or the fact that she was almost drooling. He looked at her warily until she grinned at him. He seemed to relax a little and gave her a sparkling smile in return.

She restrained herself from leaping on him and wrapping herself around him like an octopus. That wouldn't be very subtle.

"Good morning," he said, climbing the stairs.

"Mornin'."

"Did you sleep okay last night?" he asked, lounging in the chair beside her. He propped his feet on the rail next to hers.

*Okay, here I go.* She gave him what she hoped was a languorous sidelong look. "I slept okay. And you?"

He shrugged. "Okay."

They were both lying through their teeth and she knew it.

She nodded toward her cup. "I made coffee, if you want some."

He sprang from his chair. "Sounds good. Do you want more?" he asked, holding out his hand for her cup.

The idea of Mark waiting on her amused her. "Sure. I take it black."

"My kind of woman," he said, grinning, and went into the cottage.

Probably not, but who cared? She'd been given a golden opportunity for Mark to be the first man she made love with. Not that she intended to tell him, of course. She'd pretend to be experienced and sophisticated about the whole thing in order to convince him that she had no problem having a short-term affair.

"Here you go," he said, handing her a filled cup.

"Thank you," she murmured, her gaze running over his body. "Despite sitting behind a desk all day, you've managed to stay in shape, haven't you?"

He shrugged. "Exercise is too ingrained in me to stop, I guess. I find it releases stress."

She placed her hand on his bicep and gently squeezed, causing him to choke on his coffee.

"Is something wrong?" she asked.

He shook his head and coughed. "Just swallowed wrong, that's all."

She reached over and patted, then stroked his back.

He gave her a sharp look and she smiled at him. She figured batting her eyes would be a little too much. He glanced at her breasts beneath her jacket and then quickly away to her legs before he shut his eyes and took a deep breath.

They sat in silence for several minutes and then Mark cleared his throat. "I, uh, I'm really sorry about last night," he said. "I was way out of line and I apologize for coming on like a caveman."

"You didn't," she replied, her voice husky. "As a matter of fact, I enjoyed kissing you and hope we'll do it again, sometime."

He swallowed. Sounding a little hoarse, he said, "The thing is…I don't want to give you the wrong idea about me."

"And what would that be?"

"Uh, that I'd take advantage of you in any way."

"You needn't worry. I'm quite comfortable with you, Mark. There isn't anything that you could do to make me feel that you're taking advantage of me."

She returned her gaze to the ocean. The sun was up and the air grew warmer.

She crossed her ankles and stretched. "I believe that after breakfast I'll get one of the umbrellas the resort has for their guests and lay out on the beach. Maybe read a little, nap a little and just be a slug. What are your plans for the day?"

"Haven't made any. Mind if I join you?"

"Not at all," she replied, hiding her pleasure at the way her plans were shaping up. Proximity was a vital part of her first steps. "I don't know about you, but I'm hungry." She stood and as she lifted her leg to step over his, he quickly put his feet on the floor. "Thanks," she said, and went inside.

Mark felt like groaning out loud. Why had he asked to spend the day with her when he was already fighting all kinds of impulses where she was concerned? If he had any doubt about those impulses, it disappeared when she put her hand on him in a couple of places—innocuous places, at that—and he became instantly rigid.

Last night had been a disaster. Now he knew exactly how she tasted. Her response was everything he could have wanted…if he'd planned to take her to bed. He had to keep reminding himself that Kayla wasn't the kind of woman who would be interested in a no-strings-attached affair, which was the only kind he wanted with anyone.

He never lied to the women he dated about his unwillingness to make a long-term commitment. Those were his rules, up front…but he couldn't suggest such a thing to Kayla! If Karyn had told him the truth and Kayla did have a crush on him at one time, he didn't want to take advantage of any feelings for him she might have.

No. He needed to exercise some constraint where she was concerned. How hard could that be, after all? They were only here for a few more days and he wasn't some oversexed adolescent.

What he needed to do was to set some rules for himself.

Top of the list—no more kissing her, for any reason. He'd made it much more difficult for himself by initiating the kiss last night. She'd felt so good in his arms and her luscious mouth had been too much of a temptation to resist. Definitely no kissing.

No more holding her hand, feeling her warmth, thinking about how those hands could pleasure him. Wait. Even better. No touching her at all.

He would be friendly, he'd be casual and he'd enjoy her company, but he would not touch her.

Yeah, that ought to do it.

"Mark, could you rub some sunscreen on my back for me?"

He looked at Kayla, dismayed by her request. Such a simple request, really, and perfectly natural, given they had just settled themselves on a beach blanket beneath an umbrella.

Sunscreen was a must—otherwise she'd burn—and there was no way she could reach that area.

All right. He'd make an exception to his rule where sunscreen was concerned. He'd hurry to get some on her back and not think about the fact he was touching her.

She handed him the bottle, slipped off the beach cover and shorts she'd worn and turned her back to him.

Her disrobing took his breath away. He hadn't taken into account his reaction to seeing her in a skimpy swimsuit.

He muttered an obscenity beneath his breath, looked at the bottle in his hand and then to her back. Her skin looked like alabaster and was probably soft to the touch.

Before he could pour the lotion into his hand, Kayla stretched out on her stomach and propped her chin on her folded arms, watching the waves roll in.

That's when he got a good look at what she was almost wearing. Strings were the only thing holding her suit together. What was she thinking, wearing something like that on the beach? Why, anyone strolling by could see her lying there, practically nude.

He glanced around at the other people around them who were enjoying the sun and saw some equally revealing swimwear. He didn't give them a second glance.

Mark supposed this sort of thing was what women wore these days, but he had this insane urge to wrap the blanket around her and hide her from every male on the beach.

He poured the lotion into his hand and stared at his palm. There was no help for it. He had to do it. He spread the lotion evenly on his hands and placed them on her back.

Oh, yeah. Definitely soft to the touch. He closed his eyes. He could do this. He wasn't a barbarian. He stroked his hands up and down her back, feeling her warmth. Unable to stop, he poured more, this time directly from the bottle onto her back, and rubbed his hands over her shoulders and the nape of her neck.

She felt so good to touch; her skin silky smooth beneath his fingertips.

"Ohh, that feels so good," she murmured. Oh, yeah. He'd drink to that. For that matter, he might need several drinks to get his mind off her. "Could you do the back of my thighs, too, please?" she asked.

Of course he could. No problem. He unobtrusively tugged at his swimsuit around the groin area before transferring more lotion to his hands. He started at her knees and slowly worked up...and up...kneading the muscles and breaking out in a cold sweat.

His hands shook.

"Mark?"

He jerked his hands away from her. "What?" he said, sounding hoarse.

"Can you believe that Karyn would give up the chance to come down here? I find it mind-boggling. No doubt there's snow and ice in New York and she could have avoided the mess and the stress, had she chosen to. I'll never understand her decision."

She rolled over onto her back, her eyes closed. Her suit barely covered her nipples. He didn't remember her having noticeable breasts the last time he saw her. She certainly had some now.

He almost whimpered in his distress. She had a beautifully shaped body—slender with curves in all the right places. He was close to salivating. It was all he could do not to lean down, nose the material away and wrap his tongue around her....

He scooted back from her and, sitting cross-legged, casually placed his hands in his lap.

She slowly opened her eyes and turned to face him, a move that put her closer to him. "Do I need more lotion in front?"

"Probably not," he managed to say. He cleared his throat and fought to keep his eyes on her face. Her breast was only a few inches from his knee. He could casually stretch and move his leg so that—

Stop it!

"This is so nice," she murmured, her eyes drifting

closed. "Why don't you lie down?" she asked, patting the space next to her.

Because I've got to get my mind off of grabbing you, throwing you over my shoulder and hauling you back to the cottage, where I'd want to keep you in bed for the rest of the time we're here.

"Not right now, but thanks." He cleared his throat. "I think I'll go for a swim." He stood and turned away from her. He would put some distance between them for a while. He'd also figure out a way for her to get sunscreen on her back without his help.

"Sounds like fun," he heard her say from somewhere behind him. "I think I'll join you." He glanced over his shoulder and watched with something close to horror as she stood, adjusted her top and began to walk toward him.

Why couldn't they be in Alaska, where she'd be forced to wear some clothes!

He loped out to the water, splashing as he continued moving until he could dive into an oncoming wave.

He finally admitted to himself that he was in deep trouble.

# Chapter 4

Kayla stood in the shallows and watched him swimming as though his life depended on it.

Hmm. He'd been aroused, so that was a plus. The fact that he'd run to get away from her wasn't.

She looked down at herself. This suit was never intended for water. If it shrunk by one thread, she'd be arrested for indecent exposure.

Now what? Should she go swimming with him or return to the blanket and wait? She looked at the sun and decided she might have another thirty minutes before she needed to cover up. She wanted to get a tan, not a burn.

If proximity was the key, she needed to stay close

to him. With her decision made, Kayla waded out into the water and began to swim. She was a good swimmer, but he had a head start, so she wasn't sure she could catch up with him. If not, she'd enjoy her swim on her own.

He must have seen her behind him because he slowed down until she caught up with him.

"Oh, this feels so good," she said, treading water so she could catch her breath. "No wonder you were out first thing this morning."

"How are you holding out?"

"Great. I swim a lot at home. It helps to take the kinks out after several hours of hard studying."

"You're good."

She allowed the water to carry her closer to him. "So are you." She smiled. "I hope you're enjoying yourself as much as I am."

She watched several expressions play across his face before he said, cautiously, "Uh, yes. Yes, I am."

She draped her arms around his neck and leaned forward slightly. "That's good," she whispered before she kissed him, "so am I."

From the way he stiffened at her touch, she thought he was going to shove her away, but then he pulled her hard up against him and she discovered he was still aroused, despite the cold water. Her last thought as she gave herself over to his kiss was to hope they didn't drown.

They were both gasping for air when they finally broke away.

"If we don't watch it, we're going to drown ourselves out here," he said, sounding winded. "We need to head for shore."

She laughed. "I was thinking the same thing. And I need to get out of the sun. I've been in it long enough for today."

They swam in silence while Kayla relived the kiss. He'd kissed her as though he were desperate for her, almost as desperate as she was for him.

Thank goodness. By tonight, she knew he'd make love to her and she could hardly wait.

When they reached the shoreline they stood and waded out of the surf. Still without speaking they went over to their towels and her beach bag, gathered everything and walked toward their cottage.

"I don't know about you," she said lightly, "But I'm ready for a nap. That was quite a workout. For a while there, I thought you planned to swim the forty miles over to St. Thomas."

"Sorry. I get into a rhythm and don't notice how far I'm swimming."

Once inside her room, Kayla took her shower and afterward put lotion on her skin. She hoped she hadn't overdone the sun exposure. There was nothing romantic about a seduction scene if she was the color of a lobster.

She fell asleep and this time rested peacefully, waking up a couple of hours later. She dressed and went into the living room. Mark's door was open but there was no sign of him anywhere.

Not that his whereabouts mattered. He had to come back here sooner or later. When he did, she would be waiting for him.

Mark deliberately stayed away from the cottage for the rest of the day. He spent most of his time arguing with himself.

He'd kissed her again, blast it. To be fair, he hadn't had much choice, but he could have stopped it a hell of a lot sooner than he had. He couldn't seem to control himself when he was around her. Kayla was being playful when she kissed him. She didn't mean for him to grab her and practically devour her.

If anyone had told him that he would spend his vacation constantly aroused, he would have laughed in his face. He was a normal, red-blooded male with a strong sex drive. He didn't allow himself to get all hot over someone unless he planned to get her in bed as soon as possible.

Only he couldn't do that. Not with Kayla.

Why did she have to be so alluring? She'd become a vibrant and very sexy woman and if she were anyone else, he wouldn't hesitate. Instead, he ached, a condition he didn't expect to go away any time soon.

They went to dinner together that night. Neither of them had much to say. Once dinner was over, they returned to the cottage and Mark made certain he didn't touch her.

She didn't seem to notice. Just because she'd kissed him a couple of times didn't mean she would want to take the next step.

Once back at the cottage, Kayla paused and looked at him. He gave her what he hoped was a friendly smile. She didn't return the smile as she said good-night and went into her bedroom.

Once her door closed, Mark relaxed a little. He'd managed to get through today, but how was he going to resist making love to her in the coming days?

He reminded himself that she was too good a friend for him to use her that way. She was the kind of woman a man married, not played around with. Kayla was a love-me-forever sort of person, something he wasn't.

Someday Kayla Parker would make some lucky man a wonderful wife.

He wasn't sure why that thought didn't please him.

Mark went to his own room and went to bed, where he spent the rest of the night having erotic dreams starring Kayla.

By the next evening, Kayla knew she would have to take more drastic measures if she was going to get Mark into bed. He'd spent the day watchful of her every move. Whenever she'd moved closer to him, he'd immediately moved away.

Now what?

That night, she waited until they finished their meal and then said, "I hear live music coming from the lounge. I think I'll go listen to it. Care to join me?"

He studied her thoughtfully before he replied, "Okay."

Once inside the dim and crowded room, they found a table in one of the corners. The cocktail waitress took their orders and left.

"I never have time to go out to listen to music," she said eagerly, leaning toward him so he could hear her. "This is fun." Her lips brushed against his ear.

The dance floor was crowded, the dancers enjoying the fast beat of contemporary music. They sat and watched them and Kayla couldn't stop her foot from tapping with the rhythm.

After his second drink, Mark asked if she'd like to dance. She nodded. So far, the evening was going the way she'd hoped.

They reached the dance floor as an up-tempo number ended and a slow one began. Mark froze. Kayla slipped her arms around his neck before he could change his mind. He placed his hands on her waist with obvious hesitation.

"You're still a good dancer," she murmured into his ear.

"And you've improved tremendously since your senior prom," he replied, causing her to laugh.

"Taking me to the prom was the kindest thing anyone has ever done for me. You knew I'd sit home, otherwise."

"No, I didn't. I just really enjoy attending senior proms and Karyn refused to allow me to go with her."

"You're such a liar," she said, chuckling.

"I'm not lying now. You're an excellent dancer and you're one of the most beautiful women in this room. Did I mention how great you look in that dress? Every man here has kept his eyes trained on you since we walked in."

"Such flattery will go to my head quicker than the wine I've been drinking."

He sighed. "I wish things were different."

She lifted her head from his shoulder. "What things?"

"Just…things."

"Oh." She didn't pursue the subject because she knew what he referred to. The sexual tension that had been between them all day had risen dramatically once they began to dance.

By the time they walked back to the cottage, Kayla was so turned on by the night, the mood and the music that all she could think about was getting Mark undressed and into bed as soon as possible. She hoped he had the same thing in mind because she was running out of ideas on how to seduce him.

They arrived at the cottage a little past midnight. Once inside, Mark, faking a yawn, said, "I'm ready to turn in. How about you?"

She gave him a long look. Drat. He showed no signs of making a move on her. "I suppose," she finally replied.

"Well." He paused in his doorway a little awkwardly and looked at her. He wasn't even going to kiss her! "Then I'll see you…in the morning," he said.

"Good night, Mark," she replied and retreated to her room.

It was time for drastic measures. Subtlety hadn't worked. If she wanted Mark to make love to her, she would have to be the aggressor, like it or not.

She shivered. What if he turned her down? Could she deal with his rejection?

She didn't know, but she would have to make the first move since he obviously wasn't going to.

After looking through her wardrobe, Kayla slipped into one of her sheer nightgowns and studied herself in the mirror. This was it. She was either going to make a complete fool of herself and be soundly humiliated or…tonight she and Mark would make love.

# Chapter 5

"Come in," she heard him say gruffly when she tapped softly on his bedroom door. It wasn't as though he didn't know who was there.

Kayla took a deep breath and opened the door. He hadn't gone to bed. Instead, he stood looking out the window with his hands in his pockets. Without turning around, he asked, "What do you need, Kayla?"

"You."

He turned slowly until he faced her, his hands hanging at his side. He saw how she was dressed and in a strained voice said, "Kayla, I—"

"Please don't send me away, Mark." She clasped her hands to stop them from shaking. "Can't we pretend that there's no history between us? Let's enjoy the time we have together with no strings attached."

He frowned at her use of one of his phrases. "There are always strings, Kayla," he said slowly. "Always."

"Does that mean that every woman you've made love to—"

"I can't use you in that way. It isn't right."

"Oh!" she said, walking toward him. "Well, if that's the only thing holding you back, we don't have a problem. You see, I want to use you."

She stopped in front of him and reached for the buttons on his shirt. She was encouraged when he didn't stop her. Instead, he closed his eyes. "I don't want to destroy our friendship and this could very well do it, you know."

She slipped her hands beneath his shirt and slid it off his shoulders until it dropped to the floor. "I think this will strengthen our friendship," she said, kissing him lightly on the mouth. "I trust you. You aren't taking advantage of me. And I want you so badly I ache with it."

Her words seemed to break through his defenses and he eased his arms around her and held her, one hand pressing her head against his chest. His heart raced beneath her ear and he was trembling. But then, so was she.

She turned her head and touched his nipple with her tongue, causing him to jerk in reaction.

She hoped he would take over now because she

didn't have a clue what to do next. Tear off her clothes? Hop into bed? Peel off his clothes and kiss every inch of his body?

Kayla was relieved when he shifted slightly and slid his hands down her hips, gathering the material until the hem of her gown was in his hands. Then he stroked the tops of her bare thighs, not stopping until he pulled her gown over her head.

Not fair. He still wore his khakis and there she was without a stitch on. She could feel embarrassment race through her body. Instinctively she raised her hands to cover herself.

"Please let me look at you," he whispered. "I want you so much and I want to savor each step of making love with you."

Just like that, her embarrassment fled and her heart soared.

He drew her to the side of the bed and quickly dispensed with the rest of his clothing before he gently lowered her onto the mattress. He pulled his billfold out of the back pocket of his pants and removed a foil-wrapped package, which made her realize she hadn't given protection a thought!

Mark stretched out beside her, facing her, and Kayla placed her hand on his stomach, moving slowly down toward his aroused shaft.

"Wait," he said, "I, uh, I'm afraid that if you touch me right now, I'll explode." He took her hand and kissed her knuckles. She'd never seen an erection before and was surprised at its size, but reminded herself that she needed to act experienced in these matters.

The lamp by the bed made his skin gleam as though gilded with gold. He turned her hand over and placed a kiss on her palm.

"You've been driving me crazy from the moment you arrived," he said.

"In what way?"

"In every way. I was turned on as soon as I recognized you the other evening and I've been in a painful state ever since."

She wished he wouldn't talk so much when all she wanted was for him to—

He leaned over and kissed her on the breast. The intimate touch sent tremors through her body and when his tongue stroked one of the hardened nipples she almost gasped out loud.

She was so aroused she shook with need. Everywhere he touched ignited fires within her and she shifted restlessly on the bed. She should be doing something for him, shouldn't she? Her thought processes had long since disappeared. All she could do was respond to his touch.

By the time he knelt over her, she was close to frantic for relief. Instinctively she wrapped her legs around his thighs.

He pushed inside her and she immediately stiffened, causing her lovely sensual haze to disappear. He was so large.

He stopped moving. "Am I hurting you?"

She nodded slightly. "A little."

"You're so tight. I'm sorry. I should have waited until you were ready."

"I'm ready. Believe me, I'm ready. Just…you know…go ahead."

He pulled away from her and sat back on his heels. With one arched brow, he repeated, "Just go ahead?"

She gave him a vigorous nod and sobbed, "Yes, please!"

"Kayla?"

"What?" she replied impatiently.

"You've never made love before, have you?"

She opened her eyes and stared at him in dismay. "Well, I—it isn't like I don't—" She closed her eyes. "Was I that obvious?" What had she done or not done that gave her away?

The bed shifted and when she opened her eyes she saw Mark standing by the bed, pulling up his pants. She realized with horror that he didn't intend to make love to her. How could he just stop like that?

She sat up, grabbed the sheet and pulled it over her breasts. "What's wrong?"

He turned and glared at her. "You have to ask? You

were going to make love without telling me this was your first time. That's what's wrong."

She blinked. "Was I supposed to have attended training classes first?"

He spun away and ran his hand through his hair in agitation.

"What did I do wrong?" she asked, knowing she was out of her depth here.

He turned back and faced her. "What is this all about, Kayla? I mean, really. Is this something you and Karyn cooked up as some kind of joke on me? Because if it is, I'm not amused."

Her embarrassment disappeared and humiliation set in. With as much dignity as possible, Kayla slipped off the bed on the other side, wrapped the sheet securely around her and walked out without saying a word.

When she reached her bedroom, she closed and locked the door.

She stood with her back against the door. This was awful. No, worse than awful. This was absolutely horrible. What was she going to do now? She'd been soaring, knowing that Mark wanted her as much as she wanted him. He'd been eager, darn it. He couldn't have faked that.

So how could he stop at that point, leaving them both without some kind of relief?

She knew one thing—she had no intention of

coming out of her room until it was time to catch her flight back to Oregon. She wouldn't starve to death in a few days. Even if she did, starvation was preferable to facing Mark again.

She placed her hands over her face.

How could he believe that what had almost happened between them was some sort of joke? Or that Karyn was a part of this?

Maybe she was so inept in bed that he had been turned off, a thought that didn't help her mood, any.

All she knew was the evening had turned into a disaster of major proportions.

Eventually she went into the bathroom and stepped into the shower. She would not cry, she would not cry, she would not— Damn! Hot tears rolled down her cheeks as the spray washed over her.

She had no idea how long she stayed there, but eventually she turned off the water and dried herself. One glance in the mirror and she shook her head in disgust. She was not one of those women who could cry and still look great. No. Her eyes were swollen and her nose could lead Santa's sleigh.

So much for her new look. Mark must still see her as a gawky, skinny kid because he certainly wasn't impressed with her curves. What had ever given her the idea that he wanted to get her in bed but was too much of a gentleman to suggest it? Maybe a woman in skimpy clothes easily aroused all men.

He'd wanted to make love to her and then he didn't want to make love to her and she didn't have a clue why. She'd never heard such a pitiful excuse in her life. He couldn't make love to her because he would be the first man she slept with? Give me a break. Why should he care? She hadn't been in his bed to sleep, anyway.

If this experience didn't cure her of thinking she might still be in love with him, absolutely nothing would.

She towel-dried her hair and found another night-gown. She'd no more than sat on the side of the bed when Mark tapped on her door.

"Kayla?"

She stared at the door, thankful she'd locked it. She didn't respond.

After a long pause, he said, "Kayla, look. We need to talk."

She rolled her eyes and climbed into bed. Not likely during this century.

"Come on, Kayla."

Funny he should use that particular phrase, given the circumstances. She would have been delighted to if he hadn't left her so soon. She turned off the lamp.

"Don't be that way."

Don't be what way? An idiot? Sorry, too late.

"Look. I probably didn't handle this very well."

You think?

"It's just that— Oh, hell. Open the door, Kayla. This isn't any way to discuss things."

She got out of bed, grabbed the sheet she'd left on the floor, opened the door—catching him by surprise—threw the sheet in his face, slammed and re-locked the door.

She crawled back into bed and wondered how long it would take for him to realize she did not want to talk to him or see him. Not ever. Thank goodness they lived on opposite sides of the continent.

Maybe she'd move to Hawaii to practice law in order to put an ocean between them, as well.

Mark leaned his forehead against Kayla's closed door and sighed. He'd really made a mess of things. It was obvious there wasn't much he could do about it tonight if she refused to speak to him. Maybe by morning she'd be in a better frame of mind to listen to what he had to say. He owed her an apology for his clumsy behavior.

She had to come out sometime and when she did, he'd be ready.

He went back to his bedroom and tossed the sheet on the bed. What a night. When a woman was agreeable to going to bed with him, he had never hesitated before.

But this was different.

This was Kayla.

He stretched out on the bed. Great. His pillow smelled of her light scent. How was he supposed to sleep, when he was already uncomfortable? He hadn't hurt this much since he was one raging hormone disguised as a teenager.

How could she be so cavalier about her virginity? She'd lived to be twenty-five without having sex. Why suddenly decide to make love with *him?*

And why did he care?

He wasn't sure, come to think of it. He hadn't seen her in years and had lost contact with her, but that didn't mean that he didn't think of her as part of his family. He loved her like a—

Wait a minute.

He loved her?

Well, of course he *loved* her. She'd been a part of his life for more than half his life. Wasn't it bad enough that he'd lusted after her ever since she arrived?

Now he'd hurt her, the very last thing he'd wanted to do. He was confused about his contradictory behavior. No wonder she'd gotten upset with him. He was upset with himself.

Once he apologized tomorrow, he'd explain why they shouldn't make love so that she would understand. He wanted to make it clear to her that it wasn't because he didn't want to, because he did. Very much.

He just couldn't. Not and be able to face himself in the mirror each morning for the rest of his life.

# *Chapter 6*

Kayla got up the next morning with new resolve, after a restless night with very little sleep.

She would not allow Mark Stevenson to ruin her holiday. He wasn't worth it. Just because she'd had a silly crush on him while she was growing up was no reason for his rejection to ruin the rest of her vacation.

If she'd hoped to get him out of her system by making love to him, not making love to him worked a lot faster!

He'd done her a favor, really, although she had no intention of thanking him.

She dressed the same way she'd dressed each

morning she'd been there—shorts and blouse over a one-piece swimsuit she hadn't worn before—and packed her bag with towels, sunscreen and a book she'd brought along to read.

She studied herself in the mirror, relieved to see that her eyes looked normal—well, maybe a little pink, but she could cover them with her sunshades—and her nose no longer glowed.

In short, Kayla Parker was ready to face the world. She hoped.

Instead of making coffee at the cottage, Kayla quietly left and went to the dining room for the buffet breakfast. She'd slept later than usual and by the time she reached the main building the dining room looked full.

After she filled her plate she looked around for a small table that wasn't occupied. A man who looked to be in his late-twenties or early-thirties got up from one and she thought he was leaving until she realized he was walking toward her.

"Excuse me, but I saw you standing here and I wondered if perhaps you'd like to share my table?"

He had a friendly, open countenance and she needed to find a place to eat. "I'd be delighted. I appreciate your offer. Thank you."

Once seated, her breakfast companion said, "I'm Dave Talbot from Ohio." He held out his hand.

She shook it and said, "Kayla Parker, Oregon."

He was attractive with his blond hair and green eyes and he didn't raise her pulse one beat, which was a welcome relief after the past few days.

"Are you here alone?" he asked, while they ate.

"Well, yes and no. I was supposed to meet a friend of mine who planned to fly down from New York but at the last minute she had to work. When she couldn't make it, her brother came in her place."

"How old is her brother?"

She grinned. "Old enough to be annoying."

He laughed. "I've known a few people like that. Have you made plans for the day?"

"The same plans I have for every day. Stretch out beneath one of the umbrellas, swim when I get warm and enjoy the atmosphere. Why do you ask?"

"I'm going snorkeling. I'm meeting some friends—Gene and Carol Henley and Pat and Leah Greene—after breakfast. We've been spending hours each day exploring the reefs. You're welcome to join us, if you'd like."

"That sounds like fun, but I've never snorkeled." It did sound like fun. She'd enjoy being with other people after what had happened with Mark.

"It's easy. I can show you in a few minutes. None of us are all that proficient, but we have fun, which is the purpose for being down here, isn't it?"

Kayla was grateful for the suggestion. She wanted

to report back to Karyn that despite her not coming, she'd managed to have a good time.

During breakfast they exchanged a little history about themselves. She was amused to discover he taught psychology at a college in Ohio. His friends were also teachers. Why was it she seemed to be most comfortable with academics?

As soon as Dave and Kayla arrived in the lobby, Dave spotted the Henleys and the Greenes. After general introductions, the six of them found transportation and left the resort.

Carol and Leah were friendly, teasing Dave by pointing out that he'd gotten tired of being the fifth wheel in the group. Carol said, "I told him he should have brought someone with him, but no, he wouldn't hear of it."

Dave glanced at Kayla and slowly smiled, causing her to blush. Maybe this would work out okay. She would make herself available to join the group for the next day or so and then go home.

She dismissed Mark from her mind.


Where was she?

Mark had thought she was still in her room when he came back from his morning swim and saw that there was no coffee ready. He made some and decided to take her a cup as a peace offering.

When she didn't answer his knock, he tried the

door and discovered it was unlocked…because she wasn't there.

Had she gone to breakfast without him?

He looked at his watch. That was possible. He'd overslept since he hadn't fallen asleep until almost dawn. By this time she was probably already on the beach.

Mark returned her cup to the kitchen, then showered, shaved and dressed before he went to eat.

There were a few latecomers, like him, but otherwise, the place was empty. After a hearty breakfast Mark went looking for Kayla.

He'd never noticed how many people were on the beach until he tried to find one particular person. He peered beneath every umbrella and eyed every woman with Kayla's hair coloring.

A couple of the women smiled as if to say he was welcome to stay and visit if he wanted. He was glad to know there were some people who wouldn't mind his company, because it became obvious as the day went on that Kayla was avoiding him. And doing a fine job of it, at that.

He stayed on the beach until lunch, when he went looking for her in the restaurant again.

He saw no sign of her.

After he ate, he decided to return to the cottage to see if he might have missed her, but from the looks of things, she hadn't been there since he'd left.

All right. He'd wasted enough of his time. If she didn't want to be adult about the situation, he saw no reason to attempt to find her and apologize.

She'd been adult enough last night, hadn't she? Wasn't that what had been eating at him for most of the day? Eventually, he got around to asking himself why he'd stopped so abruptly last night.

He'd wanted her badly, there was no doubt about that. She *was* an adult and she'd made it clear she wanted him. So what, exactly, had been his problem?

Maybe it was because the feelings he had for her were considerably deeper than he'd thought, and they had shocked and scared him. His urgency to claim her last night hadn't been because he was looking for temporary pleasure but because she was the young girl he'd escorted to her senior prom, all innocent and trusting, looking at him with sparkling eyes of anticipation and making it clear she wanted him.

Of course he'd wanted her, but he'd also felt tender toward her, protective of her. And he'd stopped in order to protect her from himself.

Instead of having casual sex with a willing participant, Mark had wanted more. He'd wanted to hold and treasure her forever, to love and cherish her until—

Wait a minute.

Where had that come from? Those words sounded suspiciously like wedding vows.

He must really be losing it. He couldn't imagine being married to—

But he could. He could see himself living with Kayla, sleeping with her each and every night and having the right to do so. He could see her pregnant with his child; nursing his baby. He could see a little girl with flyaway hair wearing glasses and braces and smiling at him with her mother's smile. He could—

That did it.

He slammed out of the cottage and loped to the water's edge, not stopping until he was forced to swim. At the moment he felt he could actually swim the forty miles to St. Thomas, anything to take his mind off the dawning realization of his true feelings for Kayla Parker.

Kayla arrived back at the resort midafternoon. She couldn't remember a time when she'd laughed so hard and had so much fun. The two couples and Dave were easy to be around, the married couples telling funny stories about their kids and the school where they taught while she regaled them with stories about her parents and all their causes, which elicited laughter, as well.

She waved goodbye to the two couples and Dave walked her to the cottage.

"Thank you for including me in your group today, Dave. I had no idea what I was missing until I was underwater looking at the reef. It's spectacular. I would never have gone out by myself."

"The buddy system is a must when you're around water." He grinned at her. "Thanks for being my buddy." He stopped on the path and turned to her. "I've really enjoyed your company today. Maybe I can see you tomorrow. Didn't you say you're flying back the next day?"

"Yes. I can't believe how fast the days have flown by. It seems like I just got here." They continued toward the cottage. "I'll have to let you know about tomorrow, Dave. I need to do all those last-minute things we do before heading back to the real world."

He laughed. "Great way to put it." He glanced toward the cottage she'd pointed out was hers and said, "Looks like your friend's brother is at your cottage," Dave said, nodding his head toward Mark.

She looked and saw that Mark sat on the porch with a drink in his hand, his bare feet propped on the railing, watching them walk toward him.

Kayla felt a quiver of unease. Maybe her reaction was because this was the first time she'd seen him since she'd walked out of his bedroom last night.

Don't think about that and ruin the day.

Why was it that she could be so relaxed and comfortable with one man and be so agitated around another? The heated look Mark gave her as his gaze wandered over her body made her shiver.

When they reached the bottom of the steps, Dave said, "Hi, there. I'm Dave Talbot. You must be Kayla's friend's brother."

Mark ignored him. He looked at Kayla. "Have a good day?"

She forced a smile. "Yes." She looked at Dave and said, "This is Mark Stevenson, the man I mentioned to you." She glanced back at Mark. "Dave taught me how to snorkel today."

Mark took another swallow from his glass before he muttered. "Good for Dave," into his glass.

Dave turned to her and said, "Thanks again for going with me today. I enjoyed it. Let me know about tomorrow."

She nodded. "I will."

Kayla turned her back on Mark and watched Dave walk away, cowardly wishing she could go with him. Finally, she turned and looked at Mark. "Did you have to be so rude?"

"Yes. Care to join me in a drink?"

She glanced at the glass of amber liquid and ice he held. "What are you drinking?"

"Bourbon and water."

She lifted an eyebrow. "I didn't know you drank bourbon."

He held the glass up in a toast before emptying it. "Now you do," he said. Mark got up and opened the door for her. When she stepped inside, he followed her. He continued to the kitchen where she saw a liquor bottle sitting on the bar.

*I wonder how long that's been going on?* She had no intention of asking him. Instead, she went into her bedroom and shut the door.

Mark had the ability to get under her skin faster than anyone she knew, male or female. He could be so infuriating. Why hadn't she remembered that? There were several times when they were growing up that Karyn had wanted to kill her brother. At the moment, Kayla could have cheerfully throttled him, herself.

She stripped off her clothes and went in to the bathroom for her shower, still seething at Mark's high-handedness. There was no excuse for his rudeness. None at all. He'd made it clear that he didn't want her, hadn't he? So what difference did it make to him who she saw or what they might do?

Once she calmed down a little, Kayla rinsed off the soap on her body, stepped out and reached for her towel. She yelped in surprise. Mark stood in the doorway leaning against the jamb, a fresh drink in hand.

"Get out of here!" she said, grabbing her towel. "What do you think you're doing?"

"I've seen you in that state before, you know," he pointed out. She clutched the towel to her breasts. "I see no reason for you to pretend to be outraged now." He raised his glass and sipped. After a moment, he said, "I've been doing a lot of thinking today."

She turned her back on him and quickly dried off. After wrapping the towel firmly around her she squeezed past him and stalked into her bedroom. As though she were alone, she quickly put on her panties and bra, a pair of shorts and sleeveless top.

When she turned around she saw that Mark was still in the doorway to her bathroom, the only difference being that he had turned to face her. He finished his drink without saying anything else.

She narrowed her eyes. "How long have you been drinking?"

He shrugged. "Officially, since I was twenty-one, although I did manage to sneak a few drinks before then."

"I meant today, numbskull."

"Didn't notice."

She left the room and went into the living room. He wanted to talk, did he? Well, she had a few things she wanted to say, as well.

He followed her. She sat down and nodded toward the chair across from her. "If you have something to say," she said, "then say it."

"Does that mean that you want to know what I've been thinking?"

"I have a hunch I'm going to hear it whether I want to or not, so how about getting it off your chest?"

He nodded. "You know, you were always a smart kid. As well as a smart aleck. I've always liked that about you. Some things never change, I guess."

"This is what you've been thinking?"

"Why did you go off today without telling me you'd be gone for most of the day?"

She frowned. "I didn't think about it, I guess."

"You know, I find that hard to believe. I think you gave the matter a great deal of thought, Kayla. So be honest with me."

She studied him for a moment and then said, "Okay, I will. I didn't want to see you again. Is that honest enough for you?"

"Because of what happened last night," he stated, as though for clarity.

"Because of the way you behaved toward me last night, to be precise. I've heard of a woman being a tease. I guess I was a little surprised to discover that a man can be one, as well."

"Is that how you recall it?"

"That's what happened, Mark. One minute you're making love to me. The next minute you're up and dressed. There's no other way to describe it."

"Well, I recall last night a little differently. I recall discovering that I had a virgin in bed with me."

She scowled at him. "Don't worry. It's not contagious."

He stared at her and from his expression she could almost believe that he was concerned about her, which was a crock. "You could have told me," he finally said.

"What possible difference does it make?" she asked.

"Well, it told me that at twenty-five you'd never been with another man."

"Brilliant deductive reasoning."

"It also made me realize that I was glad that you've waited for a man who deserves you. That's the way it should be. The problem is that I'm not that man."

She stared at him in disbelief. "Are you saying that you stopped because your intentions aren't noble enough?"

He scowled. "Listen to me, Kayla. We've been friends for years and I value that friendship. I will not do anything to jeopardize what we have because it's very special to me. You're very special to me."

"Oh, I see. You've decided that I'm too special for you to take to bed."

"Yes. That's exactly what I've decided. Look, Kayla, I'm doing you a favor here. I don't have a good track record with women and I don't want to hurt you, of all people."

"So you decided to save me from myself last night, is that it?"

He sounded testy when he replied. "If that's the way you want to look at it, then yes, I think somebody needs to protect you!"

"And you've appointed yourself my guardian, huh?"

"Somebody needs to! What you did today was foolhardy."

She crossed her arms. "In what way?"

"You allowed some stranger to pick you up. You went off with him when you don't know anything about him. He could have raped you!"

"Underwater? That would have been quite a feat, now, wouldn't it?" She stood, her irritation getting the best of her. "You've had too much to drink."

She went outside, no longer able to stay in the room with him spouting his noble nonsense. A man who deserves her, indeed.

At least they agreed on something. He certainly wasn't the one.

Kayla walked along the shore, letting the ripples of foam flow over her feet.

What was the matter with Mark, anyway? Hadn't Karyn said that he never dated a woman for long? This setup should have been perfect for him, then. They had a couple of days to enjoy each other and then they could return to their own lives.

She believed him when he said he considered her a friend, but what was wrong with being friendly lovers?

Once the sun set, she returned to the cottage and found Mark once again on the porch. "Just so you know, I'm going to dinner," she said on her way by him.

After she changed clothes, she came out of her room and found that he, too, had changed.

"May I join you?" he asked quietly.

"I have no problem with it as long as we discuss something other than my lamentable lack of a sex life."

They ate dinner in silence. Mark wished he knew how else he could have dealt with this situation without making her angry. He couldn't think of any other way than what he'd done, given the fact she hadn't given him a clue beforehand.

He could understand that her feelings were hurt. More than his feelings had ached most of the night. He'd never stopped in the middle of lovemaking before and he was the first to admit he never wanted to do so again.

He couldn't imagine himself doing that for another woman. This was Kayla and he refused to harm her in any way. He wanted her to return to Oregon in the same condition she was in when she arrived at the cottage.

His sister had a great deal to answer for and he intended to have their next conversation in person.

They returned to the cottage in silence. When it was obvious to Mark that Kayla wasn't going to say anything more to him, he asked, "Are you going to see that guy tomorrow?"

She'd reached the doorway to her bedroom when he asked. She turned and looked at him. "I might. Why?"

"Just be careful, okay?"

"I'm always careful, Mark. You're the only man with whom I've let my guard down…for all the good it did me."

Some restraint within him snapped at her cool demeanor. Damn it. Why should he bother protecting her when she'd made it clear she wanted something else from him?

He strode over to her and took her by the arms. "All right, Kayla. I got your point loud and clear. You're ready to spread your wings and experience all that life has to offer, which in your case includes sex. Well, that's fine with me." He pulled her to him and said, "In that case, I might as well be the one to teach you what you're so eager to learn!"

## Chapter 7

She stared at him as though he'd spoken a foreign language she'd never heard.

He wanted her so badly he could scarcely hang on to the small amount of restraint he had left. Her attitude toward him since last night had taunted his decision to leave her alone. Why should he care about taking advantage of their situation if she didn't?

"Mark?" she said softly. "Are you serious?"

"I never kid about something like this. I want you. If you want me, too, then let's go for it."

Kayla couldn't believe what she was hearing... and seeing. Mark's heated gaze made her shiver. He really wanted her.

She threw her arms around his neck and kissed him with, perhaps, a little too much enthusiasm, she decided, when he stopped her by the simple act of cupping her face in his hands. "Let's take this a little more slowly, okay? Now that I know this is new to you, I want to take my time."

"After last night, it's certainly no longer new to me. I've been practically clawing the walls since then."

He grinned. "Good. Then you know how I've been feeling."

He lifted and carried her to her bed. They repeated their actions of the night before until he lay stretched out between her legs, tugging on one of her nipples. He was flushed and his eyes glittered and Kayla had never felt so much love for him as she did at this moment.

He raised his head. "Now," he said, breathing harshly, "where were we before our intermission?"

She laughed, more out of joy than anything else. "I believe we were…right…there," she said with a sigh as he slowly pressed into her. "Oh, yes. Yes. That's exactly…"

She lost her train of thought.

He took his time, despite her efforts to hurry him, and rocked against her with deliberate movements until he was—finally!—fully inside.

"I'm sorry if I hurt you," he said, panting.

She shook her head, smiling up into his adorable face. "No. I never noticed." She raised her mouth to his and he took her offering, passionately kissing her, his tongue keeping the same rhythm he'd set below.

Kayla clenched around him, feeling that she was about to explode. She wanted to hang on, but it was too late. With a cry she succumbed to the myriad sensations that overwhelmed her.

Her climax triggered his. He groaned and his tempo increased until he collapsed beside her, gasping for air.

She lay there for the longest while and knew she wore a silly grin on her face. After all the fuss, Mark had made love to her and it had been better than she could have possibly imagined.

Eventually, he turned his head and looked at her.

She grinned at him.

A slow smile finally formed on his face. "Are you okay?" he finally asked.

She sighed blissfully. "More than okay. Thank you, Mark."

"Please believe me when I say that it was my pleasure."

She turned to face him and put her hand on his chest. "Your heart is racing."

"Not surprising."

"Are you sorry you made love to me?"

"I'd be lying if I said yes. You're certainly old enough to know your own mind, but I feel like I've let you down, somehow. You deserve more than a casual affair."

She traced his nose and brows with her finger. "Oh, I don't know. I think I got just what I deserved."

He took her hand and placed a kiss in her palm. "You gave me an invaluable gift. I'll never forget it."

She left the bed and went into the bathroom. "Wow," she whispered to her mirrored image, "Dreams really do come true."

She turned the water on in the shower and stepped inside. Every muscle in her body was relaxed and her bones were almost liquefied. She leaned her palms against the shower wall and closed her eyes.

She jumped in surprise when she felt a hand glide down her back.

"Didn't mean to startle you. I thought you heard me," Mark said, picking up the soap and washing her back. "Are you sore?"

"A little."

"We'll take it easy, then."

She turned so that she was facing him and immediately noticed that he was already aroused again. "I didn't think a man could, er, recover so quickly."

He gently kissed her. "Believe me, this is far from normal for me. For some reason, all I have to do is think about you and I immediately grow hard."

He bent over to her breast and, cupping it in his hand, tugged on the nipple with his mouth.

Kayla had trouble thinking when he did things like

that. Especially when he lifted her against the shower stall and pulled her legs around his waist.

"Comfy?"

She could feel him touching her on that delicate spot between her legs. She smiled and closed her eyes, her arms draped around him.

"Umm-hmm."

"Good." He slowly lowered her onto his shaft until she was fully seated against him, his arms holding her close.

She heard the soap hit the floor and bounce, but who cared? She was fully open to him and pushed ever closer, while he moved swiftly inside her, bracing her against the shower wall.

Without warning, she exploded in a thousand different pieces, unable to stop herself. She tightened her arms and legs around him, feeling the deep pulsating of her climax within her. A few moments later he groaned and buried himself deep inside her.

Somehow they managed to dry off and return to bed, both of them too limp to move. Kayla fell asleep with her head on Mark's shoulder.

Sometime during the night Mark woke himself up reaching for Kayla, who had turned over and was no longer touching him. The sudden knowledge that he'd missed having her close to him even when he was asleep shocked him into full wakefulness.

He carefully got out of bed and returned to his own room, where he lay awake for the rest of the night.

Something was happening to him that he didn't like. Something that was a threat to his way of life.

He didn't want to say goodbye to Kayla in a couple of days. He didn't want to say goodbye to her at all.

He'd known when he gave in to both their desires and made love to her that things might be different. He figured there'd be some awkwardness, but there hadn't been. He felt so much in tune with her, it was almost as if he knew what she wanted or needed from him before she did.

All the aspects of who she was, from a child to this moment, had come together for him and he admitted to himself his worst fears.

He was in love.

He didn't want to be. He'd made it a practice for years to run from even a hint of the feeling. He loved his independence and love made him too vulnerable. He didn't want to be vulnerable with anyone.

But it was too late to change things because he knew that he was in love with Kayla Parker. He'd loved her for years, but somehow becoming intimate with her had forced him to admit what he'd gone to great lengths to hide from himself since she'd first arrived.

So now what?

Nothing had changed between them. He'd done a

fine job of convincing her that he wasn't looking for a serious relationship. Too bad he hadn't been able to convince himself, because admitting he loved her didn't change anything.

He lived in D.C. She lived in Oregon. He worked long hours. She was in law school, studying for long hours. How could they possibly maintain a relationship with those odds against them?

He didn't know. All he knew was that for the rest of his life he would be miserable without her.

# Chapter 8

Kayla was alone when she woke up the next morning.

She wasn't certain why she was surprised, really. Theirs wasn't some big love affair. In fact, with only another two days left, she could scarcely call it an affair at all.

So now she knew what it was like to make love to Mark. She thought about the night before wistfully. He'd been so gentle with her, so intent on not causing her pain.

She knew she'd carry the memory in her heart for a long time. She wasn't at all sure she'd ever want to go to bed with another man.

So, maybe he'd been right to tell her to wait for a man who deserved her. They differed on whether or not he deserved her and he'd made *his* feelings clear on the subject.

Lying there wasn't getting her anywhere. Today was her last full day in St. Croix and she intended to make the most of it. By the time she showered and dressed, Kayla had decided to adopt a casual attitude to their situation. She'd be friendly but would in no way act as though anything extraordinary had happened.

She was an adult. She could do this.

Kayla opened her bedroom door and stepped into the living room, ready to greet Mark with a friendly hello.

The room was empty.

Oh. Right. He always went swimming first thing in the morning. Just as well. She'd do better greeting him after a cup or two of coffee, anyway.

Once the coffee was made, she took her cup out to the porch and sat down. She was going to miss this view. She wasn't looking forward to returning to the cold and damp of Oregon.

She looked at her legs stretched out in front of her, where her feet rested on the rail. They looked tanned. As did her arms. She sighed with satisfaction. She would return home rested and resolved to get on with her life.

Regardless of what happened from now on, she would never regret making love to him.

She finished her first cup of coffee and stood to get another one when she happened to notice a man walking along the edge of the water, dressed in a shirt and long pants, which were rolled to his calves. He walked slowly, his head down, and she thought at first that it was a new arrival to the island looking for shells.

But there was something familiar about him. She was startled when she realized the man was Mark, who hadn't gone swimming after all. She waited for him with what she hoped was a pleasant smile on her face.

Her smile faded when he grew close enough for her to see his face. He looked exhausted and he wore the same clothes he'd worn to dinner last night instead of his usual beachwear.

He didn't see her until he started up the steps and when he did, his face lit up. That was the only way she knew to describe the glow that suffused him. When his smile held all the intimacy they had shared, she couldn't help the rush of love and desire that washed over her.

"Good morning," he said, pausing in front of her. "Did you sleep all right?"

She nodded, studying the lines around his eyes and the one between his brows. "You don't look like you slept at all. Is anything wrong?"

He dropped his arm around her and hugged her to him. "No serious conversations until I've had some coffee." He rubbed his bristled face. "A shave and shower wouldn't hurt, either."

Once inside the cottage, she said, "I'll get you some coffee. If you want to shower, go ahead. I'll bring the coffee in to you."

He nodded and she watched him walk into his bedroom, unbuttoning his shirt.

Something was wrong. Really wrong. She hoped he wasn't already regretting what had happened. Oh, please, don't let that be his reaction.

She carried his cup into his room and heard the shower running. Aha. She set his cup down and quickly undressed. He glanced around when she opened the shower door and stepped inside.

"I decided that as tired as you look, you probably need some help with your shower. I'm volunteering."

She met his gaze while she busily lathered him with soap, smoothing it over his chest, arms and shoulders. The intensity in his eyes was intoxicating.

She continued down his body, soaping his legs and feet before straightening and taking him in her hand. She was amazed that anything on the human body could be so hard and yet feel so smooth to the touch.

He hissed through his teeth. This time she met his eyes and let him know she was as aroused as he was. He lifted her and she wrapped her legs around his hips. The water had washed the soap off him. She nibbled his ear and he quivered before he positioned her so that he could slide into her.

She rode him, lifting her hips and sliding back down in a rapid rhythm that threw them both into a blistering release. Mark's arms shook where he'd been leaning against the shower stall. She slid her feet to the floor.

Showering had never been so much fun.

She stepped out and grabbed a towel for her hair and handed him another one. While he dried he watched her towel her hair and body. How could she feel shy when he looked at her as though she were the most magnificent woman he'd ever seen?

When she began to wrap the towel around her, he stopped her by encircling her wrist with his thumb and finger. "Don't. Please. I can't seem to get enough of you. The more I make love to you, the more I desire you. It's almost like an addiction.

She kissed him lightly. "I feel the same way."

He took her to his bed.

They were late for breakfast.

When they walked into the restaurant, Kayla spotted Dave having coffee at the table they'd shared the day before. Had it only been twenty-four hours since she'd wanted to stay as far away from Mark as possible?

"I'll meet you at the buffet," she said to Mark, and continued to where Dave sat. He immediately stood.

"Oh, don't get up. I just want to tell you that I won't be able to do anything with you today. I hope I haven't kept you waiting."

He sat down. "It doesn't matter. I'm sorry, though. I was looking forward to spending more time with you."

"The thing is," she began, searching for words, "I—"

"You've made up with your friend's brother. I know."

"You know?" she echoed, surprised.

"Whisker burns along your neck are a fairly accurate indication. So what was yesterday about? Did you hope to make him jealous?"

"No. I really didn't want to be around him yesterday."

"Then I'm happy that you chose to be with me." He glanced past her. "If those daggers he's shooting at me were real, I'd be dead by now," he said conversationally.

She didn't have to look to know that Mark wasn't pleased with their visiting. She held out her hand. "It was great to meet you, Dave."

"Same here," he replied.

She joined Mark at the buffet. "What was that all about?" he said gruffly.

She picked up a plate and began to fill it. Without looking at him, she said, "Why do you ask? Are you jealous?"

"Of course I'm jealous. Am I going to be censored for that?"

She looked at him and batted her eyes. "My hero. Ready to do battle on my behalf."

He finished filling his plate and grumbled, "You know, you're getting way too much enjoyment out of this."

She spotted a table by the window. Once they were seated, she reached over and took his hand. "You needn't worry, you know. You've already put your mark on me."

He frowned. "What are you talking about? Did I bruise you?"

She ran her fingers along her neck from her ears to her throat. "Whisker burn. Dave noticed."

Mark's face flushed. "I'm sorry, Kayla. I, uh, I planned to shave but somehow I got sidetracked." He looked over to the table where Dave had been sitting. It was now empty. "So he noticed?"

She laughed. "You look inordinately pleased with yourself, you know. All you need is to beat your chest and let loose with a Tarzan yell."

He grinned. "Yeah, well, this is all new to me, okay?"

Her smile faded. "You don't need to pretend, Mark. I know you've been with other women."

They'd been eating between the snippets of conversation. Now he placed his fork on his plate. "I'm pretending nothing, Kayla. I have never felt this way before. Hell, I've never been capable of such a marathon of sex before. You're going to kill me if we keep up this pace for much longer."

"Poor baby. You'll have plenty of time to recuperate once you return home."

He pushed his plate away and folded his arms on the table. "That's one of the things I want to talk to you about. I figured it would be easier to have a heavy-duty conversation on a full stomach."

She leaned back in her chair. "I'm afraid I'm not following you, Mark. Are you talking about your recuperative powers or something else?"

"I'm talking about going back home."

She looked down at her plate before she answered him. "Don't worry, Mark. I'm not asking for anything more than what we have right now. I meant what I said earlier. There are no strings attached, just the way you want it."

"Now, see, that's where you're wrong. Because I want to attach all kinds of strings around you. I know I don't deserve you but despite reminding myself of that over and over, I still want you so badly I ache. And I'm not just talking about the physical aspect of what we have together. I've had to face the fact that despite all my protestations, I do want to get married, but only to you. I want to live with you and love you and help you produce that family you've always wanted."

"I don't know what to say," she replied, her heart pounding so hard she was having trouble breathing. "I never—not once—expected you to see me in your life that way."

"Well, it's been a pretty big shock for me, too. I've been arguing with myself since you got here. The only conclusion I came to was that, like it or not, I'm crazy in love with you. I know I sound like a jerk, dumping this on you like this."

He looked around the now empty restaurant. "Let's get out of here."

They walked along the beach for a while in silence. Finally, Mark said, "Are you interested at all in pursuing a relationship with me?"

"Oh, Mark. I've been pinching myself since breakfast to make sure I'm not dreaming. Of course I want a relationship with you. I've been in love with you for years."

He came to an abrupt halt. "You have?" He looked at her with amazement.

She closed her eyes. Men. How could they be so obtuse?

"Do you really think I would have worked so hard to get you into bed if I wasn't in love with you?"

"I thought you were looking for some exotic vacation to remember and I happened to be available."

When she frowned at him he grinned at her. "Okay, so I'm teasing. But just a little. You had me convinced you weren't looking for any sort of commitment from me."

"That's because I wasn't. I was willing to have this time with you even if this was all we'd ever have."

"Well, I want more."

"So I'm beginning to understand."

"Does this mean you'll marry me?"

"I can't, Mark. Not any time soon. I want to finish law school and—"

"Georgetown University has a great law school. I don't live all that far from the campus."

"You mean, I should transfer?"

"I don't see why not. You'd have to apply, of course, but knowing you, your grades are high enough you won't have any trouble being accepted."

She turned and began to walk again. "Maybe by next fall."

He put his arms around her and hugged her close to him. "Would you consider laying out this semester and moving…oh, say…in two weeks?"

Kayla looked up at him and blinked. "Are you serious?"

"Very. I don't think I could possibly function without you if I had to wait for you to finish this coming semester."

"I don't believe this. What happened to the careful, rational Mark who plans every step of his life before embarking on something new?"

"He's running scared, Kayla. You're the most important thing that has ever happened in my life. I think I knew that by the time I was thirteen years old. Being with you has reminded me of some of the hopes and dreams I used to have before I got caught up in the whirl of big law firms and prestigious clients."

They reached the cottage and by silent and mutual consent sat down on the porch.

"I thought that was what your goal was?"

"So did I until I got a chance to work in the atmosphere there. Karyn was right about—" He shrugged, "Actually, she was right about a lot of things, but she told me that I was becoming cold and cynical. If I have, it was in order to survive."

"Is there a chance you'd want to practice someplace else?"

"Possibly. Who knows, maybe we could open our own practice together someday, maybe in a small town where we can be a part of the community and help friends and neighbors with their legal problems. No big cases with legions of lawyers working night and day. Just the two of us and some office help. Of course once we start our family, we might have to make adjustments, but we can figure all that out, can't we?"

"You've given this a great deal of thought, haven't you?"

"You bet I have. I've looked at options and various scenarios and I knew that none of it would work unless I could get you to move closer and give me a chance to convince you to marry me."

"I'm convinced, Mark. I was convinced the moment you said you were in love with me. All the rest of it is working out logistics."

Later that night, the phone rang not long after they'd fallen asleep, still wrapped in each other's arms.

Mark picked it up and said, "H'lo?"

"Well?" Karyn asked brightly.

He turned on the lamp beside the bed and propped up against the headboard with Kayla's head next to his, the phone receiver between them.

"Well, what?" he said, stroking the arm Kayla had draped across his waist.

"Have you enjoyed your vacation?"

"Yes, I have. It's beautiful down here, Karyn. You don't know what you've been missing. Getting away was exactly what I needed…to rest, get some sun, gain a new perspective on things. It was just what the doctor ordered."

A long silence greeted him.

"And you did that all alone?" she finally asked. Kayla lifted her head so that she could see his face. He put his finger to his lips in a shushing motion.

"Of course not. The resort is crowded. Everybody must have decided to come to the islands for the holidays. I doubt there's anyone left to keep things running back in the States."

Another long silence.

"All right," she said finally. "Just answer me this. Did Kayla get down there okay?"

"Who?" he asked innocently. That's when Kayla could no longer muffle her amusement. When she burst into laughter, he joined her.

Karyn, sounding disgruntled, said, "I sincerely hope that's Kayla, you rat."

"I'm not sure who she is. I found her in my bed one day and coaxed her into staying for a while. Here, I'll let you talk to her."

"Hi, Karyn," Kayla said. "I was so disappointed that you weren't here when I arrived. I'd so looked forward to seeing you again. And why didn't you tell me you weren't coming?"

Karyn sighed. "I had this plan in my head that if the two of you spent some time together that— Oh, well. It doesn't matter. I'd hoped that once Mark saw you that he would—"

"Lose my head and forget the perfect life I'd made for myself?" Mark said.

"Something like that, I suppose," she replied, sounding disappointed. "At least you were able to catch up with each other."

"I'd say so," Kayla said. "It was good to see him again. I still miss you, though."

Karyn almost wailed as she said, "And to think that I gave up this lovely vacation so that you two could…that maybe you'd realize…that…oh, never mind!"

"Fall in love?" Mark suggested.

"Yes, as a matter of fact. That's exactly what I hoped would happen, darn it!"

"It worked."

Silence. Finally, she said, sounding cautious, "Are you saying what I think you're saying?"

"Your matchmaking scheme worked, Karyn," he said. "Right now we're dealing with the logistics of Kayla living on the opposite coast from me, and the fact that she's in law school."

"Ohmigosh, ohmigosh, you mean it's true? You guys are actually planning to get together?"

"If you mean get married, then, yes, we're planning to get married. When and where has to be worked out. We're leaving tomorrow. Kayla has to get back to Oregon and school. I have to get back to work. Those are constants. Now, we're looking at variables."

Karyn immediately burst into tears. "Oh! I'm so happy. She's been part of the family for years and years. Now it'll be official. You could get married in Connecticut at the folks' place. Mother will be over the moon. I'm so excited."

"I can tell," Mark said dryly. "Do you suppose that

while you have a good cry and start your own celebration, you could let us get back to sleep?"

"Oh. You were asleep. Both of you? I mean, are
you and Kayla—"

"You have all the information you need, Karyn.
Good night." He hung up the phone and looked at
Kayla.

"She sounds happy," Kayla said, feeling a little surprised by Karyn's emotional response to their news.

He turned off the lamp, rearranged his pillows and
settled back into bed. "Of course she is. And why not?
Her little plot worked, you see. She'll be impossible
to be around for months…maybe years." He tugged
her until she lay on top of him, looking down at him.

"What are you doing?"

"Oh, nothing, really. But since she woke us up, I
guess I hoped to find something to do to make us
sleepy." He lifted her enough that he could place his
mouth around the tip of her breast.

Kayla inhaled sharply. "That's not going to put me
to sleep!"

"Well, maybe not right away," he admitted. He
moved his hips and she could feel the hard ridge beneath her and smiled.

He'd quickly taught her what he liked to do in bed
and she had to admit she was a quick study. She went
up on her knees and settled down on top of him, loving the sound of his moan as she used her thighs to

lift and lower herself at a slow pace. Eventually her teasing broke through his restraint and he placed his hands on her hips, meeting her quick thrusts with ones of his own.

Kayla couldn't keep the pace without quickly reaching her climax. She tried to hold back but when her body convulsed and spasmodically clutched him he lost control as well.

By the time they recovered, Kayla was definitely ready for sleep. Sex was better than a sleeping pill and a great deal more fun.

She was drifting into sleep when he spoke.

"Kayla?"

"Mmm?"

"I've been thinking about something."

"You think too much."

"Yeah, well, that's the nature of this particular beast. But here's the thing. Are you on any kind of birth control?"

That woke her up. "Uh, no. I never needed to be."

"That's what I figured."

"Which means?"

"As you know, I haven't always been diligent about our protection. There's a better than average chance that you may be pregnant."

She'd thought about the possibility, of course. She'd thought about it the first time he took her in the shower. There had been nothing between them, then.

"So?"

"You're not worried?"

"Worried? Not at all."

"What do you think?"

"I think we should wait and see. If it looks like I am, I'll probably be moving east very shortly."

He hugged her to him and gave a big sigh of obvious satisfaction. "I can only hope," he said, burying his face in her hair.

\* \* \* \* \*

# HOME ON LEAVE
## Stella Bagwell

To my mother, Lucille,
for always making Christmastime a special time.
I love you.

# Chapter 1

"When are we gonna be in Texas, Mommy?"

Greta Barstow held back a weary sigh as she glanced over at her four-year-old daughter, Lilly. The golden-haired youngster had been strapped in the airplane seat for nearly two hours. And before that, the two of them had been stranded for many more hours at Chicago O'Hare as snowplows and deicing machines had worked feverishly to get jetliners back into the air. It was no wonder Lilly had asked the same question at least twenty times in the past half hour. Greta was beginning to wonder herself if they would ever see Hobby airport in Houston.

"We'll be there soon, honey. Just a few more minutes."

Lilly wrinkled her nose with doubt as she tilted her head from one side to the other. "Will we see Grandma and Grandpa when we get off this airplane?"

A spasm of guilt hit Greta and for a moment she closed her deep blue eyes as her thoughts turned to her in-laws. It wasn't their fault that Douglas had died suddenly at the absurdly young age of thirty-eight. James and Anita had been just as devastated over losing their son as Greta had been over losing her husband. Yet these past three years since the funeral services she'd seen her in-laws only once and that had been when the Barstows had flown up to Kennebunk a few months after Doug's death.

Several times since then Greta had planned to travel to Texas to visit Doug's parents. But each time the departure date had drawn near she'd always seemed to find a reason for postponing the trip. She loved Anita and James, but the warm memories she'd made with Doug at the Barstow home in Texas had been just too painful to face. And now—well, she'd forced herself to make this trip for Lilly's sake. It was Christmas, after all, and she wanted the holiday to be special for her daughter and the Barstows.

"I'm sure one of your grandparents will be at the airport to pick us up," Greta assured her daughter.

Swinging her legs like a pair of scissors, Lilly asked, "Mommy, do you think Santa will know where to find me? If he don't find me he might give my gifts to some other little girl!"

Remembering how important Santa's visits had been during her own childhood, Greta kept her smile to herself. "Santa has magical abilities. He knows where all little boys and girls are on Christmas Eve. And he also knows whether they're being naughty or nice. I hope you remember that when we get to your grandparents' house."

Lilly nodded emphatically. "Oh, Mommy, I'm gonna be good. Real good. I promise."

Another fifteen minutes passed before the stewardess came over the intercom and instructed the passengers to prepare for landing. Greta made sure both hers and Lilly's safety belts were properly fastened and her handbag was pushed under the seat.

In no time at all, the huge aircraft was banking into a tight left turn. As Greta gazed down at the endless lights of Houston, she tried not to think of the last time she'd been in Texas. She'd flown Doug's body to his homestate to rest in the Barstow burial plot near Alvin. His sudden death of an unexpected heart ailment had shocked the whole family. Yet she couldn't allow her thoughts to dwell on that now. The whole holiday would be ruined. And she couldn't do that to her daughter.

With Lilly's hand clamped tightly in hers, Greta made her way off the airplane and through the busy terminal toward the baggage claim area. Travelers were thick. Everywhere there were sights and sounds of people hugging, crying and laughing.

As they walked toward the luggage carousel, Greta scanned the crowd for Anita and James. At her side, Lilly lagged at a slower pace, her attention snagged by each shop and eating place they passed.

"Greta! Greta Barstow!"

The sound of her name had her turning, and fully expecting to see her father-in-law, her mouth fell open as a tall, muscular young man with short brown hair bounded up to them.

Dear God, it was Broderick Barstow, Doug's younger brother! She'd not known Brodie—as everyone called him—was even in the country, much less in Texas.

Her heart beating much faster than it should have been, she offered him her hand. "Hello, Brodie."

With a wide grin that exposed a mouthful of white teeth, he brushed her hand away and slipped his arms around her waist. Lifting her high in the air, he hugged her tightly, kissed her on the cheek and laughed.

"Merry Christmas, Greta! It's great to see you!"

By the time he set her back on her feet, Greta's white face had turned completely red. She'd never been greeted in such an abandoned way by anyone and to have her brother-in-law behaving so carelessly in front of so many people had more than caught her off guard. Still, she couldn't stop the corners of her mouth from tilting into a faint smile.

"Uh…yes. It's nice to see you again, too," she murmured as she unconsciously straightened her black skirt and tried to avoid staring at Brodie's tough, masculine face.

Since she and Doug had always made their home in Maine during their four-year marriage, she'd only talked to the man on a few occasions, but she'd not forgotten him. He was seven years younger than Greta and looked nothing like her late husband. Nor was his personality similar to his brother's. The two had been as different as plain and spicy. And Brodie was definitely the spicy one. He was a military man and it showed in his broad muscular shoulders and trim, narrow waist, the straightness of his back and the confidence he exuded.

Tonight he was dressed in civilian clothes—a pair of Levi's, a black turtleneck covered with a worn denim jacket and an outrageous pair of black cowboy boots made of ostrich leather. Ever the conserv-

ative, Greta hated to admit how good the flamboyant clothing looked on him, but it did.

A tug on Greta's hand reminded her that Lilly
was waiting to be included in their little meeting. She
glanced down at her daughter, who was staring up at
Brodie with fixed wonder.

Brodie's gaze zeroed in on the child, who was si-
dled up to her mother's leg and peering at him with
wide, wary eyes. "Well, who's this little beauty? It
can't be Lilly! She looks too grown-up to be my
niece," he teased.

"I am Lilly!" she proudly shot back at him. "My
name is Lilly Barstow."

Squatting down to the child's level, Brodie placed
his forefinger beneath her dimpled chin and made an
exaggerated issue of examining her face.

"Is that so? Hmm. Maybe you do look like that little girl I met a few years back. How old are you,
Lilly?" he asked.

Holding up one hand, she folded her thumb
against her palm. "I'm four! And I go to school!"

His brows arched with surprise, he glanced up at
Greta. She responded with a hesitant smile.

"Nursery school," Greta explained.

Glancing over her shoulder at the luggage carousel,
she said, "Uh, the luggage has arrived. We'd better get
our bags before someone picks them up by mistake."

Ten minutes later the three of them were seated in a dark-colored pickup truck while the luggage was safely stowed in the back. Compared to their home in Kennebunk, Maine, the weather was extremely balmy. The white cable-knit sweater Greta had worn over her skirt was almost too warm to be comfortable. Or maybe it wasn't the weather at all, maybe it was the man sitting next to her, she thought bewilderedly.

He drove south from the airport, through the busy streets of Pearland and eventually turned off on Highway 6. At some point before they reached the town of Alvin, he turned the truck onto a farm-to-market road and headed west.

Up until a few moments ago, the traffic had been heavy and their conversation had been limited, but now as Brodie drove along the narrow, country highway, he said, "We were expecting you early this morning. But Mom said your flight was delayed. I was beginning to think you weren't going to make it."

"Snow. When we finally flew out of O'Hare it had stopped, but there was several feet of it on the ground. We were lucky to make it out of there when we did." She fiddled with the suede handbag she had squashed upon her lap. "I, uh, have to admit I was very surprised to see you at the airport. I didn't realize you'd be home for the holidays."

He flashed her a grin. "Does that mean you would have stayed in Kennebunk?"

Greta's lips pressed to a thin line. It had always been hard for her to tell if Brodie was teasing or serious. "Of course not! Why would you even say such a thing?"

But to herself, Greta had to admit that if she had been aware of Brodie being home, she would have had second, even third thoughts of calling off this trip. Not that she disliked her brother-in-law. In all honesty she didn't know him that well. It was just that each time the man looked at her, she felt like a ridiculous female—a woman who couldn't tell her right foot from her left. And she didn't like that helpless, vulnerable feeling. Not in the least.

"Oh, I don't know. Just an impression I get," he said with a shrug of one shoulder. "It's been a long time since you've been back to Texas."

Bending her head slightly, Greta stared at her fingers that were clenched tightly around the black handbag. Across the seat, Brodie cast another glance at her and tried not to frown.

The woman hadn't changed a bit, Brodie thought. Still dressed conservatively, her hemline hit her midcalf and hid a pair of pale, shapely legs. The heavy white sweater covering her upper body was loose and camouflaged any curves that were underneath. The one flamboyant thing about her, a mass of fiery red hair, was pulled tightly back from her oval face and subdued into a curly ponytail at the nape of her neck.

God, the woman could have been gorgeous, he thought, with her pale, smooth skin and deep blue eyes. Instead she was dowdy. Just like her personality. Or maybe he wasn't being entirely fair to her, Brodie mused. Maybe he'd never seen the real Greta. Maybe there was a hidden fire inside her to go with all that flaming hair. The idea intrigued him. Although, he didn't understand why. He'd not come home for Christmas to analyze his sister-in-law, or any other woman, for that matter.

"Yes, I know," she quietly agreed. "But, things kept happening. I couldn't seem to find enough time to make the trip…until now."

A few moments of silence stretched between them and then he said, "I don't suppose you stopped to think that a visit from their granddaughter would have helped my parents tremendously."

Greta's mouth flew open and she realized with a shock that she wanted to yell at the man. But before she could allow herself such an uncharacteristic indulgence, her eyes darted to the back seat where Lilly was staring wide-eyed out the window. Although the child's attention appeared to be on the darkened landscape, Greta had no doubt she was listening to every word that was being uttered between the two adults.

Lifting her head and stiffening her spine, she admitted, "I'm sure I'm guilty of not thinking of a lot of things. The past three years have…passed in a fog."

Brodie's eyes remained focused on the dark road ahead. "Don't you think it's time for the fog to lift?"

Her nostrils flared as she darted an annoyed glance at his rugged profile. Who did this man think he was anyway? "I'm here, aren't I?"

Moments passed and then a provocative smile spread his lips. "Yeah. And maybe I should warn you that we have fog here in Texas, too. But it doesn't last three years. It's so hot down here, it burns off real fast."

Her cheeks red, Greta turned her face toward the window and remained silent until they arrived at the Barstows' country home.


With no neighbors in view, the rambling wooden structure sat back in a huge grove of spreading live oaks interspersed with pecan and Mexican fan trees. With Christmas only three days away, twinkling lights had been twined around the tree trunks and the posts supporting the long porch. Higher up, along the eaves of the house, icicle lights hung in a bright, white fringe.

"Mommy! Look how pretty!" Lilly exclaimed as she unbuckled her safety belt and peered between the shoulders of the two adults. "We're gonna have the bestest Christmas ever!"

Normally Greta corrected her daughter's grammar, but tonight she merely smiled at Lilly's shining face.

"I hope it's the bestest one, too, honey."

Behind the wheel, Brodie watched mother and daughter. He'd always held the opinion that Greta was a distant woman. But now he got the feeling he'd been wrong about that. She wasn't aloof. She was sad, the kind of sadness that went all the way to the soul.

Doing his best to push away that troubling thought, Brodie climbed out of the vehicle then helped his passengers do the same. The three of them were standing on the ground when the front door of the house opened and a man and woman hurried down the front steps.

"Is that you, Brodie?" Anita called.

"Yes, Mom. And I have your guests with me."

"Oh, Brodie," she scolded gently through the darkness. "Greta and Lilly aren't guests. They're family."

By then Anita and James Barstow had reached the area where Brodie had parked and immediately the older couple swept Greta and Lilly up in tight, tearful hugs.

"Are you my grandma and grandpa?" Lilly asked as the older Barstow male juggled the little girl on one arm.

Everyone laughed, except Greta. The fact that her daughter didn't know her own grandparents wasn't a bit amusing to her. It was terribly troubling. Yet she had no one to blame but herself.

James, a big, burly man, who'd worked some thirty-five years as a carpenter, grinned at Lilly with outward adoration. "We sure are, honey. But Grandma and Grandpa are words that are just too big for us to answer to. Why don't you call us Granny and Gramps?"

For an answer, Lilly flung her little arms around James's neck and squeezed tight. He patted her back and tried to clear the knot of emotion from his throat, while standing next to him, Anita dabbed at her eyes with the tail of her shirt.

Greta looked away and swallowed as memories of Doug threatened to overcome her. He should be here with them, she thought sadly, to share the joys of Christmas with his family. But their life together had ended abruptly. She'd never share another Christmas with her husband.

"Well now," Anita said through her happy tears, "why don't we all go in and have something to eat.

I'll bet you two are starved after the ordeal you've been through today."

With Lilly still in her grandfather's arms, James and Anita started toward the house. Brodie quickly called after them, "I'll help Greta get their bags. We'll be right in."

As the three of them headed on toward the house, Greta glanced at Brodie and felt her heart began to pound with heavy, unfamiliar thuds.

"Are you wanting to say something to me in private?" she asked.

Taking her by the upper arm, he led her over to the door of the truck where they were completely swallowed by shadows.

"I don't know what made you finally decide to come back to Texas for a visit," he said in a low, husky voice. "Probably Lilly. You never seemed to care for the rest of us that much. But whatever brought you here—I'm glad."

Greta hadn't realized she'd been holding her breath until it whooshed past her lips.

"Oh."

He moved a step closer and Greta breathed in the warm, male scent clinging to his clothes. He was big and strong and as sexy as sin and she'd never had a man like him so physically near to her. To say Brodie shook her was understating things.

"Oh," he repeated. "What does that mean? Are all you New Englanders so cool and unemotional?"

Cool? Greta was on fire. His strong fingers clamped around her flesh were sending shards of heat radiating down her arm and into her whole body.

"I—no! I'm not being—cool," she finally managed to utter. "I—I'm—you've just taken me by surprise, that's all."

His fingers eased upon her arm, yet they didn't pull away entirely. Instead, they began to move up and down in a gentle, enticing motion.

"How did I do that?"

She didn't know why he still had a southern drawl to his words. The man had been stationed all around the world for long periods of time. The thought made her wonder where he was off to next. The volcanic Middle East again or some humid, Philippine island? The question made her inwardly shudder to think of the danger he often faced.

"First of all you accused me of not caring anything about your family," she answered. "That isn't at all true. And secondly, I expected you to scold me for coming. Instead, you seem glad about it."

Her eyes were beginning to adjust to the darkness. At least, enough to see the crooked grin spreading across his lips. The sight warmed her, in spite of her efforts to resist him.

"I am glad about it, Greta. For the past three years, I've prayed you would come to see my parents. They've needed you and their granddaughter."

And what about him, she wondered. Had he needed to see her? No! What a ridiculous question, she scolded herself. Brodie Barstow didn't need anyone—except the U.S. Army. As for women, she was just the opposite of what he found attractive.

"I haven't stayed away to—to hurt your parents, Brodie. After Doug died I could hardly bear to think of this place. Your brother and I had such pleasant times here when we would fly down from Maine to see your family. And I knew all of that would come back to me once I got here."

Brodie's hand lifted from her arm and it was all she could do not to flinch as he touched his fingertips to her cheek.

"I thought you'd be over losing him by now."

Her eyelids fluttered downward as a surge of strange emotions caused her to outwardly tremble.

"Does anyone ever get over losing the person they love?" she asked in a thick voice.

Slowly, his fingers smoothed over her skin. "I don't know, Greta. I've never loved anybody like that."

Startled by his admission, her eyes flew up to his. The wry twist to his lips wrung a tear from her heart.

"Brodie—"

"Let's forget all this somber talk," he suddenly interrupted, "and get the bags. You and Lilly are here for a holiday. And I'm going to make damn sure that by the time you leave here there'll be a smile on your face."

"Mommy! Wake up! Wake up, now!" Lilly's hand frantically shook her mother's shoulder until Greta cracked a sleepy eye.

"Lilly," she protested with a sleepy groan. "Why do I have to wake up now?"

Lilly bounced on her toes as Greta slowly pushed herself to a sitting position in the bed.

"Because Uncle Brodie is taking us to get a Christmas tree! A real tree! And he has to have me and you to help him pick the right one!"

By now Greta was awake enough to see that morning sunshine was pouring through the bedroom window and her daughter was already dressed in red leggings and a chartreuse sweatshirt. The loud colors of her daughter's clothing clashed like the cymbals banging inside Greta's head. She felt as though she'd had thirty minutes of sleep instead of the few hours she'd slept from midnight until this morning.

Shoving her disheveled hair away from her face, she swung her legs over the side of the bed and reached for her watch on the nightstand. "Have you eaten breakfast yet?"

Lilly began to do pirouettes around the small bedroom. "Yeah! Granny gave me some grits and some eggs. And Uncle Brodie taught me how to eat sorghum on a biscuit. It was good, good!"

Seeing she'd slept much later than she first thought, Greta rose from the bed and pulled on a blue velour robe. As she tied the sash at the waist, she asked her daughter, "When did you get up anyway?"

"Mommy! You know I can't tell time! It was kinda dark, though. Uncle Brodie was in the kitchen. He called me a good trouper. 'Cause all good troopers get up while it's still dark."

Well, Greta had certainly not been a good trouper this morning, she thought groggily. The long delays at O'Hare and the flight had obviously hit her hard, but then she wasn't accustomed to traveling.

Lilly danced across the floor on her toes until she was standing in front of her mother. It was then Greta noticed the child's long, blond hair was pulled back into a single braid. Other than a few stray hairs curling around her ears, the braid was tight and neat and was tied at the end with a black bow.

"I see that your granny combed your hair. It looks very pretty."

Lilly shot her a toothy grin and giggled. "No,

Mommy! Uncle Brodie combed my hair. He said he was gonna fix it like a racehorse when it runs through the mud."

*Uncle Brodie. Uncle Brodie.* How on earth was she going to make it through the next few days? Greta wondered miserably. Just thinking of the man caused all sorts of sinful thoughts to run through her head and she didn't know why. Before, when she'd been married to Doug, she'd never looked at another man in a carnal way, especially Brodie Barstow. He was her brother-in-law, for Pete's sake! Besides that, she didn't go for the young, reckless type. Not the least little bit.

"Sounds like you and Uncle Brodie have had a grand time this morning," Greta commented.

"Oh, we have! And Uncle Brodie says we're gonna have more fun, too. He says Christmas is a time for cele-cele-bration," Lilly finally managed to get the word out.

Greta wasn't going to lie to herself. For the past three years, she'd simply been going through the motions of celebrating the holidays, pretending to be happy, for Lilly's sake. Now that her daughter was a four-year-old and more capable of picking up on her mother's moods, Greta was more determined than ever to put her heart into the festivities.

Walking across the room, Greta reached for her

hairbrush lying atop a polished oak dresser. As she hurriedly pulled it through her thick, curly hair, she asked, "What about Gramps? Have you seen him this morning?"

"Uh-huh. But he's already gone. He had to go to work. To build a house, he said. Did you know Gramps could build houses, Mommy?"

James Barstow could not only build houses, he could build anything he wanted, including beautiful furniture. Before he'd put his carpentry skills to work, however, he'd spent ten years in the army and did two tours of duty in Vietnam. Greta was certain Brodie had gotten his inspiration to become a military man from his father. As for Doug, he'd not been like his father or his brother. He'd been a quiet, bookish man, who'd worked as a money investor for a major brokerage firm in Portland, then later on in Boston. He'd abhorred anything to do with guns and violence and had practically refused to talk about his brother's career as an officer in the army. Greta had never pressed him to do so, but she'd often wondered if her husband had been jealous of his strong, charismatic brother.

"I sure did," she answered her daughter's question, then turned away from the dresser as a knock sounded on the door.

Expecting it to be her mother-in-law, she called, "Come in?"

The door swung open and Brodie, with a steaming cup of coffee in his hand, stepped into the room. His gaze swept furtively up and down her slender body wrapped in the ankle length robe. Greta could feel her cheeks warming as his eyes lingered on her breasts and the loose red hair flying around her shoulders.

"So you're up, sleepyhead," he said with a grin. "I've brought you a cup of coffee to get you going. Did Lilly tell you about the tree?"

Her eyes met his as she accepted the coffee, then dropped furtively to her bare toes as she answered, "Yes, she did, but your mother—"

"Mom has gone to the grocery store. She won't be back for two or three hours," he interrupted. "You need to drink up. We're burning daylight."

Cupping both hands around the warm mug, Greta breathed in the aroma of the fresh coffee while she cocked at an eyebrow at him. "I didn't realize a person was supposed to be up at the crack of dawn around here. Maybe you should have played reveille this morning."

He chuckled and the deep warm sound vibrated through Greta's body. It was so good to hear laughter. Especially a man's laughter. Doug had been such a serious man. He'd never been one to joke and laugh. It had taken something very amusing to make him chuckle and these past three years had been totally empty of those occasions.

"That's a good one, Greta. You've surprised me. I didn't know you had any humor in you."

She'd not exactly been trying to be humorous, but she was glad he'd taken her words that way. He'd gone to the trouble of bringing her the coffee and she didn't want to appear ungrateful. Moreover, she didn't want to admit that she was as stiff as he believed her to be.

"Thank you for the coffee, Brodie."

With a brief smile, he turned and started out of the room. "You're welcome. Whenever you're ready to go, I'll be waiting outside, in the backyard." He glanced at Lilly who was watching the interplay between the two adults with rapt attention. "Want to come with me, honey? I'll show you Gramps's workshop."

Racing to his side, Lilly grabbed hold of his hand and eagerly followed him out of the room. Staring at the empty doorway, Greta suddenly wondered if her daughter was that hungry for male companionship or had the child simply fallen in love with the man.

She prayed not. It wouldn't do for her daughter to get too attached to Brodie. He might be a Christmas soldier right now, but in a few days, he'd go back to being a real one. Lilly would have to go back to Maine and forget him. And so would she.

# Chapter 2

The day was sunny and warmer than most summer days in Kennebunk. Brodie drove them to nearby Alvin, a small town with all the amenities of a larger one. In the parking lot of one particular shopping area, a nursery had set up a huge circus-type tent filled with fir trees of all kinds and shapes.

Brodie pulled into the parking lot and stopped the truck. Once he killed the motor, he glanced across the seat and gave Greta a conspiring wink. "This looks like a good place to find the perfect tree. Are you ready, Lilly?"

"Yeah! Yeah!" Lilly squealed loudly from the back seat.

He chuckled at the child's excitement as he turned a wry grin on Greta. "What about you, Greta? Are you ready for this outing? Or is picking out a Christmas tree old hat to you?"

Her brows arched with faint surprise. "Nothing about Christmas could ever be old hat. Not to me," she said with conviction, then glancing away from him, she shrugged one shoulder. "Actually, this is the first time I've ever been on a trip for a real Christmas tree."

Brodie stared at her. The woman represented hearth and home and family. He'd figured Christmas tasks had always been a routine thing for her.

"You're joking, aren't you?"

She turned her face back to his and he noticed her blue eyes were strangely shadowed.

"No."

Twisting slightly toward her, he said, "But—I'm sure you and Doug had a Christmas tree in your house. You had to get it somewhere."

"From a department store. He had allergies so we used artificial," she explained.

A frown creased his face. "I'd forgotten my brother was bothered with allergies. But, surely as a kid you—"

Greta shook her head. "We, uh, couldn't afford a real tree." Quickly, she began to fumble with the latch on her seat belt. "Shall we go now?"

Brodie wanted to say no. He wanted to tell her he wasn't going to let her out of the truck until she answered everything he wanted to know about her. But that was crazy. As crazy as the attraction he felt stirring deep in his gut every time he looked at the woman.

This morning she'd allowed her red hair to swing loose about her shoulders and, even more to his surprise, she was wearing a pair of snug blue jeans that revealed a pair of long, shapely legs and a pert little behind. The gray turtleneck she'd topped them with was even more clinging and several times he'd caught himself studying the small rounded shape of her breasts.

Brodie had to admit he didn't feel guilty about his physical attraction to Greta. His brother was gone and that part of her life was over. But the whole thing did surprise him. She was the exact opposite of every girlfriend he'd ever had.

"Sure," he replied and hurriedly climbed out of the truck to help his two passengers out of the cab.

By now the sun was climbing high in the sky and a strong southerly breeze whipped Greta's hair into a mess of curls. As the three of them walked toward the tent where the trees were displayed she fought with her hair until Brodie said, "Relax. Don't worry about it. You look very pretty just like that."

His compliment very nearly caused her to stumble. She wasn't pretty and he knew it. Why did the man have to say such things anyway? Was he just a habitual flirt, she wondered. The notion displeased her and, as the three of them entered the tent, she tried not to think about Brodie Barstow or his silver tongue.

A few minutes later, Lilly pointed toward a scotch pine that had to be one of the tallest evergreens in the entire tent.

"This one, Mommy. It's pretty. Real pretty!" Lilly exclaimed.

"Well, it is pretty," Greta reluctantly agreed. "But it's very…big, honey. Maybe you'd better pick out something smaller."

Standing close to Greta's side, Brodie spoke up, "Now why does she need to do something like that? Who wants a little ole scrawny tree that Santa will need glasses to see?"

"Brodie!" Greta interjected, her gaze swinging up to his face. "This tree will fill up half of your parents living room. Anita and James will have a fit if we bring this tree home with us. Besides, Santa already wears glasses."

Brodie noticed a slight tilt to her lips as she spoke

the last and he found himself surprised and warmed that she appeared to be thawing toward him.

"Well, yeah, Santa does wear glasses," he conceded with a grin. "But a big tree will give him plenty of room to put all the presents he brings to the Barstow house."

Lilly suddenly turned away from the tree and tugged on Brodie's hand. "Will some of those presents be for me?"

The grin on Brodie's face softened to one of tender affection as he squatted on his heels and pressed Lilly's tiny hand between his two big ones. "Have you told Santa what you want for Christmas, little lady?"

Lilly nodded emphatically. "Mommy wrote him a letter for me. 'Cause all I can write is my name."

Brodie glanced up at Greta and winked. "Did you mail it for her?"

There was a wicked playfulness to his expression that caused something to stir deep within Greta and she felt her cheeks grow warm as she answered, "Of course I did. Straight to the North Pole."

"Well, then," he said as he turned his attention back to Lilly. "It sounds like you'll have presents under this tree. But first we've got to get it home and get it decorated. Ready?"

Lilly clapped her hands with glee and danced from one foot to the other. "Ready! Ready! Let's go!"

Seeing she'd totally lost her argument about getting a smaller tree, Greta smiled and held her palms up in a gesture of surrender. "Okay, you two win. I'll stay here and make sure no one gets this tree," she told Brodie, "while you go pay."

Brodie chuckled. "Somehow I knew I'd get that part of the job."

Minutes later, with the tree completely filling up the bed of the truck, Brodie drove the three of them away from the parking lot and headed the vehicle onto a major thoroughfare that cut through town.

"Anyone hungry yet?"

Lilly was too busy staring out the back windshield at the tree to answer Brodie's question. As for Greta, she wasn't a big eater, but since she'd already missed breakfast this morning, her stomach was beginning to growl in protest.

"I am," she answered. "Is it lunchtime yet?"

Brodie glanced at his wristwatch. "A little after eleven. But since Lilly and I had a very early breakfast and you had none at all, I thought we could all do with a little refueling. Fast food good enough for you?"

Doug had never been keen on eating fast food and had discouraged Greta if she'd mentioned stopping at one of the major chain restaurants for a burger. Because he'd paid close attention to his diet, she'd learned to cook lean, healthful meals and she'd continued on that same track even now that Doug was gone. But in all honesty, her and Lilly's meals were usually uneventful. The sound of a huge, greasy hamburger sounded wonderfully delicious to Greta.

"That would be fine with me," Greta told him and then with a sudden lifting of spirit, she added, "Would you go someplace where they serve ice cream? It's so warm today Lilly might enjoy ice cream for dessert."

"I'm on my way, ma'am."

A half hour later, Lilly was concentrating on the pile of French fries in front of her. Ketchup was smeared on the corners of her mouth and chin and for probably the fifth time since they'd sat down to eat Greta reached across the small table to wipe her daughter's face clean.

Sitting next to her, Brodie gently laid a hand on Greta's forearm. She paused and arched a questioning brow up at him.

A tiny frown marred his forehead. "Why don't you just let her eat and do all that when she gets finished?"

Greta hadn't stopped to think she was overdoing things with Lilly. Continually keeping her neat and tidy was a habit, she supposed.

"This is good stuff, Mommy," Lilly said as she crammed another stick of fried potato into her mouth. "Can we eat it again?"

Seeing how much Lilly was enjoying herself, Greta forgot about using the napkin in her hand. Brodie was right this time. She needed to let Lilly relax and be a child.

"I'm sure we can."

Lilly looked at her mother. "When we go back home, too?"

"Not all the time," she answered her daughter. "But sometimes we will."

Brodie turned his eyes to Greta. "She acts like she's never eaten French fries before," he said with surprise.

Greta's gaze dropped from his face down to her own meal. "She hasn't. Not that I remember."

Brodie cast a quick glance at the child. Her long golden hair had loosened from the braid he'd made for her this morning and now little curls framed her face. Her eyes were dancing with excitement and he could plainly see the girl was experiencing things she'd never encountered before. The fact made him wonder even more about the lives Greta and Lilly had been living since his brother's death and even before.

"Well, I'm glad she's enjoying herself," Brodie said. "All kids need treats once in a while."

Greta cast him a brief, slanting glance. It was unsettling to have him sitting just inches away from her side. He was so potently male that just looking at him sent fissures of heat throughout her body. Having him close enough to smell and touch was just about more than she could handle.

"She gets treats. I just haven't taken her to places like this before."

"Was Doug a spoiling father?" he asked, then quickly shook his head. "I suppose he wasn't with her long enough to do much spoiling."

Lifting her head, she looked at him squarely. Her heart stumbled then took off in a dead run the moment her eyes connected with his. "She was only a bit past a year old when Doug died. He wasn't with her long enough to make any sort of impression on her."

His gaze didn't waver from hers. "I'm sorry about that, Greta. I truly am."

"Mommy, I'm full. Do I have to eat it all?"

Distracted by Lilly's questions, Greta glanced at her daughter. "No, sweetheart. If you want to, you can go over there and play where the other children are." Greta motioned to the play yard just a few feet away from their outdoor table. "But first take off your shoes and leave them here at the table with me. Shoes aren't allowed on the carpeted playground."

Lilly didn't have to be told twice. She jerked off her shoes and raced off to where several other children near her age were sliding down slides and climbing through colorful blocks and barrels.

"She's happy about that," Brodie commented.

Greta smiled as her gaze followed his over to where Lilly was already climbing a ladder.

"I want her to have a good time while we're here in Texas. That's what this trip is all about. Lilly. And giving her time to be with her grandparents. And you," she added honestly. "I didn't realize you were going to be here, but I'm glad that you decided to come home for Christmas. Lilly needs a masculine hand in her life—even if it is just for a few short days."

Surprised by her admission, he turned on the bench seat they were sharing and leaned even closer as he studied her flushed face. She wasn't wearing much makeup, but the southerly breeze had nipped her cheeks a soft, rosy color to match the color of her lips. Sunlight danced in her eyes and he realized that at this moment she looked more alive than he'd ever seen her.

"Hmm. You surprise me, Greta," he said as the corners of his lips slowly spread upward. "I figured you thought of me as a bad influence."

She breathed deeply and tried to tell herself that he was just a man. Sitting next to him was no different than sitting next to her father-in-law. But inside she was trembling and all she could think about was the way his brown eyes looked like warm chocolate, the way his cheek dimpled at the side of his mouth and the way that mouth curved upward in a slow, sexy smile at her—plain, simple Greta.

"I don't know where you got that idea," she said.

He chuckled lowly and the warm sound washed over in a way that made her want to close her eyes and smile along with him.

She had to get a grip on herself, she thought with sudden clarity. This man was her brother-in-law. He was spending time with her because she was family and it was his duty, not his choice.

"You're so funny, Greta."

"I'm not trying to be."

He chuckled again. "I know. That's why you're so funny. And you know, it won't be a crime if you decide to laugh at me or yourself or anything—if you get the urge to."

She sighed and swallowed and Brodie cringed as a far-off look suddenly came into her eyes.

"I guess I must be pretty boring company compared to the women you know," she said after a moment.

He reached over and took her hand. The sudden contact of his flesh against hers very nearly made her groan out loud.

"You're not boring. You're just—different," he said.

"I'm sure," she murmured.

He rubbed his fingers across the top of her hand with slow, thoughtful movements. In a matter of seconds, Greta realized she should pull away from him. She should let her actions tell him that he shouldn't be stroking her in such a familiar way. But something inside her didn't want to give up the pleasure she was getting from his touch.

"Why haven't you married, Brodie?"

As soon as the question was past her lips, Greta wanted to kick herself. But it was too late to take it back. And anyway, she was curious about him. She couldn't seem to help herself.

A wry smile slowly spread across his face and Greta was relieved that he was taking her question lightly.

"I don't know exactly. So far I'd have to say I've never met a woman that I've found more interesting than the army."

Her eyes dared to flick over his handsome face. "I guess I wasn't thinking. I should have realized that you're married to the army."

A playful scowl pulled at his features. "I wouldn't say that—exactly." He scooted a fraction closer to her side. "Actually, most of the women I've known are more concerned about having a career than they are about becoming a wife." He shrugged the shoulder touching hers. "A sign of the times, I guess." Tilting his head down toward her face, he added, "What about you, Greta? Are you obsessed with a career?"

In the back of her mind, Greta knew she should scoot down the seat and put a decent amount of distance between them. But it was so exciting just to be sitting with their thighs touching, their arms brushing. He made her feel alive and special somehow. That was enough to scare her, but not enough to send her to the opposite end of the bench.

Her physical relationship with Doug had been gentle and pleasant. Their marriage had been warm and solid. To put it simply, their life together had been nice. But the feelings she got when she was close to Brodie were far from nice. They were passionate. And irresistible.

"I don't have a career," she said. "I have a job, that's all."

"What kind of job?"

Her heart was beating way too fast, but she couldn't seem to reason with it or make it see that the man beside her was just making ordinary conversation.

"I'm an office manager for an insurance firm in Kennebunk. It pays well—enough to support Lilly and I. And I'm comfortable there. I guess that's a lot to be thankful for."

Brodie hadn't known she'd had a business education or that she'd even worked outside the home. He'd figured these past three years since Doug had died that she and Lilly had been living off the life insurance settlement. Before his brother had died, Doug hadn't talked much about his wife to Brodie. But then the two of them had not been that close, he thought regretfully. Once the two of them had become adults, Doug had chosen to build his life in New England and Brodie had entered the army. The two men had never really connected. Not as brothers should.

"So now it's my turn," he said. "Why haven't you remarried, Greta?"

Stunned by his question, she stared at him. "I can't believe you're even asking me that question," she finally replied.

His brows lifted to two faint question marks. "Why not? You're a young, lovely woman. You should have a husband. And Lilly needs a father."

Even though she'd known Brodie was a straight-speaking man, she couldn't believe the bold, frankness of his words. She'd been married to his brother for goodness sake!

"I—I would never marry just for the sake of giving Lilly a father. It wouldn't be right for me—or for her!"

He didn't say anything. He didn't have to. The expression on his face said he clearly didn't understand.

A frustrated sigh pushed past her lips. "Brodie, I haven't bothered to look for a husband. Because I know it would be futile. I could never find another one like Doug."

He grimaced. "Why would you want to find one exactly like him? If you ask me, that would be creepy, trying to replace a husband with a duplicate."

She scowled at him before she turned her gaze to the playground where Lilly was climbing through a series of bright red rings. "I'm not trying to replace him," she said firmly. "And I'm *not* going to replace him! I just meant that…well, I could trust Doug, completely. I don't think I could ever trust any man like that again."

Brodie's brow furrowed as he carefully studied Greta's face. He wanted to prod her to explain. Trust a man to do what? Or not to do what? What was she afraid of anyway?

The questions lingered on the tip of his tongue, but from the closed look on her face, Brodie realized they'd be better left to a later time. Even though he didn't quite understand why he felt this incessant need to know what was going on in Greta's head. He wasn't looking at the woman as wife material for himself. He wasn't searching for a wife, period. No, that wasn't entirely right, he corrected himself. This past year he'd begun to dream of more than just a casual date. A brief sexual romp with a willing woman no longer left him feeling contented. Maybe that's why Greta's image of love and family had done something to him. Now he just had to figure out what that something was.

That night, after a meal of smoked brisket, cole-slaw and pinto beans, Anita urged Lilly and Greta to join her on a jaunt to the attic to collect all the ornaments and trimmings she'd stored from previous Christmases. Brodie was left to deal with putting the evergreen in a stand and hauling it into to the house.

Later, in the living room with Christmas music playing softly on the stereo, Greta was content to sit back with her father-in-law and watch as Anita and Brodie showed Lilly how the twinkling strings of lights were strung through the branches and then the silver garland draped in scallops from bough to bough.

"I think it's time to start hanging the glass balls," Anita announced as Brodie finished fastening the garland at the top branch of the eight-foot tree. "Here Lilly, you can start with these."

She handed a box of shiny red ornaments to Lilly, who in turn looked at her grandmother with amazement.

"I get to hang 'em?" Lilly asked in disbelief.

"Sure you do," Brodie flashed the child a grin. "You're just the right size to do the bottom limbs. Let me show you."

He set the box of ornaments in a safe place and carefully explained to Lilly how to attach the slim wire hanger to the bulb and then hook it on the tree.

Greta was proud to see how well her daughter followed instructions. Yet the sight of Brodie and Lilly together, their heads close, their laughter mingling, brought a bittersweet pang to her heart. The two of them looked so right together, almost as though Brodie was her father. But he wasn't. Lilly's father was gone. Greta's husband was gone. And like she'd told Brodie, she couldn't replace him.

From his easy chair, James glanced over at Greta. "I think my granddaughter is enjoying herself," he said, his faint smile full of fondness.

"Very much," Greta agreed. "This is all new for her. And believe me, once we get back to Maine, she won't forget any part of her Christmas holiday."

James opened his mouth to say something else, but at just that moment the telephone sitting near his elbow shrilled loudly.

Frowning, he reached over and picked up the receiver. After exchanging only a few words, he covered the mouthpiece and called to his wife.

"For you, Anita. You'd better take it in the kitchen. It's Sonja and you know she doesn't talk loud enough for anyone to hear her."

"Oh, sorry everyone," Anita apologized for the

interruption. "Sonja's wanting to discuss the party for Christmas Eve. I'll try to get off as quickly as I can."

"Don't worry about it, Mom," Brodie told his mother. "Greta will take your place."

As Anita hurried out of the room, Brodie looked over at Greta and curled his finger. "Come on," he ordered playfully. "You've rested over there long enough."

"I'm keeping your father company."

Brodie grinned as though he knew she was stalling. "Dad's tired. He's worked all day. He doesn't need a beautiful woman stirring him up."

"Speak for yourself, Brodie," James joked.

Her cheeks red, Greta left the armchair and walked over to the Christmas tree where Lilly was in deep concentration over where to hang her next ornament.

"I'm not really good at this," she said to Brodie. "Maybe you should wait until Anita finishes her phone call."

"Moss will be growing on the branches by the time that happens," Brodie assured her. "And you don't have to be good at this to get the job done. There's only one requirement you need for tree trimming."

"Oh? What is that?" she asked warily. "I probably don't have it."

"I think you have it somewhere in there," he said, his gaze flicking up and down the length of her. "If you'll just let it come out." Bending around, he retrieved a box of ornaments from the floor and handed them to Greta. "All that's required is fun. Smiling, laughter, giggling, even dancing. You know about all those things, don't you?"

Did she? Of course, she laughed and smiled. And she'd experienced fun times with her husband. But not in the carefree, reckless way Brodie was talking about. The idea troubled her greatly.

Her gaze dropped to the box of ornaments she was holding. "You don't have to make fun of me just because I'm not a socializer, like you."

Groaning softly, he stepped forward and lifted her chin with his forefinger. "Greta, look at me. I'm not making fun of you. I'm just teasing. Don't you know that's just a part of having fun?"

Her blue eyes were filled with doubtful shadows as they scanned his face. How could she tell him that the only teasing and laughing she remembered in her life had come from her father? She didn't want to admit to that. If she did, then she would have to explain that by the time Greta had turned six and started to school, Michael O'Brien had left the family, never to return.

"Uh, yes, I do know. And, believe it or not, I do laugh and smile on occasion," she attempted to tease back.

One dark brow arched with amusement as he studied her face. "Really? What about dancing?"

Greta shook her head. "Never. I don't even know how."

He pretended to look shocked. Or maybe he really was shocked. With Brodie it was hard to tell, she realized.

"That's absolutely awful," he declared. "We've got to do something about that. Right now."

"Brodie!" she exclaimed with a gasp as he reached for her hand and tugged her into the circle of his arms. "What are you doing?"

"I'm going to show you how to dance," he said with a wicked grin.

Her heart thumping wildly, Greta tried to pry her hand from his and ease herself away from the rock-hard wall of his body, but her struggle only prompted him to pull her closer.

"I don't want to—this is not the time, Brodie!" Swiveling her head in search of Lilly, she found her daughter still standing next to the tree. Apparently the ornament in her hands had been forgotten as she gazed impishly at the two adults.

"Dance, Mommy! Dance!" she prompted with a giggle. "Like this!"

Immediately, Lilly went into a waltz-like skip around the living room floor. From the corner of her eye, Greta could see James watching the whole scene with a wide smile on his face. But then he would be enjoying the sight, Greta thought. James was like Brodie. He believed in letting loose and having fun. Something that had taken Greta by surprise the first time she'd met her father-in-law. Doug had been so quiet, so no-nonsense, so opposite of his family.

Brodie chuckled next to Greta's ear. "See, your daughter already has the picture of things. And when would be a better time to dance than at Christmas? It's a time for celebrating—in all sorts of ways," he said as he slid one hand to the middle of her back.

Yes, but she wasn't a celebrating sort of woman, she wanted to tell him. "We're supposed to be trimming the tree," she reminded him.

"We've got all night to do that," he pointed out.

Her breath caught in her throat as he took her free hand and placed it on his shoulder.

"There now," he said with a grin that sent funny little curls through her stomach. "We're all ready. Just follow my footsteps," he instructed.

Willie Nelson was doing a version of "Pretty Paper" on the stereo. Greta didn't know whether that constituted dance music or not. But Brodie seemed to think so. He began to move their bodies forward and back and from side to side.

At first Greta was immersed in watching her feet and concentrating on matching him step for step. But then slowly, as the awkward rhythm of their bodies began to take shape, she became acutely aware of his warm hand against her back, his fingers wrapped tightly around her fingers and the heat of his body radiating into her breasts and belly and thighs.

Dear heaven, she'd not known that dancing could be such a sensual act. At least, it was sensual for her. As for Brodie, he'd no doubt danced with dozens of women before. Most likely, this was just entertainment to him. They were celebrating, as he'd called it. And that was the way Greta needed to think of it, too. Except that her legs were shaky, her mouth dry, and she had the most incredible urge to rest her cheek upon his shoulder.

They made several circles around the small, open area of the living room. During one of them, Greta noticed her father-in-law's chair was empty. James must have slipped from the room sometime during the dance. She was glad. It would be embarrassing if the older Barstow read something on her face that shouldn't be there. Yet, on the other hand, she realized Brodie's parents were open-minded people. They wouldn't condemn her for being attracted to their younger son.

All of a sudden the music stopped and their footsteps came to an end. Brodie said in a low voice next to her ear, "Well now, that wasn't so bad, was it?"

Clearing her throat, Greta attempted to laugh and

make light of the moment. "I'm sure it was much worse for you than me. I stepped on your toes. You'll probably be crippled after this."

A faint smile creased his cheeks. "Not hardly. You did fine. A few more circles around the floor and you'd be a pro." Releasing his hold on her, he stepped back to give her a little bow. "Thank you, ma'am, for the dance."

Her throat was suddenly so thick, her voice came out hoarsely when she spoke, "You're welcome, Brodie."

Just as her eyes dared to meet his, Lilly chose that moment to come running up to them.

"Me, too, Brodie. I wanta dance."

The child held her arms up to Brodie in a pleading gesture for him to pick her up. Smiling indulgently, he reached down and lifted her up into the crook of his arm.

"All right, young lady," he told Lilly as he settled the child's weight in a more comfortable grip, "hold on and we'll take a little waltz around the floor."

As Lilly giggled with delight, Greta moved slowly back to the Christmas tree and picked up a box of the ornaments. She was shocked to find that her fingers were trembling and her face felt flushed with heat. Even as a teenager, she'd never reacted like this to the opposite sex and as she began to hang a shiny bulb upon the tree, she silently swore to get a grip on herself before this visit with the Barstows ended in disaster.

# Chapter 3

Nearly an hour later, Anita returned to the living room from her phone call. She was carrying a tray loaded with mugs of steaming hot chocolate and a plate of cookies. Everyone took a break and sat back and admired the tree that was now loaded with lights, ornaments and candy canes.

Every few minutes Lilly would go over to the decorated spruce and try to guess where Santa might place her gifts and, of course, every few minutes the child would change her mind and choose a different spot. Greta had never seen her daughter so animated and eager about anything. And though she had to admit that all children were excited about Christmas, there was more to the smile on Lilly's face. She was thriving on this new family around her and Greta was actually seeing her daughter blossom before her very eyes. It was a gladdening sight, yet it also made her wonder if their life back in Maine had really been that lacking.

By the time the cocoa and cookies had disappeared, Lilly's head was drooping. Greta excused the two of them and ushered her daughter back to the bedroom where she helped her get into her pajamas and made sure she thoroughly brushed her teeth. After she'd listened to Lilly's prayers, tucked her under the covers and returned to the living room, she found it empty.

She was standing in the arched doorway leading into the room, gazing at the twinkling lights of the Christmas tree, when she heard a quiet step behind her.

Turning, she gasped softly as the blurred sight of Brodie's face crossed her vision and then his lips connected with the smooth curve of her cheek.

"Mmm. That's nice," he murmured close to her face. "Maybe I should check out the other side."

Before she could protest he pushed back her loose hair and planted a lingering kiss on the opposite cheek. Greta's breath caught in her throat and heat suffused her from the top of her head to the soles of her feet.

"Wh-whaat? Are you doing?" she finally managed to stutter the question.

Chuckling quietly, he lifted his head to look at her shocked expression. "You're standing under the mistletoe, my dear. I wouldn't be much of a man if I didn't take advantage of the situation."

Not at all sure he was telling the truth, Greta quickly tilted her eyes toward the ceiling. Sure enough there was a cluster of the green leaves and white berries attached with a big red bow to the top of the doorway. Why hadn't Greta noticed the decoration before, she wondered. Why was it taking this army captain to open her eyes?

Breathing in a deep, bracing breath, she turned and hurried across the room. Once she'd taken a seat on the couch, she asked, "Where are your parents?"

Brodie sauntered casually into the room. Before Greta realized what she was doing, her gaze was traveling up and down his long legs and marveling at the way the faded denim clung to his muscled buttocks.

"They've retired for the night," he answered. "Dad was tired after working all day. They didn't think you'd mind if they turned in a little early. They told me to tell you they'd see you in the morning."

"Of course I don't mind," she assured him. "Neither one of them should feel like they have to entertain me while I'm here. They need their rest. The holidays can be exhausting."

To Greta's dismay, Brodie sank onto the cushion next to her and squared his knee around so that he was facing her in a casual, yet intimate way.

Propping his arm along the back of the couch, his fingers were resting just an inch or so from her shoulder. Greta felt both cornered and wildly excited by his nearness and she struggled to hide it all from him.

"Exhausting and fun," he added, his brown eyes crinkling into a smile at her. "Tell me, Greta, are you having any fun at all? Or are you just…tolerating everything?"

Pressing her lips together, she scowled at him. Why was he always prodding her like this? And damn it, why did she even care what the man thought about her?

"In spite of what you think, Brodie Barstow, I do know how to have fun. And I am enjoying being with your family. What do you think I am, anyway," she asked crossly, "stiff-necked?"

He lifted her hand from her lap and drew it toward him. "No. I think—you've been living in a vacuum, Greta. I don't believe you know what it's like outside of your safe little world."

Gasping, she tried to jerk her hand from his, but his fingers held tightly onto hers, his eyes gripped her shocked gaze.

"Doug's death—" she began only to have him interrupt.

"Has nothing to do with it."

Her jaw dropped and she unconsciously leaned toward him as her blue eyes searched his face for some sort of reasoning. "I can't believe you said that! What are you trying to tell me, anyway?"

"Don't get all huffy on me, Greta. I'm not insulting you. I'm just pointing out that you need to break down those walls you've built around yourself so that you can live—really live."

She continued to stare at him as though he was speaking a strange language. "What are you talking about? I *am* living!"

His response was a mocking snort, which in turn caused rosy red anger to color Greta's cheeks.

"Who made you such an expert on life anyway?" she tossed at him.

He smiled as though he was right and she was wrong and nothing could change the fact. "No one. But I'm smart enough to see some things about you."

Curiosity rushed in to replace her anger and she stared at him with parted lips. "Oh. Being a soldier has taught you how to analyze women?" she asked tartly.

Laughing, Brodie squeezed her hand. "Not exactly. But I've met a few down through the years."

"I'll just bet," Greta muttered. "Well, I don't like you comparing me to them. If that's what you're doing."

The humor quickly fell from his face. "I can't compare you to them, Greta. You're the most…different sort of woman I've ever known."

Suddenly she felt very awkward and very sad. From the time she'd been a young girl of six and just starting school, she'd felt different. Her life wasn't like most of the kids around her. Her father hadn't wanted her or her mother. He'd walked out on them without a backward glance. And when he'd left, Teresa O'Brien had been forced to work three jobs just to keep a roof over her and Greta's head and to put food on the table. Greta had watched her once beautiful mother turn into a worn, wisp of a woman. As for herself, Greta had grown up basically on her own while her mother was out working.

"I realize that I must seem prudish and dull to you. But I'm not a wild and loose sort of woman. It's just not in me to be that way."

"Thank God," Brodie murmured with a gentle smile.

Her eyes blinked with confusion. "I don't understand. I thought you— Haven't you been trying to tell me I need to loosen up, turn into some sort of party girl and find myself a man?"

He grimaced. "Uh, not exactly."

A pent-up breath slowly passed Greta's lips as she pulled her hand from his and threaded her fingers together upon her lap.

"You're not being very good at explaining yourself," she said.

He didn't reply immediately and she glanced his way to see that he was studying her with narrowed brown eyes. The idea that he was scrutinizing her so intently heated her almost as much as their awkward dance had.

"You're right. I'm trying to be subtle when I should just come out and say it. I think you're using Doug's death as a way to avoid having another man in your life."

Outrage pushed her to her feet. It wasn't his right to be getting so personal with her!

"You really are incredible!" she practically growled at him, then determined to put an end to their conversation, she walked over to the stereo and began to search through a stack of CDs. She was pushing a Christmas selection into the player when she felt Brodie standing just behind her shoulder.

"Why won't you admit that I'm right?" he asked softly.

His voice was deep and roughly masculine, just like the rest of him. She shivered inwardly.

"Because you're *not* right," she said while deliberately keeping her back to him. "But then, I don't expect you to know anything about love or marriage. I doubt you've ever experienced the first and it's obvious you haven't the latter."

"I'm not sure you have either," he countered smoothly.

Of all the things he'd said, this shocked her most and she whirled around to face him. "What are you trying to say now?" she demanded. "Everyone knew that I loved Doug."

"I'm sure that you did—in your own way."

Her nostrils flaring, she stepped around him. "And just in case you didn't know," she flung over her shoulder. "Doug loved me."

"Is that what you call it?"

Furious now, she turned and stomped back to within inches of his taunting face.

"You're making me mad, Brodie. Really mad," she said through clenched teeth.

"Good. At least you're getting passionate about something."

The anger burning her cheeks was directed more at herself than him. She was too strong a woman to allow this man to affect her in such a powerful way.

"You know nothing about your brother's marriage to me," she argued. "How could you? You never both-

ered to come up to Maine to visit him—you were always away on some tour of duty. Love of your job
as a soldier seemed to always outweigh any need to
be with your brother."

His features were suddenly rigid. "I suppose that's
what Doug always told you," he said wryly. "Did he
tell you that I didn't want to come around? That I'd
always been consumed with being a soldier?"

Greta's defensive stand suddenly faltered as she
recognized a thread of truth in Brodie's questions.
"Uh, yes, Doug did tell me those things. But wasn't
he speaking the truth?"

"No," he answered, then with a frustrated shake
of his head, he went on, "but before you think I'm
trying to call my brother a liar, let me explain. In
Doug's opinion, I was consumed with the army. He
never understood why I could love my job when he
abhorred the very idea of carrying a weapon of any
sort. He believed anyone who'd trek for miles
through blistering heat and rain and cold, had to be
crazy. Doug liked his life nice and easy and safe. He
didn't like surprises. That's why he married you."

Her earlier anger totally disappeared as a cold
chill filled her through and through. "Oh. You have
a theory about that, too?" she asked stiffly.

The rigid lines of his face relaxed and he studied
her with a regret that chilled Greta even more.

"Yes," he said softly. "Doug was a predictable man. He craved routine and security."

Greta drew in a shaky breath as her mind's eye flashed backward to when she'd first met Doug. Doug had received a scholarship in accounting at the University of Southern Maine at Portland, where Greta had been attending classes for her business degree. The two of them had literally bumped into each other in the cafeteria. He'd been apologetic and embarrassed and she'd been charmed by his quiet reserve. And later, as they'd gotten to know each other, she'd felt safe and comfortable with him. Had she construed those two emotions as love? Had Doug saw the very same two things in her?

"There's nothing wrong with that," she said rigidly. "I want the same thing for myself and for Lilly."

Brodie's expression was suddenly tinged with sadness. "Think about it, Greta. Doug recognized you wanted those things. He could see you were a quiet, submissive woman, one who would always be steadfast and true. I'm sorry, but he didn't marry you because he fell madly in love with you. He wasn't capable of being that impetuous."

Greta wanted to scream that he didn't know what he was talking about, that she and Doug had been wildly in love. But the words wouldn't come. Because somewhere, deep down inside her, she had to accept that Brodie was right.

Turning her back to him, she said in a tight, low voice, "I don't know how you could say such horrible things about your brother. Especially since he's not here to defend himself."

His hands came to rest on the back of her shoulders. "Greta," he scolded softly, "I wasn't badmouthing Doug. I loved my brother very much. There wasn't a mean bone in his body. And if he'd lived to be a hundred, he would have been a good husband to you—in his own way. But he's gone and now you're on your own and I'd like to see you have something more than safe and comfortable in your life."

Emotions she couldn't decipher suddenly clogged her throat. She closed her eyes and swallowed. "I don't want *something more*," she whispered hoarsely. "And I don't want you telling me what I need!"

"Greta—"

The rest of his words were never spoken as she pulled away from his touch and hurried out of the room.

The next morning as Greta finished the last of her coffee, Anita rose from the kitchen table and began to gather the dirty dishes. Immediately Greta started to rise to her feet to help the woman, but her mother-in-law waved her back down.

"There's no hurry," Anita insisted with a happy smile. "You finish your coffee and relax. We can visit while I do this."

Except for the two women, the house was empty. Brodie and his father had decided to go out this morning for a little last-minute gift buying and both men had insisted on taking Lilly along with them. Greta couldn't help but notice how quiet the house seemed without Lilly's chatter and how empty it felt without Brodie hanging around, tossing her a wink here and a grin there.

Damn the man, she thought crossly, she was thinking about him even when he wasn't near. It was a good thing her time here at the Barstows' would be coming to a close shortly after Christmas. Otherwise, he was going to turn her into a complete fool.

"I'm glad James could take off work until after Christmas," she said to Anita. "Lilly is definitely enjoying being around her grandfather. She's still talking about his workshop and all his hammers and tools. She believes he can make anything with a piece of wood."

"And he very nearly can," Anita said with a fond chuckle as she placed several plates on the cabinet countertop. "I've noticed Lilly likes being around her uncle, too. It's probably obvious to you that both men are spoiling her. But—that's what children are for sometimes. At least, I did my share of spoiling when Doug and Brodie were children."

Her hands wrapped around her coffee mug, Greta thoughtfully studied the other woman. "Being around Brodie makes it hard for me to believe that he and Doug were brothers. The two men are—were as different as different can be."

Walking back over to the table, Anita picked up a few more dishes. "That's true. Brodie took after his father and paternal grandfather. Doug was more like my two brothers. They were both quiet, reserved men."

Greta traced the rim of the coffee cup with her forefinger as she carefully contemplated her next words. "This will probably sound like a strange question, but was Doug sometimes jealous of Brodie?"

Turning away from the kitchen sink, Anita wiped her hands on a dish towel as she looked at Greta. "Oh, probably no more than most brothers are," she said with a shrug of one shoulder. "Doug was our only little boy for nearly eight years before Brodie came along. For a while, I expect he resented being rooted out of that number one position. But all kids are like that."

"Actually, I wasn't thinking about when your sons were little children," Greta explained. "I meant after they were grown."

Anita looked faintly puzzled. "Oh. Well, to be

honest with you, I never noticed any particular jealousy. Why are you asking?"

Feeling suddenly awkward and foolish, Greta quickly rose to her feet and began to scrape the food scraps from her plate. "I don't really know," Greta said as she stifled back a sigh. "Except that Doug sometimes seemed to resent Brodie's career in the military. If I had such a decorated brother, I would be very proud. I'd brag to everyone about him. Doug didn't talk about Brodie much at all, to anyone."

The knowing smile on Anita's face said that she understood everything Greta was trying to put into words.

"You have to remember that Doug was not a physically strong man, Greta. Oh, I'm not implying he was a milksop, but he just never was the strong, strapping guy that Brodie was. He had to focus his interest on different things in life than something as rough and tough as a career in the army. That had to have left him with some major disappointments, especially when his father was a decorated hero from the Vietnam War and his grandfather an army lieutenant during World War II. I believe Doug wanted to be like his brother and his father, but he just didn't have the makings for it. But none of that means he wasn't special though," she added tenderly. "He was a good man."

"Yes," Greta said with a quick smile. Doug had

been good. He'd been just what Greta had wanted. Or so she'd thought. Until last night when Brodie had filled her head with all that nonsense about love and passion. What did he know about it, anyway, she asked herself. Stable security was much more important to her than the thrill of a kiss.

But even as she was trying to convince herself of that fact, her fingers were lifting to the spot where Brodie had kissed her cheek.

Later that morning, Greta and Anita were at the kitchen table wrapping gifts when Lilly and the two men returned from their shopping excursion. While Lilly and her grandfather carried their wrapped packages to the Christmas tree in the living room, Brodie lingered in the kitchen.

"Mom, you'll never guess who I ran into this morning down at the shopping center," Brodie said as he poured himself a cup of coffee.

Anita didn't bother to glance at her son. Instead, she focused her attention on the red ribbon she was attaching to a shiny silver package. "You're right, I'll never guess, so tell me."

"Patsy Wallis. Remember her? She was in my high school class."

Anita darted a look at her son as she continued to fidget with the ribbon. Across the table, Greta was doing ___ her best to act as though she wasn't listening to a ___ d being said.

"___ ___ ourse I remember," Anita declared, "she was ___ ___ nd cheerleader. Didn't you date her at one ___

B___ ___ckled and took a seat next to Greta's right ___ ___ Lifting her head, she gave him the same cool ___ ___e'd given him at the breakfast table, but it di___ ___m to affect him. He grinned and patted her ___ ___iat was lying atop the table.

"___ ___m. That was her friend, Kelli. Patsy was the ___ ___e that drove the white Mustang."

"___ ___. Very pretty girl. I'll bet she still is," Ani___ ___d aloud.

B___ ___continued to study Greta. "I suppose." His gaz___ ___ appreciatively over Greta's fiery red curls. "If ___ ___e brunettes."

G___ ___cowled at him and Brodie smiled suggestivel___ ___k at her. Thankfully Anita missed the excha___ ___ompletely.

"___ you two have a nice visit?" Anita asked her son.

B___ ___ie sipped his coffee before he answered and Gre___ ___t there imagining the whole scene with him and ___ ___high school cutie. No doubt this Patsy had faw___ ___ all over him, she thought nastily. She'd probably stroked his arm and batted her lashes up at him and he'd melted all over her.

As soon as the image settled in her head, Greta immediately slapped herself. She couldn't be jealous over Brodie Barstow! He'd be one of the last men on earth to take a second, serious look at her.

"Very nice," Brodie answered his mother. "She told me they were having a big Christmas dance down at the VFW tonight. Her husband is a veteran and helps organize the thing. Why hadn't you mentioned the dance to me? Aren't you and Dad going?"

Finished with the package, Anita pushed the box aside and went over to the sink to wash her hands. "Sorry, Brodie, there's been too much happening and the dance had slipped my mind. Sometimes your father and I attend. But we hadn't planned on it this year. Not when we've got to go to the Morraleses' tomorrow night for their party." Turning away from the sink, she suddenly clapped her hands together. "I just had a marvelous idea. Why don't you take Greta to the dance? It would be a wonderful outing for her and you'd get to see some of your old friends."

Shocked, Greta stared at her mother-in-law. "Oh no!" she burst out. "I can't dance. Brodie can attest to that."

Anita waved her hand in a dismissive way. "Pooh, who cares? All you do is hold on to each other and move your feet a little. Brodie can show you what to do."

Greta's gaze flew over to Brodie. His expression

was thoughtful and, in Greta's opinion, just a little too dangerous for her liking.

"Mom, that is a great idea!"

Feeling as though the two of them had already backed her into a corner, Greta rose to her feet and moved away from the table. "You're both forgetting Lilly," she said quickly. "And I'm sure the dance will be for adults only."

"Naturally. It's an adult party. That's why it would be good for you," Anita told her. "James and I will keep Lilly. In fact, there's an animated Christmas movie for children showing at the theatre. I'm sure she'd love it."

She couldn't go to a party with Brodie, Greta thought desperately. The two of them would be alone. He'd be close to her and he'd be touching her. She couldn't deal with that. Not when he was already making her quiver with a desire that was strictly forbidden, as far as she concerned.

Shaking her head, she moved over to the cabinet counter and began to clear a bit of clutter. "I'm sorry. I'm just not the partying type. I wouldn't know a soul and Brodie would have much more fun if he went without me," Greta said.

"Nonsense," Anita said firmly. "Brodie will introduce you to his friends. Besides, Christmas is a time for joy making and you need to make the most of your vacation before you go back to Kennebunk."

Oh dear, oh dear, how could she get out of this, Greta wondered desperately. She couldn't! Not without making a big issue and looking stiff and ungrateful in the process.

"Mom's right. It won't be long before you'll be heading back to Maine. And then you wouldn't have the chance to do a Texas two-step," Brodie said, then quickly corrected, "well, I guess you might have a chance, but it just wouldn't be the same as doing it here."

It was all Greta could do to keep from groaning out loud and rolling her eyes toward the ceiling. He was doing this on purpose! He was forcing her to go places and do things that she would never do otherwise. Couldn't he see that she didn't want to change her quiet, simple existence?

"I don't know how to do a Texas two-step," she pointed out to him.

Rising from the table, Brodie went over to where she stood rigidly by cabinets. "You will after tonight," he promised with a cunning tilt to his lips. "And anyway, it's like Mom said, all we have to do is hold each other and move our feet."

*Hold each other.* Surely Brodie realized that was the last thing the two of them should be doing. Or did he?

## *Chapter 4*

That night, as Greta searched through the clothes she'd brought from home, she asked her daughter, "Are you sure you don't mind Mommy going to the dance with Uncle Brodie?"

With an emphatic shake of her head, Lilly pointed a tiny forefinger at a piece of red fabric. "Wear that, Mommy. It's pretty. See, I'm gonna wear red, too. Like Santa does." She held the skirt of her dress out so that Greta could take a close look.

"Oh my, you do look beautiful tonight," Greta exclaimed. She passed a hand over Lilly's shiny crown of blond hair. "Are you excited about going to the movie with your grandparents?"

Lilly nodded, then with a grimace, she tilted her head to one side. "But I'd like to go with you and Brodie," she said in a slightly sulky voice. "I wanta dance, too!"

Greta patted her daughter's head, then walked around the bed and took a seat next to the stack of clothes she'd laid out on the mattress. "You can't go both places, sweetheart. And the dance is only for grown-ups. Besides that, Granny and Gramps would feel awful if you didn't go with them."

Lilly thought about this for a few moments before she hopped onto the side of the bed and bounced herself up and down. "I don't wanta make Granny and Gramps sad. I wanta be good. Or Santa might not come. And then I wouldn't get any toys."

Greta cast her daughter an indulgent glance. "That's very logical of you, honey."

The bouncing paused as Lilly's small features wrinkled up in confusion. "Lolli-cal? What's that, Mommy?"

"Oh, it just means that you're a smart little girl."

Leaping off the bed, Lilly raced around to where her mother was sitting on the opposite side of the mattress and tightly hugged Greta's neck.

Smiling with comical affection, Greta asked, "What was that for?"

Lilly grinned at her mother. "That's 'cause you're smart, too!"

Greta didn't think so. A smart woman didn't allow herself to be led into dangerous temptation. And a night out with Brodie was going to be exactly that.

She was a beautiful woman. Why hadn't Brodie realized that before, he wondered. Or was he just now seeing her through different eyes?

"You look very lovely tonight, Greta."

The two of them had arrived at the dance just moments earlier and were now standing a few feet away from one of the many decorated Christmas trees scattered around the massive room of the VFW building. The ceiling was draped with tinsel and poinsettias took up any space that couldn't be used for dancing. Hundreds of people were milling about, eating barbequed brisket and all the trimmings from long buffet tables, and dancing to seasonal music being played by a local band. The scents of evergreen and delicious food saturated the air and the festive atmosphere had Greta's blue eyes shining.

"You sound surprised," she said wryly.

Brodie looked down at her, his gaze focused on the low neckline of her red top. The fabric was glittery and the hint of décolletage was definitely risqué for her taste in clothing. Her appearance bowled him over and he was shocked at how much he wanted to hold her in his arms, strip the luxurious pieces of clothing from her body and make slow love to her.

The silent admission of his feelings darkened Brodie's eyes as he continued to study Greta. "I am. Surprised that you own such a garment."

Greta cheek's flushed as she glanced down at the red top and black velvet skirt she was wearing. The outfit had been an impulsive purchase right before she and Lilly had left Kennebunk. Now, seeing the appreciative light in Brodie's eyes, she was glad she'd allowed the sales clerk in the department store to talk her into something sexy instead of sturdy.

"I thought I'd better be prepared. Just in case your parents wanted to go out to a nice restaurant—or something."

His fingertips slid seductively across the ridge of her exposed collarbone and she hoped he couldn't see the goose bumps racing down her arms or the rapid thump of her heart beneath the red fabric.

"I'm glad," he said softly. "This is the way I always knew you should look."

Just the idea that he'd thought about her appearance was disconcerting, but to have him looking at her now, as though she were a luscious grape he wanted to peel, was enough to make her insides shake.

"Uh, why don't we see if we can find something to drink?" she suggested.

With a brief but knowing smile, he moved his hand to the back of her waist and guided her toward the refreshment area. Along the way, the two of them were stopped several times by acquaintances of Brodie's. Everyone seemed surprised to see him and all wanted to know how long he'd be staying home this time. Greta had been wondering the same question herself and was disappointed when he answered with the elusive response that he hadn't received his new orders yet.

But then, it shouldn't matter to her, she reminded herself. She'd be going back to Maine in a matter of days. Where Brodie went from here was no concern of hers. Yet she couldn't deny that forgetting him was going to be a difficult task.

Once they reached the buffet tables, Brodie gestured toward an array of drinks. "Looks like we have the choice of sodas, coffee, tea, beer and Christmas punch—spiked and regular. Which do you prefer?"

He was obviously expecting her to choose something bland and safe, Greta decided. And for some reason it was suddenly important to her to show him that he didn't know her quite as well as he thought.

"I'll try some of the spiked punch," she told him. "After all, it is Christmas."

His brows lifted with mild surprise. "All right!" he happily approved. "Let's make a toast."

He filled two plastic glasses with the cherry-red drink and handed one of them to Greta.

"What are we toasting to?" she asked.

As he started to answer, several partygoers arrived at the refreshment table. Brodie took Greta by the arm and murmured, "Let's get somewhere out of the way."

Greta allowed him to lead her to a small bench at the opposite end of the room where the area was less crowded and the noise more muted.

"This is much better," he said as the two of them took a seat on the bench. "Now to the toast, what would you like to drink to? Health? Wealth? Love? Happiness?"

Because the bench was short, Greta was forced to sit close by his side. As she studied his rugged face, she couldn't help but think she was with the sexiest man here at the dance. He was young and tough and physically fit and the glint in his eyes and the dimples in his cheeks made him pretty much irresistible, even to her.

"Why don't we just drink to happiness. That encompasses most everything," she said. "After all, if a person isn't happy none of the other things matter."

Lifting his glass, his eyes caught hers. "Here's to our happiness," he said softly.

Greta's hand quavered as she touched her glass to his. *Our happiness.* He made it sound so intimate, as though the two of them were actually connected in a romantic way and, just for a moment, she allowed herself to wonder what it would be like to be loved by a man like Brodie. Everything he went to do in life he did with passion. No doubt he would treat love and marriage in the same way. An intimate relationship with Brodie would be fiery and all-consuming. Not the nice, calm companionship she'd had with her late husband.

"You've surprised me again, Greta," he went on after each of them had taken a long sip from their drink. "You didn't choose the one I thought you would."

The alcohol in the punch burned her throat, but the pleasant warmth that spread through her stomach made up for it and she took another careful sip before she answered, "What did you think I'd choose to toast to? Wealth? All men seem to think us women are focused solely on money."

Brodie shook his head and then suddenly his solemn face dipped closer. "Not you, Greta," he said lowly. "I thought the thing you'd want most for yourself would be love."

Shaken by his statement, she glanced around her to see who might have overheard his comment. Thankfully, the only people nearby were the dancers skirting the floor some few feet away.

"I've already had love," she reminded him.

"Have you?"

She clutched the plastic cup tightly as her gaze swung accusingly back to his. "Brodie, how could you say—"

He didn't allow her to finish. "I'll bet Doug never saw you looking like you do tonight. I'll bet the two of you never even went to a dance together."

Greta stared guiltily down at the red liquid in her cup. "That wasn't necessarily Doug's fault. I should have tried to put some fun and passion into our marriage. But to be honest with you, I didn't know how. And even if I had, I would have been afraid to."

Scooting closer, Brodie slid his arm around the back of her shoulders. "Greta, why?"

"It's—" she stopped and shrugged, then started again, "I guess coming from an unstable home has always made me long for security."

"Unstable," he repeated the word with disbelief. "I've never heard you mention your family. I always figured you were brought up in one of those strong, New England families."

The corners of Greta's lips turned downward. "I

rarely talk about my family. I guess that's because we're not a family anymore. My father left my mother and I when I was only six years old."

Long moments passed as his gaze roamed her face. "Why? I mean, why did he leave?"

Lifting her eyes to his, Greta said, "I've wondered about that for years now, Brodie. But I don't suppose I'll ever know. When I was small, I used to think it was because he didn't like my mother or me. But later, after I became an adult, I've thought back to the times before Michael O'Brien left our home and I remember that he appeared to be a happy man then. At least, he seemed happy most of the time. He liked to laugh and joke. And one time I heard him telling Teresa, my mother, that she was too damn serious for him and she was making me just like her. I didn't know what he meant at the time, but later I figured it out."

"Do you ever see your father now?" Brodie asked as he tried to imagine losing his own father in such a way. It just wasn't fathomable.

Greta shook her head. "I haven't seen or heard from him since I was six. I presume that once he decided to leave, that was it, he didn't want any part of us anymore." She drew in a rough breath and let it out. "He wanted to go somewhere that he could be happy. And apparently it wasn't with us."

With a tight grimace, Brodie asked, "What about your mother? Do you see her often?"

Shaking her head once again, Greta said, "No. A few years ago, she moved away and married again. She doesn't often get in touch. Sometimes I believe she blames me for Daddy's leaving."

Brodie moved his arm from her shoulders and clasped his hand around her cool fingers. "That's ridiculous. You can't be blamed for something that happened between your parents."

Lifting the cup to her lips, Greta swallowed the last of the cherry-red drink. "I know," she conceded, "but I can't stop the thought from going through my mind. And once Daddy left, she had to work really hard just to keep a roof over our heads. There were times we barely had enough food to eat. Things would have been easier if she hadn't had me to take care of."

"Things would have been easier if she'd had a responsible husband," Brodie countered.

Nodding grimly, Greta stared down at their entwined fingers. "That's why I made sure I got a college education so that I could always support myself. That's why I felt so comfortable with my marriage to Doug. He was all work and no play, the complete opposite from my father. I knew he would never get some wild whim to search for greener pastures."

Suddenly there were so many things Brodie wanted to say to her, so many things he felt she needed to hear. Since that night he'd picked up her and Lilly at the airport, his emotions had run the gamut from unexpected attraction to something far, far deeper. More and more he was realizing that he wanted her to be a part of his life now and forever. He wanted the chance to make her happy, to make the three of them a real family. But now was not the time or the place, so he simply rose to his feet. "Come on. The band is starting to play 'Blue Christmas.' Let's dance and be happy."

Glad to put all of the sad thoughts of the past behind her, she allowed him to tug her to her feet and into his arms. In a matter of moments Greta forgot all about making her footsteps match perfectly to his and forgot, too, about the people swirling around them. Having Brodie's body pressed tightly to hers was filling her body with heat and her mind with all sorts of improper images.

"You're getting good at this. You're a quick learner," Brodie whispered close to her ear.

Her cheek was resting against his shoulder and she breathed in the uniquely masculine scent clinging to his shirt. "It's the punch. I feel as limp as a rag. Maybe you should take me home," she suggested.

Brodie's hand tightened at the side of her waist. "Not on your life. The night has just started."

* * *

Nearly three hours later, Brodie pulled the truck to a stop in front of the Barstow home and killed the engine. Across from him, Greta roused up in the seat and reached for her high heels.

"Oh goodness," she said with a groan as she pushed her aching feet into the heels. "I must have dozed off, I didn't realize we were so close to home."

Leaning his left arm on the steering wheel, he turned slightly to look at her. The soft glow of a nearby yard lamp illuminated her tumbled red curls and sleepy face. Brodie realized he'd like nothing more than to draw her into his arms and taste her lips. "You were tired," he reasoned. "You needed a little snooze."

"That punch didn't help matters," she said. "I wonder what was in it?"

He chuckled softly. "Vodka probably."

"Oh." She touched fingertips to the crease in the middle of her forehead. "Well, I can assure you I'm feeling the aftereffects."

His expression turned to one of concern. "Just sit there a minute and take a few deep breaths," he suggested. "There's no hurry to get into the house. The night is warm."

He was right. The night was balmy and being enclosed in the interior of the truck with Brodie was making her feel downright hot. She couldn't wait around for her head to stop spinning. As long as he was near, that would never happen.

"I'm all right. Really," she said and with a deep breath she reached for the door latch.

"Greta?"

Pausing, she forced herself to glance his way and her heart lurched into high speed as she found his gaze in the gray shadows.

"Yes?"

"I just wanted to tell you what a good time I had tonight. Thank you for going with me."

Surprised, she searched his face. "You sound like you really mean that."

With a hasty groan of frustration, he reached over and clasped his hand around her upper arm. Greta felt every nerve in her body suddenly stand on its end.

"I mean that and a whole lot more."

"Brodie, what—"

Sliding to the middle of the bench seat, he tugged her into his arms. "Damn it, Greta, do I have to spell it out to you?"

Her heart was pounding now and her breaths were coming fast as the heat of his body began to seep into hers. "Yes," she murmured, "because I don't know what this is all about."

He didn't answer with words. Instead he lowered his lips to hers.

The intimate contact stole Greta's breath and for a moment she was frozen motionless as his lips worked a magic spell upon hers. In a matter of moments a flame flickered deep inside her and burst through her body like a golden beam of hot light. Slowly, her hands crept to his shoulders and slid around his neck. Her body instinctively arched into his.

Pushing his hand into her tumbled curls, Brodie lifted his head and gazed down at her. "I've been wanting to do that for a long time."

"No," she whispered in an awed voice.

A wry smile touched his face. "Why do you find that so incredible?"

"I—because I'm your sister-in-law!"

"Not anymore. You're my brother's widow."

She stirred, hoping he would release her, but, if anything, his hold on her tightened.

Aghast, she asked, "Doesn't that mean anything to you?"

His fingertips smoothed the soft skin at her temples. "It means that part of your life is over. And it has nothing to do with the feelings I have for you."

She managed to ease back from his chest, but still he kept a tight hold on her shoulders. "Brodie, I don't know what it is you're feeling for me, but we both know it's not permanent. And it's definitely not serious."

One hand moved away from her shoulder to cup the side of her face. He could understand why she would think of him as a bit of a playboy. He'd never had a serious relationship in his life. But that was only because he'd never met a woman who'd made him long for a cozy home with a wife and children. And even if he had met the right woman, he couldn't have expected her to follow him around from one base to another. But now things were different. A few months ago he'd put in for a position that would keep him rooted to one spot. Any day now he expected to hear whether or not the army had granted his request. "You really don't understand what I'm feeling for you. For us," he murmured. "You can't tell how much I want you."

The sharp intake of her breath hissed against her teeth as she tried to calm her roiling emotions.

"And you want me just as much," he went on before she could make any sort of reply. "You just don't want to admit it. To yourself or to me."

With a tiny groan, she pressed both palms against her cheeks. "Maybe I do want you," she whispered fiercely. "But I'm not stupid. I know you don't have a serious bone in your body. Not where women are concerned. And I have no intentions of becoming one of your victims!"

His jaw dropped. "A victim! What do you think I am anyway? And what am I doing to hurt you? Kissing you? Telling you how much I want you?"

Greta suddenly felt so trapped and exposed that all she could do was lash back at him. "Yes! When we both know you don't mean any of it."

"Oh, whoa now," he ordered. "Maybe we'd better just do all this over. You've missed something."

Seeing his face was aimed straight at hers, she tried to dodge away from him, but his arm slid tightly around her shoulders while his thumb and forefinger gently caught hold of her chin.

"Brodie—don't—"

"Don't what? Kiss you?" Lifting her chin, his fingertips traced loving patterns over her face and outlined her quivering lips. "Tell me, Greta. Tell me you don't want me."

"I can't," she murmured, her voice strained.

A desperate groan rumbled deep in his throat and then his lips were back on hers, tasting their sweetness, searching for a sign that she needed him as much as he needed her and when her arms locked tightly around his neck and her tongue began to mate eagerly with his, Brodie felt a surge of triumph.

"Now," Brodie murmured once the kiss finally ended, "did that feel like I didn't mean it?"

Her face on fire, her body trembling with aftershocks, she jerked back from his hold. "Look, Brodie, I've already had my hopes and dreams crushed once. I can't go through it again. Not with you. Not with anybody!"

"Greta—"

Whatever else he said was lost to her as she quickly flipped the latch on the door and slid to the ground. Without looking back, she hurried into the dark house and didn't stop until she was safely behind her bedroom door.

The next evening, Greta was in the kitchen helping Anita wrap several party dishes with cellophane. Brodie's mother was already dressed in an emerald-green skirt and sweater with a rhinestone studded reindeer pinned to her shoulder. The older woman had fussed with her hair for more than an hour and Greta could see the coming party was very important to her.

"I am really sorry about this, Greta," Anita said as she and Greta placed the wrapped dishes into a cardboard box. "I hate that James and I have to leave you and Lilly tonight, of all nights. But the Morraleses' have been lifelong friends, not to mention that Martin is a partner in James's construction company. Normally we have our little Christmas get-together with the crew before now. But this year Sonja planned it for Christmas Eve."

Greta waved away her apology. "Don't worry about it. Lilly and I will be fine. I actually need the rest and Lilly is going to be anxious to go to bed early. So Santa will get here quicker, you know," she explained with an indulgent smile.

Anita leaned over and kissed Greta's cheek. "Thank you, honey, for being so understanding. We'll have all day tomorrow together," she promised. "And you won't have to worry about being here alone tonight. Brodie will be here with you."

The woman didn't have to remind her of that, Greta thought. She'd been worrying about the fact all day long. And after falling into his arms last night, she'd been trying her best to avoid the man and so far he'd made it easy by being gone on some outing with his father all day. But tonight would be a different matter and she was already determined to put up a steely resistance to his charms.

Anita went on as though she hadn't expected a response from Greta. "I've left plenty of eggnog in the fridge. There's a couple of cold cut and vegetable trays in there, too. You might want to snack on them. Or you could have the tamales."

"Don't worry. We'll find plenty to eat," Greta told her.

Footsteps sounded behind them and Greta turned to see James entering the kitchen. He was dressed in starched khakis and a nice white shirt and Christmas tie. He looked very nice and Greta didn't hesitate to tell him so. Something she would have felt shy about doing three days ago.

James smiled and gave her a brief, one-armed hug. "Did you hear that old woman?" he directed at his wife. "I still haven't lost it."

Anita laughed. "You'll never lose it, darling. Not in my eyes. Now, before your head gets too big to fit through the door, would you carry this box out to the car? I'll follow you."

Minutes later, Greta was waving the couple off when Brodie stepped out on the back porch to join her.

"My parents are already leaving?" he asked.

Rather than look at him, Greta followed the wink of the taillights as the car made its way down the long drive toward the highway.

"Your mother wanted to get there early to help Sonja set everything up," Greta explained. "They said not to wait up, it'll be late when they get back."

Turning, she stepped around him and entered the kitchen. He followed on her heels and joined her at the cabinet as she began to prepare a fresh pot of coffee.

"I've hardly seen you today," he said.

She glanced sideways to see he was standing with his hands shoved in the front pockets of his faded jeans. A gray sweatshirt with a small military insignia on the left breast covered his broad shoulders. She wanted to tell herself that his long, lean body didn't excite her, that the dark hair falling onto his forehead and the dimples bracketing his lips didn't do a thing to her constitution. But she couldn't lie to herself. Not when every particle of her wanted to reach out and touch him.

"You've been out," she said as she pushed the basket of coffee grounds into place on the coffeemaker.

"Something tells me I wouldn't have seen much of you even if I had been here."

Ignoring that comment, she asked, "Where's Lilly?"

"Watching a cartoon about Rudolph. I think she wants a reindeer for Christmas. Or at least, a pony."

"Dear heaven," she exclaimed, "Texas must have put a spell on her. She's never wanted an animal before."

He inched closer to Greta's side and said in a low voice, "I wish it would put a spell on you."

Finished with her task, she glanced up at him. "Why? So I wouldn't be able to see what's right for me?"

"Greta, I—"

Brodie's words were suddenly interrupted by the pitter-patter of Lilly's footsteps as the young girl skipped into the kitchen.

"When are we gonna eat, Mommy? I'm hungry."

"In just a few minutes," Greta answered. "Would you like to help Mommy set the table?"

The golden curls on the girl's shoulders bounced as she quickly shook her head. "No. I wanta go see what happens to Rudolph. Everybody is laughing at him cause his nose is red and he's feelin' really sad." She turned with a flounce and started out of the room. "You can call me when it's ready to eat, Mommy."

Once the child was gone, Brodie stepped closer and trapped Greta's body against the row of white cabinets.

"What are you doing?" she demanded, her voice low and just a bit panicky.

His hands ran over her shoulders and down the sides of her arms as the lower portion of his body pressed suggestively into hers. Instantly, Greta could feel a wanton heat rising up in her, urging her to lean into him, to press her breasts against his chest.

"I'm doing the very thing I've been wanting to do all day," he answered simply.

Groaning, she bit her lip and glanced away from him. "You didn't listen to a thing I said last night, did you?"

His hands moved up and down her rib cage before coming to rest at the sides of her breasts. Greta's legs began to tremble.

"I listened. Just not to your words."

Her nostrils flared daintily as she tried to draw in a greatly needed breath. "You're not playing fair, Brodie."

A faint smile tilted his hard, masculine lips. "I'm not *playing* at anything, Greta. I'm serious."

With a muffled oath, she pushed at his chest, but she might as well have been trying to roll a giant boulder from her path. "Brodie, I didn't come down here to Texas to have an affair with you! I'm here to celebrate Christmas with your family and nothing else."

His brows lifted ever so slightly as his gaze roamed her face. "I came here to be with my family, too. I didn't know this was going to happen."

*This?* Just what did he mean by *this?* Greta was too afraid to ask. The way she felt at this moment, it wouldn't take too many sweet words from this man to have her falling straight into his arms.

Her palms flattened against his chest, as though the puny effort could keep him at bay. "Brodie, we both know that I'm not your type of woman. In fact, I'd venture to say I'm quite the opposite. Are you feeling an itch and I just happen to be the nearest scratching post?"

He scowled at her. "That's cold, Greta. And how could you know what type of woman I like, anyway?"

Lifting her eyes to the ceiling, she moaned with desperation. "I'm not stupid, Brodie. You're a young man, much younger than me. You're good-looking and you're outgoing. I'm sure you don't have to beg women to go out with you. You're not going to be attracted to a conservative widow, seven years older than you, and with a child to boot."

"If you'd told me that very thing a few days ago, I probably would have agreed with you." His palms tenderly cupped her face. "But now I have to say you're all wrong. I *am* attracted to you. Very attracted. Last night, after I went to bed, all I could think about was kissing you and what it would be like to make love to you."

Her face hot with fire, she turned her eyes away from him. "Brodie, don't say such things to me," she whispered in a barely audible tone.

His knuckles smoothed across her cheekbone. "Why? There's nothing wrong with me telling you how much I want you. How much I want to kiss you right here—right now."

Her eyes flickered back to his and her heart bolted into a wild gallop. Desire was simmering in his warm brown eyes. Desire for her.

Intoxicated by the thought, Greta's head unconsciously tilted back, her lips parted. Brodie's fingers slid into her hair and cradled the back of her head as he lowered his lips down to hers.

To taste his kiss again was something Greta had

been desperately wanting, but trying her best to fight against. Now the fight was over and, though she might have lost, she didn't care. To be in Brodie's strong arms, to have his hard lips exploring hers was the most glorious feeling she'd ever experienced.

"Mommy! Come here! Come see Rudolph. He's pulling Santa's sleigh through the air!"

Lilly's voice drifted loudly from the living room and the sound of her daughter was enough to make Greta instantly jerk back from Brodie's embrace.

"I'll be there in just a second, sweetheart," Greta called to her.

Greta moved to step around him, but Brodie caught her by the shoulder. Pausing, she looked up at his dark, serious face.

"We'll take this up later, Greta."

He was making a promise. And Greta could only wonder how long it would be before he kept it.

# Chapter 5

Homemade tamales were a Christmas tradition in south Texas and Anita had made sure that plenty were stocked in the refrigerator for Brodie to enjoy.

He heated a platterful for their supper and then they topped the meal off with huge wedges of pecan pie that Anita had made from nuts gathered in the backyard. Greta could feel her waistline expanding by the minute. But that was the least of her worries. The growing attraction she was feeling for Brodie was getting downright decadent and as the evening passed she could only hope he forgot about that promise he'd made earlier in the kitchen.

Otherwise, she might end up making a real idiot of herself.

After their meal was finished, the three of them went to the living room where Lilly sat cross-legged at the coffee table and used a small box of crayons to draw Christmas pictures on tablet paper. Soon Brodie joined her and Lilly giggled as Brodie sketched a picture of Santa sporting a black beard and mustache and wearing a pair of cowboy boots.

From her seat on the couch, Greta found herself smiling at the picture the two of them made together. She couldn't deny that Brodie was wonderful with her daughter. And the fact continued to amaze her. From what she'd gathered, the man had not been around children all that much. Furthermore, his job dealt with rough, tough issues. Gentleness or tenderness didn't come into the life of a soldier. Yet when Brodie was near Lilly, the tough man in him turned as soft as butter.

Once their drawings were finished, Brodie used a set of colorful magnets to plaster them to the refrigerator. Afterwards, he suggested to Lilly that it was time they set out milk and cookies for Santa's visit.

Greta helped them gather the treats and put them on a plastic tray. Brodie placed the snack on a small table near the Christmas tree and then he carefully went around the room and lit several fat, holly-scented candles. To help Santa see and not stumble around in the dark, he explained to Greta and Lilly.

"I like the candles, don't you, Mommy?" Lilly asked as she climbed onto the couch next to her mother. "I'll bet Santa will think they're pretty. Do you think he'll be here soon?"

"I don't know, sweetheart." Greta stroked her daughter's head. "Santa has lots of houses to visit tonight."

"Maybe we should turn on the news and see if we can get an update on where Santa is right now," Brodie suggested.

He turned on the television and tuned it to a local station. A female reporter was broadcasting from downtown Houston where some sort of Christmas celebration was going on. Lilly watched carefully for signs of Santa and after a few moments she squealed with delight when the camera scanned to a different view where another reporter was holding a microphone in front of the jolly old man himself.

"Well, that's good news," Brodie said as he tossed Greta a conspiring wink. "Looks like Santa has already made it to Houston. You know what that means, Lilly?"

Her eyes alight with wonder, the golden-haired child shook her head. "What does it mean, Uncle Brodie?"

Grinning, he gently tweaked the girl's nose. "It

means that Santa has already made it to south Texas and he's headed this way."

Lilly was consumed with excitement as she jumped from the couch to face the two adults. "Oh, boy! Oh, boy! Mommy, I gotta go to bed," she said in a rush. "Santa won't bring presents unless kids are in bed. That's what the reindeer said."

Looking over, Greta caught Brodie's eye. The corners of his lips were tilted to an indulgent smile and she felt a surge of anticipation that had nothing to do with Santa's arrival.

Rising from the couch, she said, "Excuse us, Brodie. I'll be back after I help Lilly to bed."

"I'm not going anywhere," he drawled.

Shaken by the suggestive tone of his voice, Greta took Lilly by the hand and quickly led her out of the room.

A few minutes later, as Lilly pulled on a pair of flannel pajamas, the girl asked, "Do I have to brush my teeth tonight, Mommy?"

"You always brush your teeth before bedtime," Greta reminded her. "Why wouldn't you brush them tonight?"

Tilting her head to one side, Lilly rolled her eyes at her mother. "Because it's the night that Santa comes!"

Hiding a smile, Greta said, "Oh. I guess I wasn't

thinking. But just because it's Christmas Eve doesn't mean you get out of brushing your teeth. So hurry to the bathroom," Greta instructed. "And then I'll tuck you in."

Lilly diligently cleaned her teeth, then put away her toothbrush. Water had splashed the front of her shirt in several spots and white toothpaste was smeared at the corner of her mouth. Greta wiped her daughter's mouth with a washcloth and dried her pajama top with a towel.

"Don't forget, Mommy, I've got to say my prayers," Lilly reminded her mother as Greta turned down the covers on the twin-size bed.

"Of course you do," Greta told her. "So I'm going to stand right here at the end of the bed and wait."

Kneeling at the side of the bed, near the pillow, Lilly began to thank God for all the good things in her life and then she asked Him to bless her mommy, her grandparents and especially Uncle Brodie.

"And thank you very much God for Christmas, 'cause Christmas makes everybody happy. Amen," she added with a flourish. "Oh, and God, I didn't tell Santa what I wanted the most. So I'm gonna tell you. I'd like a real daddy for Christmas."

Rising to her feet, Lilly jumped into bed and snuggled down in the pillow. She grinned broadly as Greta bent over to tuck the covers around her shoulders.

"Mommy, do you think I'll get what I asked for?"

The lump in Greta's throat made her voice husky as she tried to answer her daughter. "Well, Lilly, sometimes we have to wait on the things we want the most."

"But I might wake up and have a new daddy. Brodie says Christmas is a mirror-call."

Smiling gently, Greta pushed the golden curls from Lilly's forehead. "Christmas is a miracle. That's true."

Lilly's nose wrinkled with deep concentration. "What is a mirror-call, Mommy?"

"Well, it means that something wonderful can happen."

Lilly let out a long, contented sigh and closed her eyes. "Good night, Mommy."

"Good night, sweetie."

Greta adjusted a tiny night-light on the bed table. Then easing out of the room, she shut the door behind her.

As she walked back to the living room, Lilly's Christmas prayer warmed her through and through. Her daughter's innocent plea had suddenly peeled the cold layers away from her heart and now it was throbbing to live and to love.

When she returned to the living room, Brodie was squatted on his boot heels going through the wrapped gifts beneath the tree. He grinned at Greta as he gave a small package a shake.

"Can't hear a thing. It must be socks or a tie."

She smiled at him as unexpected joy swept through her. Having Brodie near her this Christmas had changed everything. Only three days had passed since she'd arrived in Texas, but somehow she felt very different.

"You're not supposed to be shaking the gifts, Brodie," she softly admonished.

Grinning mischievously he put the package back under the tree and rose to his feet. "Did you get Lilly to bed okay?"

Drawing in a nervous breath, Greta nodded. "She's very excited about Christmas, but I think she'll go right to sleep. She's had a very busy day."

Brodie walked over to where she stood at one end of the couch. "What about the things Santa is supposed to bring her? I'll help you put them out now, if you'd like."

"They're in the garage. I had everything shipped down here a few weeks ago, just to make sure there wouldn't be any last-minute problems getting the things here."

"Good. Let's go get them and then I'm going to make us a treat."

She looked at him with raised brows, but he merely smiled and nudged her toward the doorway.

"You'll see," he promised.

\* \* \*

The Santa Claus gifts were packed in a huge cardboard box. Brodie decided to carry the box inside so they could easily unpack everything in the living room.

For the most part, Lilly had asked for the traditional things that most little girls want during their early years. Brodie was completely taken with the lifelike infant doll and baby stroller.

"You know," he said thoughtfully as he stroked the doll's soft hair, "I've got to confess. My knowledge about children is about enough to put in your eye. But I've always wondered what it would be like to have some of my own. Being around Lilly this Christmas—" Pausing, he turned his head to look at Greta who was standing a few steps away. "It's been very special for me, Greta."

To see his big, strong hands gently holding the doll and to hear the affection in his voice for her daughter was enough to melt Greta's heart. "It's been very special for Lilly, too," she murmured. "I've never seen her so happy and you're a big reason for that."

Brodie placed the doll beneath the tree, then turned back to Greta. His eyes were shining as he reached for her hand. "We're finished here so I want you to sit on the couch while I go to the kitchen. I'll be back in two minutes," he promised.

Greta took a seat and he disappeared from the room. She hardly had time to wonder what he was doing, when he reappeared carrying a tray with two goblets.

"What is that?" Greta asked as he placed the tray on the coffee table. "It looks like eggnog."

Brodi took a seat next to her. "It is eggnog. Only this is special. It's laced with brandy."

"Brodie!" she gently scolded. "I had all the alcohol I needed last night at the dance."

"It's Christmas Eve," he reminded her as he leaned forward and picked up the goblets. "And this bit of spirits isn't going to hurt you."

He handed her one of the drinks and then with a snap of his fingers, he quickly rose to his feet and went over to the light switch. "This will make it taste a lot better."

When the overhead lights went out, the room dimmed to the flickering candlelight. Instantly, Greta's pulse lunged into overdrive.

"I'm not sure I can see my glass," Greta told him.

Brodie's lips twisted to a sexy grin as he slipped back into place beside her. "If you have any trouble finding your lips, I'll help. And if you think I'm trying to seduce you, you're right."

The past few days had taught her that Brodie was a man who didn't hold back on speaking his thoughts, but she never expected him to come out with something as blunt as this.

"Brodie, I—"

"Try your drink," he ordered.

She lifted the glass to her lips. "Why? Is this part of the seduction?"

A low, raspy chuckle passed his lips. "Of course."

Greta sipped the drink and was pleasantly surprised by the flavor. Yet she could hardly concentrate on the warming effect of the drink when Brodie was leaning ever closer, his eyes refusing to leave her face.

"Mmm. It tastes very good," she murmured.

"So do you."

Her eyes fluttered up to connect with his. "You don't have to say that sort of thing to me, Brodie."

"Why not? I want to tell you how I feel about you, Greta. I think you need to understand that you make me feel things and think about things that never crossed my mind before."

Greta could feel herself trembling as he took her glass and placed it alongside his on the coffee table.

"I wasn't finished with the eggnog," she said in feeble protest.

"There's plenty more to be had later. And I don't want to waste the time we have tonight."

If Greta planned to stay on the sensible path she'd taken all the years, she would leap from the couch and put a safe distance between her and Brodie Barstow. But he'd done something to her these past few days and she realized with a sudden surge of recklessness that she didn't always want to be sensible and safe.

Thoughts of resisting never entered Greta's head as he reached over and pulled her into his arms. And as he nestled her head against his shoulder, she reached up and touched her fingertips to his cheek.

"Brodie, I told you a few minutes ago that you've made this Christmas special for Lilly. Well, you've made it special for me, too."

His features softened to a look she'd never seen on him before. It was tender and serious and promising and her hands shook as she clutched the tops of his shoulders.

He tangled his fingers in her red hair as his eyes worshipped her face. "Greta, when I first saw you at the airport…I couldn't bear the sad loneliness I saw on your face. But now that's all gone. And I'd like to think that I'm partly responsible for putting a smile on your face."

As Greta continued to look up at him, she realized with a sudden start, that maybe for the first time in her life, she had become truly happy. Perhaps the joy she was feeling would only last a day or two more before she headed back to Maine. But at least she was experiencing it now.

"It's not your job to keep a smile on my face," she whispered.

His forefinger traced the quivering curves of her lips. "Oh yes, it is, honey. It's a job I plan to keep."

Doubts and questions tangled up inside her, but she didn't have the chance to utter more than his name before his lips settled softly, temptingly over hers.

A surge of sweet joy filled every particle of her being and she didn't try to hide her desire as she curled her arms tightly around his neck and opened her mouth to his.

Greta's response urged him to take everything he wanted from her soft lips and the gentle curves of her body pressing against him. Heat exploded inside him and spread like boiling liquid along his veins as his tongue teased hers, his teeth nipped her giving lips.

Up and down, his hands slid from her waist to the flare of her hips and up again to where her small breasts pushed against the cashmere sweater she was wearing.

Kneading the firm little mounds with his fingers, Greta rewarded him with a low groan of pleasure that fed his hungry arousal. Thrusting his hands beneath the hem of her sweater, his palms closed around her breasts while his thumbs slid outward to rake across her nipples.

The reaction to his touch was instant as he felt the

center of her breasts tighten into two hard buds and he quickly lowered her back to cushions of the couch.

"Let me taste you, sweet Greta," he whispered hoarsely. "Let me see how beautiful you are."

Greta's head moved side to side. "I'm not beautiful, Brodie. But I do want you. I want you so much."

Her whispered declaration was enough to make him pause and glance down at her. "Oh my darling. My Greta."

Before she could guess his intentions, he was off the couch and lifting her into his arms. Shadowy walls and doors flickered in her peripheral vision as he began to carry her through the quiet house.

"Where are we going?" she whispered close to his ear.

"To my bedroom. Do you think Lilly is asleep?"

"Yes. But put me down and I'll go check," she told him while the back of her mind was screaming with fear. Once she made love to Brodie he'd hold her heart right in the palms of his hands. And after tomorrow they would be parting. She couldn't bear such pain. But her body wouldn't begin to listen to the warnings dancing around in her head.

He set her feet upon the hallway floor. "Just a minute," he said with a low growl and then covered her lips with a long, hot kiss that turned Greta's knees to mush. "I don't want you to forget to come back to me," he added once he broke the contact between their lips.

As if she could forget anything about the man, Greta thought wildly.

She tiptoed into Lilly's room. The night-light shed a soft, yellow glow across the bed. Lilly was curled up on her side, her face serene in sleep. A yellow teddy bear was hugged to her tummy.

Lilly was probably dreaming about Santa bringing her a new daddy tomorrow, Greta mused, and she wondered how she was going to explain to her daughter that Santa didn't grant every wish a little girl made at Christmas.

When Greta reemerged from Lilly's bedroom, Brodie was waiting outside his bedroom door. Quietly, she walked to his side and once again he scooped her up in his arms and carried her across the threshold, to a wide bed positioned near a huge paned window.

Once he eased her down on the mattress, he went to the door and carefully closed and locked it.

"Just in case Lilly wakes and comes looking for you," he explained his actions. "You'll have time to get dressed and go to her."

Her breaths were more like shudders as she sucked air in and out of her lungs. "What about your parents?" she asked, knowing she sounded like a worrisome teenager, but unable to help herself. She'd never done such an impulsive, naughty thing in her life. "They might come home early."

Chuckling softly, he eased down beside her on the bed. "Not on your life. Dad and Martin always get a poker game going. They won't be home until the wee hours of the morning. Aren't we lucky?"

She swallowed as all sorts of emotions threatened to choke her. "I don't know. I really shouldn't be here. But you have a way of messing up my thinking."

His eyes on her face, he reached for the hem of her sweater and gently eased it upward. Rising to a sitting position, Greta lifted her arms so that he could pull the garment over her head. After the garment was out of the way and she was resting once again against the mattress, Brodie's hands slid over her bare arms and down her sides as his gaze took in the satiny flesh spilling over the cups of her lacy pink bra.

"Slender women have never turned my head. But I'll never be able to touch you enough. And redheads were never on my dating list. But your hair is glorious, Greta. It smells like roses and it feels like silk against my fingers."

Lifting a long curl from her shoulder, he rubbed it across his lips. Greta reached out and wrapped her fingers around his forearms.

"No man has ever said such things to me,

Brodie. Please don't say the words if you don't really mean them."

"Greta, Greta, whatever you do, don't ever doubt me."

Her guarded heart wanted to believe him. And for tonight she would. She would take every kiss, every touch, every moment in his arms and bury it in the deepest part of her.

Easing him out of the way, she kneeled in front of him and reached for the buttons on his shirt.

"Let me love you, Brodie," she murmured thickly. "Let me show you that I'm not the little mouse you think I am."

Sliding his hands around to her bare back, his fingers released the catch on her bra. The garment slid down her arms and his gaze devoured her perky breasts with their pale pink nipples.

Greta should have been embarrassed to have her nakedness exposed to a man who was supposed to only be her brother-in-law. She should have been shocked at the wicked heat pooling between her thighs, but she was neither. Brodie had unleashed something wild and wonderful inside her and she wanted to savor every moment before this night ended.

Slowly, purposely, her fingers worked loose the buttons on his shirt. She pushed it off his shoulders and down his arms. All the while, the dim light filtering through the windows bathed the hard muscles of his shoulders and chest and illuminated the rugged profile of his face.

As Greta's gaze took in the sight of his beautiful, masculine body, her breath caught in her throat and for a moment she thought she might stop breathing entirely.

"Oh, Brodie. Brodie," she whispered, her hands running rampant across his chest. "This must be a dream. This can't be me...feeling like this."

Bending her head, she pressed her lips against the slope of his shoulder. His skin was warm and smooth and faintly scented with sandalwood. The mixture stirred her senses even more and she moaned with sheer pleasure as she planted small kisses across his collarbone, up the side of his neck and along his jaw.

Brodie's hands caught her around the waist and tugged her forward until her nipples were squashed against his chest.

"This is real, honey. It's you and me. And you're making me crazy," he said with a soft growl.

Emboldened by his words, her hands worked their way down his chest until she found the waistband of his jeans. When she started to search for the zipper, he flopped back against the mattress to make her task easier.

"Did I really call you a mouse?" he asked with a grin. "I must have been out of my mind."

Feeling like a playful vixen for the first time in her life, she slid the zipper apart and tugged the jeans down over his hips. "You didn't say it outright. But I always knew what you were thinking about me."

"Really?" he goaded huskily. "What was I thinking?"

"That I was a cool, dowdy northerner."

The downward progression of his jeans stopped when they reached his cowboy boots. One by one, Greta quickly removed the boots and then tossed his jeans aside.

"You're right," he agreed, a smile lacing his voice. "And I couldn't understand what I found so attractive about that."

Greta stood at the side of the bed long enough to remove her slacks before she rejoined him on the rumpled covers. As he pulled her slender body close to his, she argued, "You didn't—you couldn't have been attracted to me."

"I was, my little mouse. I am. Just let me show you."

Greta didn't bother to say anything else. If he was trying to make her feel beautiful and sexy and wanted, it was working and she'd be crazy to argue with that.

Over and over he kissed her lips, while at the same time, his hands explored the warm hills and valleys of her body. Need, hot and urgent, spilled through her like a potent drink and she clung to him, shivering and panting and desperate to have him inside her.

Desire threatened to shatter him as Brodie raised his head long enough to look at her. "Are you protected with the pill or something?"

Her brain was so fogged with longing that for a moment she stared at him blankly and then when the meaning of his question finally hit her she wagged her head back and forth against the mattress.

"I—I'm sorry, Brodie. I haven't needed birth control. Do you have anything?"

"No. I wasn't expecting anything like this to happen," he said regretfully.

Her hands slid to his hips and she held him fast against her. "It doesn't matter. It's not a risky time for me right now."

Brodie had to believe her. He didn't have the strength to pull away from her now. Even the thought of making her pregnant was turning him on.

"Greta, Greta. You're too sweet. Too good." Bending his head, he covered her lips with a kiss that robbed them both of breath. Once their mouths broke apart, he framed her face with his palms and looked into her eyes. "Hold on to me, Christmas angel. Hold on and never let go."

Greta started to promise him that she would, but at that moment he entered her and the sensation momentarily stunned her with pleasure. All she could manage to do was groan and wrap her long legs around his.

Brodie had thought he could make love to her all night. He'd planned to savor her body for hours and give her the pleasure she needed and deserved. But only a few short minutes passed before the feel of her surrounding him was too delicious to bear. And when he felt her climbing to the clouds with him, he lifted her hips tightly to his and spilled himself inside her.

Long moments passed before Greta finally regained her breath and stirred beneath the weight of her body. Brodie rolled away from her but was careful to keep a hand splayed across her stomach. He didn't want to lose this connection with her. He never wanted to lose it.

"Greta?"

Her eyes on the twinkling lights beyond the window seal, she answered quietly, "Yes."

Scooting closer, his hand slid to cover one breast. She looked at him and suddenly it was all she could do to keep the mist in her eyes from turning to all out tears.

"We, uh, we need to talk."

All at once, it seemed, this man had become everything to her. How it she allowed it to happen? Now that she'd learned what it was like to be in his arms, how could she ever, ever forget?

She sighed. "Brodie, you don't need to give me some flowery speech. I'm a grown woman." Touching a hand to her forehead she suddenly laughed at herself. "That's an understatement. I'm seven years older than you! You don't have to explain to me what this was all about."

For long moments, his brown eyes studied her somber face. "Really? Since you seem to know, then why don't you tell me?"

Jarred by his retort, she frowned and looked away from him. "In one word, sex."

How many times had he just had "sex" with a woman, Brodie wondered. He didn't want to count. Not after what had just taken place between him and Greta. He'd felt his whole heart and soul pouring out to her and he knew he'd never be the same.

Propping himself on one elbow, Brodie's hand slipped from her breast up to her face, where he traced soft gentle patterns against her cheek.

"That's all you felt? Just sex?"

His question was so painful that she closed her eyes and bit back a groan. She'd never felt so much joy, so much desire and so very much love in her life. But she couldn't tell him that. After tomorrow she would be leaving and he would be going to God only knew where. It would probably be months, even years before she saw him again.

"Don't, Brodie. Don't ruin tonight. Our Christmas Eve together. I want it to stay special so I can remember us always. Like this."

Lifting her head from the pillow, she pressed a lingering kiss on his lips. Brodie smiled and slipped his fingers into her hair.

"Darling, you won't have to remember us like this. We're going to *be* like this from now on. I want you to be my wife. Will you marry me, Greta?"

# Chapter 6

Greta's heart began to thump harder and harder as she stared at him in stunned silence. Surely, she'd heard him wrong. Surely, he didn't want *her* for a wife.

"If this is some sort of joke, Brodie, then it's a very cruel one."

Suddenly feeling very exposed, she sat up on the side of the bed and wrapped one end of the bedspread around her naked body.

Brodie shifted on the bed to follow closely and he felt her body tense as his hands clasped the back of her shoulder. Nuzzling the side of her neck with his nose, he said softly, "How could you think I'm joking, Greta? I love you."

Stunned, she twisted around to face him. "Love! You don't know what you're saying," she said with a gasp. "You've never been in love!"

Her accusation caused one brow to arch up in a wry question mark. "How would you know something like that?"

Greta's eyes dropped to the tangled covers separating their bodies. "I don't. I just assumed because you've never been engaged or anything." She lifted her gaze back to his. "Have you been in love?"

His hands gently kneaded her shoulders. "No. Not until you. I didn't know it could be so…euphoric."

Inside her chest, her heart was doing a joyous tap dance, but she refused to let that weak, vulnerable part of her feelings show. Brodie wasn't serious. Maybe he was for the moment, but not in the long run. And her and Lilly's future was what she had to think about right now. Not how wonderful it felt to be loved by this man.

"You're not in love with me, Brodie, you're just feeling lots of Christmas cheer."

His mouth flattened to a line of disgust. "I never imagined you, of all people, would be sarcastic at a time like this."

Groaning with frustration, she twisted around so

that her whole body was facing his. "I'm trying to be reasonable. You don't want to marry *me!* I'm all wrong for you."

Unconvinced, he simply smiled at her. "You felt very right just a few moments ago."

Just looking at his face filled her heart with wondrous pleasure, so why was she arguing with him, she asked herself. Why wasn't she falling into his arms and promising to love him until her dying days?

"Brodie, I don't have to tell you that we're very different people. You need someone young, like yourself. Someone who will give you children."

"You're still very young. And you can have more children." His hand pushed at the cover until his fingers were spread against her lower stomach. In a low voice he said, "Maybe we've already started a baby."

Her heart thrilled to the idea of having Brodie's child, but her mind was riddled with fearful thoughts. "You don't want to be a husband. Or a father. You like to have fun."

"You can be those things and have fun, too. I'm going to make it my job to show you how."

Doug's passing had been sudden and unexpected and though their marriage had not been wildly passionate, the loss had been tragic. Brodie lived a dangerous life. His job often put him in the line of fire. If she were to marry him and lose him for any rea-

son, it would be the very end of her. She couldn't en-
dure that much pain.

Suddenly tears were pouring from her eyes and
clogging her throat.

"I can't marry you, Brodie. I'd always be worrying about you. And I don't want to drag Lilly from
one army base to another. That's not the sort of life
I want for her."

Quickly, before he could stop her, Greta slid from
the bed and grabbed her clothes.

"It might not be that way, Greta! We have to talk
about this," he argued as she jerked on her slacks and
sweater.

"There's nothing left to talk about, Brodie. I'd
never ask you to give up your career. You *are* a soldier. I wouldn't want to change that fact, but I can't
live with it, either. Good night."

On shaky legs, she bolted from the room and
prayed he wouldn't try to follow her.

Much later that night, Greta was lying in bed, staring at the shadows on the ceiling while she wondered how her Christmas Eve could have turned out
so joyous and so miserable at the same time. Making love with Brodie had been incredible. And even
though she'd lied to him and labeled their union as
"just sex," she'd known it had been love. Every ca-

ress, every kiss, every moment she'd spent in his arms had been done with love. She'd just been too afraid to admit it to him or herself. And now she had to ask herself where she was going to find the courage to tell him goodbye. How was she going to forget about all the joy he'd given her and go back to her safe, but lonely life in Maine?

With a sigh of misery, she turned on her side and stared at the red digital numbers on the alarm clock sitting on the nightstand. Four-thirty. Morning was here and she'd not slept a wink. Her thoughts had not been able to shut out the image of Brodie lying in the bed across the hall. All she had to do was go to him and he'd open his arms to her.

Oh dear God, she prayed, would that be the right thing to do? Or would she end up like her mother, eventually being abandoned and bitter. Teresa had been a stern, strict mother and an even more conservative wife. She'd tried to instill her strait-laced values into both her child and her husband. Greta had listened, but Michael O'Brien had rebelled. He'd chosen to grab what bit of joy he could in life. Even if it meant he was poor. Even if it meant he didn't have the best of everything.

After her father had left the family, Greta had been carefully molded by her mother's attitude. She could hardly remember a time when there had been laughter in the house. Everything had been about school, work, frugalness and common sense. Was that the sort of household she wanted for Lilly to grow up in?

Greta's thoughts were so at war, she could stay put no longer. Throwing back the cover, she tossed on her robe and let herself out of the bedroom.

She found the night-light still burning in Lilly's room. Greta walked up to the side of the bed and gazed down at her sleeping daughter. The child's long golden curls were spread out against the pillow, with a few resting against her pink cheek.

Greta started to reach down and brush the strands of hairs from Lilly's face, but at the last moment she pulled her hand back in fear that she might wake her. It didn't matter that Lilly's hair was tousled, Greta realized. As far as she was concerned, perfection was going to be replaced with happiness. This Christmas with Brodie had taught her that much.

*This year I'd like a real daddy.*

Suddenly Lilly's Christmas prayer whispered through her thoughts and, as it did, her heart began to weep for all the things she'd lost in the past, and all the things she might lose in the future if she didn't find the courage to live, really live.

As a child Greta had hoped and prayed for her father to return. That had never happened and the loss had scarred her. Now she had it in her power to give

Lilly all the love she deserved, the love of two parents. She couldn't deny Lilly that much. She couldn't deny herself.

With an inward smile of conviction, Greta tiptoed out of Lilly's room and walked down the hall to Brodie's door. After a slight tap, she stepped inside and carefully locked the door behind her.

"Greta?" The sheets rustled as the upper part of his body rose from the bed. "What are you doing?"

Placing a finger to her lips, she moved to his side. "Locking the door. Just in case Lilly or your parents come looking for us."

He wiped a hand across his eyes, then squinted at her with disbelief. "Am I dreaming?"

With a shrug of her shoulders, she allowed the robe to slide from her naked body before she slipped next to him beneath the covers.

"No. I'm here to apologize."

Her hands reached for him and he obliged by grabbing her by the waist and pulling her snugly to the front of his body.

"Well, honey, you sure are going about it the right way."

"I've been crazy, Brodie."

His hands roamed her back and slipped through her thick hair as he pressed needy kisses against the curve of her throat.

"I wouldn't say that," he murmured. "You're just a temperamental redhead."

"I love you. You know that, don't you?"

He rubbed his whiskered jaw against her soft cheek. "It's been feeling that way to me."

She let out a long shaky breath. "I shouldn't have said all those things about your job, your career. I won't lie and say I'll never worry or be scared to see you go off and fight some enemy in a foreign land. But I will accept it and support you. Because I love you."

He pulled his head back far enough to look at her. "Is this your way of saying you'll marry me?"

A rush of relief brought a muffled laugh to her lips. "Oh, Brodie, yes, yes, I'll marry you!"

After that, he found her lips with his and kissed her with a promise that Greta could feel all the way to her toes.

"I have something to tell you, little mouse. You're not going to have to worry about my safety. We're not going to be moving from one army base to another. And we're definitely not going to have to spend time apart. I've been waiting on my new orders and they just came through this morning. It's a position I requested and was thankfully handed."

Greta was so surprised she jerked upright and stared at him. "What sort of position? Why didn't you tell me before?"

"For sometime now I had decided it was time for me to quit roaming. To settle down and start a family. No more combat for me. From now on, my skills are going to be put to training soldiers for special combat operations. We'll be stationed permanently in Louisiana near Fort Polk."

Her mouth dropped and she gave his shoulder a little admonishing shove. "Brodie! Why didn't you tell me all of this earlier? I've been so miserable and—"

"Baby, baby," he crooned as he pulled her back down and onto his broad chest. "Forgive me. But you didn't really give me much of a chance. And besides, I needed to hear you say you loved me as a combat soldier. That I didn't have to change myself just for us to have a life together."

Sliding seductively up his torso, she placed a slow, sweet kiss on his mouth. "Make love to me, Brodie," she whispered. "Now and until our dying days."

With a low, needy growl, he flipped her onto her back. "Are you sure you can bear the mosquitoes in Louisiana, little mouse?"

"Hmmm. I've decided I can bear anything to have a family with you."

Later that morning as Lilly tore excitedly into her gifts, the adults drank their first cups of coffee and opened packages at a more leisurely pace.

Jokes were made and laughter filled the room as James opened his usual fare of socks and neckties.

"Well, what in the world is this?" With a puzzled look on the elder Barstow's face, he held up a small string tied into a bow.

Anita leveled an eye at him. "That's for you to tie around your finger so that you don't forget our wedding anniversary next week."

James chuckled loudly as he reached over and hugged his wife's neck. "Oh, darlin', I've never forgotten the day I married you. Now have I?"

Anita smiled contentedly. "No. But I don't want you to start, either."

Smiling at the loving interplay between his parents, Brodie reached into his pocket and pulled out a tiny package wrapped in silver and red. As he sat down close beside Greta and placed the gift in her hand, she looked at him with surprise.

"What's this? I've already opened a gift from you and I loved the sweater."

His brown eyes sparkled as he saw the joy of love and Christmas all over Greta's smiling face. This was the way she was meant to be. Happy and by his side.

"This is a little last-minute something. And I think it's just the right time for you to open it."

"Okay." Wary, but excited, she began to rip away the paper. The moment she saw the velvet box, she suspected jewelry was inside, but she wasn't prepared for the diamond and platinum ring winking up at her.

"Brodie!" Her hand fluttered to her chest as she gasped in surprise. "How did you know I would say yes?"

"I didn't," he answered. "I just knew I wasn't going to take no for an answer."

"What is it?" Anita quickly questioned craning her neck to see what Greta was holding in her hand.

"Give her time, honey, Greta will tell us," James piped up.

Tears began to fall from Greta's eyes and she dropped her head as she tried to compose herself enough to speak.

Brodie slipped his arm around her shoulder and looked at his parents.

"I'm giving Greta an engagement ring," he told them with a proud grin. "We're getting married next week so that we can be wed on your anniversary. Unless you object to sharing the same day with us."

James and Anita looked at each other and Greta felt an enormous rush of relief as she watched sheer joy wash over their faces. The couple obviously didn't think she should keep living in the past with Doug's memory. They wanted her to move forward with their other son.

"What a merry, merry Christmas!" James bellowed as he and Anita both jumped from their seats and rushed over to congratulate the both of them. "Yesterday when Brodie and I went to town I wondered why he stayed so long in the jewelry store and it hit me that he might be buying an engagement ring."

"We'll be more than happy to share our wedding day with you," Anita assured them both and then a sly grin spread across her face as her gaze swung back and forth between Brodie and Greta. "James and I had a feeling about you two. Both of you had that look in your eye. And Brodie had been dropping some hints about being in love. But we were afraid to do any pushing. We just hoped nature would take its course before this Christmas holiday was over."

"You two are gonna be happy, son," James said to Brodie. "Really happy."

As hugs and excited questions about the oncoming marriage flew back and forth between the four adults, Lilly wiggled her way to the center of the crowd to stand before her mother.

"Mommy, I wanta see, too! What is it?"

Greta held her hand out for Lilly to view. "It's a ring, sweetheart. It means that Brodie and I are going to get married."

Tilting her head to one side, she looked at her

mother in complete puzzlement. "Oh. What does married mean?"

Greta's heart was suddenly overflowing with joy.

"It means that Brodie is going to be your daddy. What do you think about that?"

For a moment Lilly stared at Greta wide-eyed and then with a little shout she flung her arms around her mother's neck.

"I think this is the bestest Christmas ever!"

\* \* \* \* \*

# SMOKY MOUNTAIN CHRISTMAS
## Kathie DeNosky

To my editor, Tina Colombo.
Thank you for all that you do.
You're the best.

# Chapter 1

The rented SUV's heater blasted Megan Bennett with warm air and helped chase away the outer chill of the cold December evening, but it did nothing to lessen the bleak, empty feeling inside of her. For the first time in her twenty-six years, she was going to spend Christmas alone.

She sighed heavily as she drove through the quaint little town of Harmony Falls, Tennessee. In the twilight of early evening, the twinkling lights adorning the trees along Main Street, the evergreen wreaths with big red bows hanging on almost every door and the majority of the houses with their electric candles glowing in all of the windows reminded her of a Thomas Kinkade painting.

"I came here to escape Christmas and landed right in the middle of it," she muttered, steering the SUV onto a narrow, snow-packed road leading farther up Whisper Mountain.

As the lights of town faded away behind her, Megan concentrated on keeping the Explorer from sliding off the steep, winding road and down the side of the mountain. Instead of spending the holidays secluded in a cabin in the Smoky Mountains, she could have spent Christmas back in Springfield, Illinois with one of her friends or accepted her parents' invitation to join them on their bird-watching expedition through the jungles of Costa Rica. But considering everything that had happened in the past few months, she didn't feel like socializing with anyone or celebrating anything. All she wanted to do was get through the holidays and hope that the coming year was better than the last one had been.

Calling it quits with the man she'd been seeing after realizing their two-year relationship wasn't going anywhere and being laid off from her job as a travel agent due to a downturn in the travel industry had been extremely difficult. But the unexpected passing of her beloved grandfather from a stroke had been devastating and left her with an empty feeling that would be hard to fill.

When the headlights of the SUV flashed across a wagon wheel leaning against a fence post, she slowed the truck to a crawl and turned onto a tree-lined lane that went even farther up the mountain. She'd never been to the cabin, but Grandpa Bennett had described it so well when he told her stories about his trout-fishing trips, she knew she'd be able to find it, even without a map.

Parking the Explorer in a clearing in front of a small log structure with a wide, covered porch, Megan sat motionless as she gazed at the secluded cabin she'd inherited from her grandfather. Tears blurred her vision as she thought of the man she'd spent every Christmas with since turning five years old.

Even though he didn't believe in a traditional celebration of the holidays, she'd always looked forward to her visits with him during breaks from school. While her parents were off pursuing their latest passion after exchanging gifts with her, she and Grandpa Bennett would sit in front of the fireplace in his study, drinking hot cocoa and eating the cookies his housekeeper had made. He'd entertain her with stories about his trips to the Smoky Mountains and the tranquility he always found at this very cabin. And she'd dreamed of the day she'd see it for herself.

"I hope I find the same kind of peace here, Grandpa," she whispered as she got out of the truck and climbed the porch steps.

Fifteen minutes later, Megan had a fire blazing in the fireplace, a pot of coffee started and most of her things unloaded from the back of the SUV. Standing beside the door, she looked around the cabin's cozy living area. She'd made the right choice to spend the holidays here. She'd not only be able to think about her future and what she wanted to do about finding another job, it would almost feel as if her grandfather was with her.

With a final glance around the room, she walked back outside. She hadn't known what condition the cabin would be in, as it had been over a year since anyone had stayed here. But once she found the breaker box to turn on the electricity, she'd been pleasantly surprised to find the place in excellent condition.

She'd have to look up her grandfather's friend, Lucas McCabe and thank the old gentleman for taking such good care of it before she returned home, she thought as she opened the Explorer's hatch. Besides, he was probably getting on in years and might want her to make other arrangements for overseeing the cabin. But at the moment, she needed to finish bringing in the rest of the food she'd bought on her way through Pigeon Forge. Once she'd done that, she'd pop a frozen pizza in the oven, put fresh linens on the bed, then settle down in front of the fire with a steaming cup of coffee and the novel she'd purchased in the gift shop while her flight had been delayed at O'Hare Airport.

Lost in thought, she pulled the last two bags of groceries from the cargo area of the SUV, closed the rear door and turned to go back inside the cabin. But she'd only gone a couple of steps when a shadowy figure of a man holding a gun emerged from the dense woods surrounding the cabin.

"This is private property. What do you think you're doing here?"

Dropping the bags, Megan couldn't have stopped her startled scream if her life depended on it.

Lucas McCabe hadn't known what to think when he walked out of his woodworking shop to see a wisp of smoke coming from Sam Bennett's cabin. That's why he'd immediately grabbed his shotgun and hiked up the mountain through the woods, instead of taking the time to drive his truck the distance between the two places. He could cut a good five minutes off the time it took to reach Sam's cabin and send the trespasser packing. But the last thing he'd expected to find was a petite little blonde with a scream loud enough to wake the hibernating bears in the area.

"Hey, lady. Calm down," he shouted, hoping she could hear him above her continued screeching.

"Who—who are you?" She took several steps backward. "What do you want? I don't have any cash with me, but...you can take my travelers' checks." Glancing around as if looking for an escape, she nodded. "You can even have my credit cards."

"I don't want your money, your travelers' checks or your credit cards," Lucas said, shaking his head.

Continuing to walk toward her, he tried to appear as nonthreatening as a man his size holding a double-barrel shotgun possibly could. But he figured he was failing miserably since she was still walking backward and looking as if she might start screaming again like a wildcat caught in a trap.

He blew out a frustrated breath. He didn't need this. He'd spent the past twelve hours in his workshop putting doll cradles together and cutting the wood for the toy trains he'd assemble tomorrow. He was bone tired and wanted nothing more than a cold beer, a hot shower and a few hours of vegging out in front of the television before he turned in for the night. Having to deal with a hysterical female wasn't high on his list of relaxing after-work activities.

"You must be lost," he said, trying to keep the irritation out of his voice. "There aren't any vacation rentals on this side of the mountain. This cabin belongs to the Bennett family. You'll have to leave."

The woman stopped walking backward. "You knew Grandpa Bennett?"

Lucas frowned as he closed the distance between them. "Just who are you, lady?"

The moonlight reflecting off the pristine snow cast enough light that he could tell she was trying to decide whether or not to give him her name. "Who are *you?*" she finally asked, lifting her stubborn little chin a notch.

"I asked first."

She let loose a frustrated sigh and Lucas knew she'd figured out that he wasn't going to answer her questions until she'd answered his. "I'm Megan Bennett. Sam Bennett's granddaughter."

"You can't be," Lucas said, shaking his head. "You're too old."

The woman propped her fists on her shapely hips and glared at him. "And how would you know what age I'm supposed to be?"

Lucas couldn't help it, he laughed out loud. Whoever she was, she had her share of grit. Once she'd gotten over her initial shock of seeing him walk out of the woods, she'd gotten as indignant as hell and looked ready to tie into him like a blue tick coonhound after a treed raccoon. Not many women her size would be willing to chance standing up to a man at least ten inches taller and a good seventy-five pounds heavier than she was, let alone one holding a double-barrel shotgun.

But Lucas's smile faded when he noticed the way her breasts moved up and down with her agitated breathing. "Sam talked about his *little* granddaughter all the time. She couldn't be more than ten or eleven years old. Twelve at the most."

"As you can see, I'm older than that."

"No kidding," he said before he could stop himself.

She suddenly shook her head. "My age isn't the issue here. Who are you and how did you know my grandfather?"

"Sam Bennett and I were friends," Lucas finally said, beginning to believe she might be telling the truth. "My dad watched over this cabin for Sam for twenty years. Then, after Dad died, I took over."

Apparently feeling the below freezing temperature through her thick red sweater, she wrapped her arms around herself. "Y-you're Mr. McCabe?"

"My name is Lucas." He nodded toward the house. "Why don't you go on inside and get warm, while I pick up your groceries? We'll sort this out after I carry them in for you."

"That's not n-necessary, Mr. M-McCabe." She was beginning to shiver and her teeth were chattering like a pair of castanets.

She started around him, but he stepped in her path to stop her. Taking the chance that she wouldn't shoot him with his own gun, he handed her the 12-gauge and urged her toward the porch. "Go inside before you get frostbite."

Holding his gun as if it was a snake or something women found equally as vile, she stared at him for several long seconds before she finally turned and marched into the cabin.

Lucas stared after her, then cussing a blue streak, turned and started picking up the food that she'd dropped. What the hell was wrong with him? Why was he having trouble catching his breath? And why did he suddenly feel like his jeans were a couple of sizes too small?

Picking up the last can of corn, he marched up the steps and brushed past her to deposit the groceries on the kitchen counter. As soon as he found out if she really was Sam's granddaughter, he'd either toss her out on her pretty little behind or make tracks back to his own cabin and work on forgetting that Megan Bennett existed.

"Thank you," she said, her soft voice sending a shock wave straight up his spine.

Lucas shrugged and tried his best to sound unaffected. "It was the least I could do, since I caused you to drop them."

When he turned around, she surprised him by shoving something into his hand. "Just so there's no more confusion about my identity, here's my driver's license," she said, sounding as out of breath as he felt. "I think you can see from the photo and information that I am indeed Megan Bennett."

He studied the license, then handed it back to her. "I'm sorry about giving you a hard time, but Sam let on like you were a lot younger."

She bit her lower lip and her pretty emerald eyes filled with tears. "I don't think Grandpa…wanted to admit that I'd grown up."

They were silent for several moments before Lucas offered his condolences. "I was sorry to hear of Sam's passing. He was a good man and we shared a lot of good times fishing the streams around here."

He cleared his throat and started edging toward the door. He needed to get out of here. For reasons he couldn't even begin to understand, he was having a hell of a time resisting the urge to wrap his arms around Megan Bennett and hold her close.

"I'll, uh, bring some more wood for the fireplace tomorrow."

"Do you want me to pay for it now?" she asked, reaching for her purse on the table.

In the process of opening the door, Lucas turned to face her. "No, and you won't be paying me for it when I deliver the wood tomorrow, either."

"But—"

He shook his head. "Sam and I were good friends. He'd expect me to watch out for you while you're here."

Before Megan could tell him that she didn't need anyone watching out for her, Lucas picked up his gun where she'd placed it on the floor and pulled the door shut behind him without a backward glance. Only then did she let out the breath she'd been holding from the moment he'd entered the cabin.

Aside from the fact that she'd been expecting the cabin's caretaker to be a much older man, she didn't think anything could have prepared her for the reality of Lucas McCabe. With straight, tobacco-brown hair that fell rakishly over his right eyebrow, dark chocolate-colored eyes that seemed to see into her very soul and a smile that could melt the polar ice caps, he was one of the most handsome men she'd ever met.

But it wasn't his rugged good looks that caused a tiny shiver to course through her. It was his size and commanding presence that seemed to fill the entire cabin that had her struggling to draw her next breath.

Even through his heavy fleece-lined coat she could tell Lucas had a physique to die for. Well over six feet tall, his chest was broad, his thighs heavily muscled and he had shoulders wide enough for a woman to lay her head on when the world seemed to be caving in on her.

Megan's heart skipped a beat and her breath caught. Why had that thought come to mind?

She didn't want, nor did she need, a man for emotional support. Nathan Kennedy had helped her see that. She'd mistakenly thought that after seeing the man for two years, he'd be there for her through the difficult days following her grandfather's death. But she'd quickly learned how erroneous her assumption had been when Nathan claimed emotional scenes made him uncomfortable and told her to get in touch with him once the funeral was over and everything had gotten back to normal.

That had been six months ago, and she hadn't talked to him since. He'd called a few times and left messages on her answering machine requesting that she get in touch with him. But as far as she was con-

cerned, he'd be waiting until Hades froze over before he heard from her again.

Megan shook her head and walked into the bedroom to put fresh linens on the bed. She'd wasted
enough energy on the subject of how unreliable men
could be. She was a strong, independent woman
who could stand on her own two feet and deal with
whatever life threw her way.

But later, as she closed her eyes and snuggled
down in the big log bed, images of a tall, dark-
haired man with a devastating smile and warm
brown eyes beckoned her to lay her head on his
shoulder, while he made the world go away.

## Chapter 2

The next morning, Lucas tossed another log onto the pile of wood in the back of his truck and cursed his sense of responsibility for at least the tenth time in as many minutes. He had work to do before the town party on Christmas Eve and taking the time to watch out for Sam's granddaughter wasn't going to help him get it done. But even as he fought the internal battle between his conscience and the need to finish the wooden toys he gave to the children of Harmony Falls each year, he continued to throw more logs into the bed of the pickup.

Aside from the fact that his parents had raised

him to help others, Lucas knew Sam would have wanted him to watch out for Megan as long as she stayed at the cabin. But that sure as hell didn't make things any easier, he decided as he slammed the tailgate shut on his truck, then opened the driver's door and slid behind the steering wheel.

He'd spent the entire night tossing and turning as he thought about the woman just a few hundred yards up the mountain. And by the time he got out of bed this morning, he was convinced that he'd lost his mind.

Megan Bennett was nothing like his wife. Sue Ellen had been tall, serene and attractive in a wholesome sort of way. She'd been his friend, his lover and even though their marriage hadn't been based on any kind of grand passion, Lucas had no doubt that they'd have spent the rest of their lives together if she'd lived. And that's what he was having the devil of a time understanding.

Megan was Sue Ellen's exact opposite and not at all the type of woman he was usually attracted to. She was petite, easily excitable and cute as the dickens. So why was she all he'd been able to think about since walking out of the woods to find her standing there screaming her pretty little head off?

Lucas blew out a frustrated breath as he steered the truck onto the lane leading up to Sam's cabin. He wasn't sure what had gotten into him, but he was determined to ignore it. He'd do what Sam would have expected of him and watch out for Megan while she was visiting Whisper Mountain, then he'd bid her farewell when she left to go back to Illinois and get on with his life.

Content with his decision, Lucas parked the truck close to the cabin, then got out and began stacking logs into a neat pile beside one end of the porch. Doing his best to keep his mind on the toy trains he had to work on when he got back to his shop and off of Megan Bennett, it took a moment for him to realize that she'd walked out onto the porch.

"Are you sure I can't pay you for the firewood?" she asked. The sound of her voice caused his heart to stall and sent a wave of heat coursing through his veins.

When he glanced up, Lucas's breath lodged in his lungs and he dropped the log he'd just pulled from the bed of his truck. Megan looked even better than he'd remembered. Her long blond hair looked like strands of golden silk where it rested against her navy blue sweatshirt and her perfect coral lips turned up in a friendly smile damn near knocked him to his knees. Certain parts of his jeans suddenly felt as if he'd outgrown them and he had to remind himself to take his next breath.

Cursing his lack of control, he picked up the log

he'd dropped and holding it in front of him to hide his undeniable reaction, shook his head. "I told you last night, Sam would want me to see that you had what you needed while you're staying here."

"Well, if you won't accept payment for the wood, then the least I can do is offer you a cup of coffee and some of the cookies I just took out of the oven."

When she crossed her arms beneath her full breasts, it drew his attention to their pebbled peaks and the fact that she was obviously feeling the below-freezing temperature through her sweatshirt. He swallowed hard and gripped the log so hard he'd probably leave his fingerprints in the bark.

"You must be getting cold out here without your coat," he said, thinking fast. It might be below freezing outside, but his internal temperature was rising with each passing second. "Why don't you go inside and I'll be in after I finish stacking this wood?"

"It is pretty chilly," she said, rubbing her upper arms. "How much longer do you think it will be before you're finished?"

"It shouldn't take me more than another five or ten minutes."

Smiling, she turned to go back inside. "I'll go ahead and pour the coffee."

Lucas remained silent as he watched her walk across the porch. With the amount of adrenaline he had running through his veins, he'd probably have the truck unloaded before she had time to close the door.

Disgusted with himself and his suddenly over-active hormones, he said a word that would have had his momma washing out his mouth with a bar of soap as he tossed the log he held onto the pile be-side the porch. Reaching for another one from the truck bed, he couldn't stop wondering why he was getting all hot and bothered over Megan Bennett. What was there about her that had him tied up in such a knot?

It wasn't like he'd been a eunuch since his wife's death. He'd gone out several times and, although he wasn't overly proud of it, he had found physical re-lief with a couple of the women who understood that he wasn't offering any kind of commitment. But Megan wasn't one of those women, nor was she a woman he'd normally find himself panting over.

A sudden thought caused a relieved smile to tug at the corners of his mouth. If she was baking, a fam-ily member or friend would most likely be joining her within a couple of days.

That was fine with him. If she had someone with her, he wouldn't have to worry about watching out for her. And as soon as he finished stacking the wood, he'd make his excuses, drive back to his place

and hole up in his workshop where he belonged.
Megan Bennett and her guest could fend for themselves.

Megan had just pulled a pan of freshly baked
butter cookies from the oven when she heard a
sharp rap on the door. "You'll have to let yourself
in," she called over her shoulder. Setting the cookie
sheet on the top of the stove, she turned to find
Lucas staring at her from the open doorway.
"What?"

He hooked his thumb toward his truck. "I…have
to get going. I need to get back to my woodshop."

She'd only extended the invitation for coffee as
a way to repay him for the firewood, since he refused to take money for it. She should be happy that
he was declining the offer. But she wasn't. For some
strange reason that she couldn't even begin to understand, she was disappointed to learn he wouldn't
be joining her for coffee and cookies.

"I remember Grandpa saying that you make
beautiful custom wood furniture," she said, smiling.
"Are you working on something special?"

He nodded. "I have some projects I need to get
finished by Christmas Eve."

"Are you sure you can't take the time for at
least one cup of coffee and a couple of cookies?"

she found herself asking. "I'd really like your opinion."

He looked doubtful as he removed his gloves and stuffed them in his coat pocket. "On what?"

"I need an unbiased opinion on how these cookies taste." She used a pancake turner to slide them off the cookie sheet and onto a platter. "The recipe belongs to my grandfather's housekeeper and it's the first time I've tried to make them."

He closed the door as he took a step into the room. "Why don't you wait and ask whoever you're spending Christmas with?"

Turning to face him, she frowned. "What gave you the impression someone would be joining me?"

"You're spending the holidays alone?" He sounded as if the thought was unheard of.

"Yes." She scooped the last cookie onto the platter, then turned to put another pan of dough into the oven. "It's just going to be me and my favorite author's latest novel. I've decided I'm not going to celebrate Christmas this year."

When she straightened, she noticed that he'd moved farther into the room. "You're not even going to have a tree?"

"No." She almost laughed out loud at the disbelieving expression on his handsome face. "I'm escaping Christmas this year by staying here."

"Why?"

"Why not?"

She hid a smile when he removed his insulated work vest, then draped it over the back of one of the chairs. He looked like a lumberjack in his red plaid flannel shirt, worn jeans and heavy work boots. But her easy expression faded as she watched him unfasten the cuffs of his shirt, roll up the sleeves to reveal his muscular forearms, then sit down at the table to reach for the coffee she'd poured just before he entered the cabin.

Good heavens, the man gave a whole new meaning to the term ruggedly handsome. She swallowed hard and turned her attention back to the cookies.

"Don't you like Christmas?" He looked mystified as he took a sip of his coffee.

"It's not that I don't like it," she said, shrugging. "I didn't feel like fighting the mosquitoes in Costa Rica just to get a glimpse of a scarlet macaw or a keel-billed toucan."

He looked more confused than ever. "Now, hold it. What does that have to do with you spending Christmas alone?"

Laughing, she pulled out one of the chairs on the opposite side of the table and sat down. "That's what my parents are doing right now. They decided they'd rather tromp through the jungles of Central America looking for rare or endangered species of birds than spend Christmas in Springfield where most of the birds have flown south for the winter." She reached for a cookie from the platter she'd placed on the table between them. "They invited me to go along, but the way my luck has been running, I'd catch some exotic fever that I'd be plagued with for the rest of my life."

"What about friends?" he asked, reaching for one of the cookies. "Why aren't you spending Christmas with one of them?"

"I didn't want to impose." Megan shrugged and rose to her feet to take the pan of cookies from the oven. "Besides, most of them feel the way I do about the holidays this year. A couple of weeks ago, we all lost our jobs when the parent company closed the travel agency we worked for."

When she finished arranging the cookies on the platter, she sat back down and took a sip of her coffee. "I'm not used to doing a lot of celebrating anyway. Grandpa didn't observe a lot of the season's traditions. He…always said he didn't like making a big brouhaha out of the holidays." What was there about Lucas that had her feeling the need to justify her decision or explain things that she hadn't even shared with her closest friends?

"You mean you didn't even have a Christmas

tree when you were a child?" he asked, his disapproval evident.

"Sure we did." She nibbled on her cookie. "My mom and dad always put up a tree a couple of weeks before Christmas. But as soon as school let out for the holidays, they'd give me a ridiculously expensive gift, take the tree down and drop me off at Grandpa's on their way to the airport."

"They didn't spend Christmas with you? Where did they go?" Instead of understanding, his disapproval seemed to be growing.

Before he got the wrong idea about her parents, Megan hurried to explain. "I'm afraid I gave you the wrong impression. I had a wonderful childhood. It just wasn't exactly conventional." She smiled as she thought of her unorthodox parents. "Mother and Daddy always made sure that I knew I was their top priority and that I was very much loved. But my dad is an ornithology professor and my mother is an avid bird-watcher. School breaks are the only time they have to take trips to see if they can find and photograph rare and exotic birds."

Lucas reached for another cookie as he digested what she'd said. "So you always spent the holidays with Sam?"

She nodded. "We had a wonderful time, too. We had our own tradition. We'd sit cross-legged in front of the fireplace in his den and have hot cocoa and cookies, while he told me stories about his trips here." She placed the half-eaten cookie on a paper napkin, then seemed to take interest in shredding the corner of the serviette. "This will be my first Christmas…without Grandpa."

Lucas could tell Megan was struggling to keep her composure as she talked about spending Christmas without Sam. He had to fight an almost overwhelming need to take her into his arms.

"You know what you need?" he asked, reaching out to cover her hand with his.

He'd only meant for the gesture to be comforting. But heat immediately streaked up his arm and spread throughout his chest at the feel of her soft skin beneath his calloused palm. He started to draw back, but when she lifted her gaze to meet his, the sadness he detected in her pretty emerald eyes had him giving her hand a gentle squeeze. He could well remember that first Christmas following Sue Ellen's death. It had been one of the worst times of his life and he wasn't sure he'd have gotten through it without the help of his friends.

Frowning, she shook her head. "I can't think of anything I need."

"Sure you do," he said, tugging on her hand as he stood up. "You need to start your own Christmas tradition—something completely different from what you've had in the past."

"Why?"

"Why not?" Standing up, he tugged on her hand. "Get your coat and boots on."

"Why?"

He laughed. "You sound like one of those parrots your folks are looking for in Central America. Now, stop arguing and get bundled up so you'll stay warm. It's supposed to start snowing this evening and the temperature has already dropped several degrees."

As he pulled on his work vest, Lucas was sure he'd lost his mind. He hadn't intended to have coffee with Megan, let alone get into a discussion about how she'd spent past holidays. But when he'd opened the cabin door to the sight of her delightful little backside as she bent over to put the cookies in the oven, he seemed to have lost every ounce of common sense he possessed. Then, once they'd started talking and he'd learned how much she missed Sam and that she'd never had a traditional Christmas, he just couldn't walk away from the situation.

Friends had helped him through the first holidays without his wife. It was his turn to do the same for Megan. At least, that's what he kept telling himself.

"What are we going to do?" she asked, sounding reluctant as she pulled on her snow boots.

"We're going to find a Christmas tree for you," he said, grinning as he removed her coat from the rack beside the door and held it for her.

She stopped pulling on the leather gloves she'd removed from her ski jacket to stare at him. "I don't need a tree."

"Did you bring one of those little artificial numbers with you?" he asked, opening the door.

"Well, no. But—"

Ushering her out onto the porch and down the steps before she had a chance to argue with him, Lucas grabbed his axe from the back of his truck and started toward the woods. "Then you need a tree."

"Slow down and listen to me," she demanded, struggling to keep up with him as they trudged through the six inches of snow on the ground.

"I have been listening to you. That's why we're out here now." He shortened his steps in order for her to catch up to him. "You can't have an old-fashioned country Christmas without first going out to chop down a tree. Then you'll need to—"

"You couldn't have been listening," she interrupted. She lifted her chin a notch. "Otherwise, you'd remember that I told you I'm not doing the holidays this year."

"I remember." He smiled. She might be protesting, but she'd followed him into the woods. "As I recall, you said you came here to escape Christmas."

"That's right. But I can't do that if you keep insisting I have a stupid tree." She stopped suddenly to prop her fists on her shapely hips. "Why are you being so insistent about this anyway?"

Lucas shrugged. He wasn't exactly sure why improving her mood was important to him. But it was.

"Let's just say I know what it's like going through the first holiday season after losing someone." The passage of time had take care of the pain of losing Sue Ellen, but he still remembered how he'd felt facing his first Christmas without her. "I had friends who kept me going after my wife died. Your friends aren't here, so I'm going to help you the way they helped me."

"Oh, Lucas, I'm so sorry." She touched his arm. "I didn't realize. How long has it been?"

"Five years ago this past summer." Stopping in front of a small cedar tree, Lucas stared at it a moment. Had it only been five years?

"In some ways, it seems like it's been a lot longer than that," he said, turning his attention back to the tree.

"What happened?"

"We found out that she had leukemia in May."

Lifting the axe, he placed an angled blow to the base of the tree's trunk. "By August she was gone."

"She must have been very young."

He nodded. "She died three weeks before her twenty-fifth birthday."

Megan was suddenly consumed with guilt. She'd been wallowing in self-pity over the rotten year she'd had, but she'd never had to face anything as devastating as losing a spouse or one of her parents. Lucas had experienced losing both.

"I'm sure that was an extremely difficult time for you," she finally said.

He lifted the heavy-looking axe again and placed a couple of angled blows to the other side of the trunk, then stopped to push against the upper part of the tree. The weakened base made a loud cracking sound, then the little cedar plopped over on its side in the soft snow.

"There were times when I wasn't sure I wanted to go on." Giving her a pointed look, he added, "But I survived because my friends wouldn't let me stop living. They insisted that life goes on and that I had to pick myself up and do the same." He shrugged. "They were right."

"You don't understand," Megan said defensively. "I'm not trying to hide from life. I just don't feel like celebrating."

"If you say so." He picked up the tree trunk with one hand, and holding the axe in the other, started dragging the cedar behind him as he walked back the way they'd come. "But I'm betting once we get your place decorated, you'll feel differently about it."

As she plodded along behind him, she glared at his broad back. Why did men think they always had a simple solution for every situation?

Frustrated, she reached down to scoop up a handful of snow, packed it into a tight ball, then lobbed it at him. She laughed when it hit him between his shoulder blades. "You're right, McCabe. I feel better already."

He dropped the axe and the tree as he bent down. "You know what this means don't you, honey?"

"That you'll give up on the idea of my decorating the cabin?" she asked, scooping up more snow.

"No." When he straightened and turned around, the wicked grin on his face promised retaliation. "It means war." The soft snowball he'd formed hit her stomach, then dropped down on top of her boots.

"Bring it on, big boy." She took aim and watched snow spray his lean cheek when her next effort exploded against his shoulder. "I don't want to decorate for the holidays."

He reached down for another handful of snow as

he walked toward her. "Yes, you do. You just don't realize it."

"No, I don't." Turning to run, the toe of her boot connected with something hidden beneath the snow at the same time his snowball landed against her back and she fell in an undignified heap.

Lucas was at her side immediately. "Are you all right, Megan?"

She put her arm around his shoulders as he helped her sit up. "I'm just fine," she said, sliding her gloved hand beneath the collar of his flannel shirt to release a good amount of snow down his back.

To her surprise, he didn't even flinch. "Nice try, honey. But you'll have to do better than that. That handful of snow went between my shirt and vest."

Rising to his feet, he pulled her up to stand beside him and the shadow of desire in his dark brown gaze stole her breath.

"Lucas?"

"Come on," he finally said, taking a step back. "We need to get back to the cabin and start decorating."

Sure that she'd imagined the moment, she watched him pick up the axe and the little tree. "You think you have all the answers, don't you?"

He shrugged and started walking toward the cabin. "Not always."

Megan brushed the snow off of herself and followed him through the woods. He might have won this skirmish, but he was not going to win the war. She wasn't going to do anything she didn't want to do and that included putting the tree up once they got back to the cabin.

"While I split a log to make a stand, why don't you see what you can find to decorate the tree?" Lucas asked as they entered the cabin.

"Gee, I didn't bring ornaments with me, so I guess there's no need to bother putting up the tree," Megan said, not even trying to hide her smug smile.

His grin caused her toes to curl inside her fur-lined boots. "Perfect."

"What do you mean, *perfect?*" She had a sneaking suspicion that he knew all along she didn't have anything in the way of decorations.

He helped her out of her coat, then hung it on the coat rack. "A true, country Christmas tree isn't decorated with store-bought ornaments and tinsel anyway."

She propped her fists on her hips. "And just what *is* it decorated with?"

"Sugar cookies, popcorn, ribbon—whatever's available." The hand he placed at the small of her back to guide her into the kitchen sent a delicious little shiver streaking up her spine. "You get started making more cookies, while I go out and make that tree stand."

"But what if I said I don't have the ingredients?" she asked, hating that she sounded so darned breathless.

"I wouldn't believe you," he said, laughing.

"Why not?"

"Because you have all the stuff it takes to make butter cookies." Leaning down to whisper in her ear, his low southern drawl made her heart skip several beats. "I'm betting you have enough flour, sugar and butter left over to make a batch or two of sugar cookies."

"But I don't have cutters," she said, making a last-ditch effort to dissuade him.

"You don't need them." He sounded so darned logical she wanted to scream. "Use a knife to cut out a couple of basic shapes and the top of a glass to cut out circles." He reached into the inside pocket of his jacket and pulled out a pencil. Removing the eraser, he handed it to her. "Use the metal end of this to cut out holes in the top of the cookies. When they bake, the holes will close in and be just the right size for the string hangers."

She glared at him as he turned to go outside. "You're not going to give this up, are you?"

"Nope." Grinning, he pointed toward the stove as he opened the door. "Get to work. I'll have the tree ready to put up by the time you take the first pan of cookies out of the oven."

When he closed the door behind him, Megan barely resisted the urge to throw something. She didn't want or need Lucas McCabe's interference in her holiday plans. Or more to the point, her lack of them. And she had no intention of letting him ramrod her into doing something she didn't want to do.

But as she muttered to herself about obstinate, misguided men and how frustrating they could be, she reached for the bag of flour and began measuring out enough for a double batch of sugar cookies.

# Chapter 3

"You're nine kinds of a fool, McCabe," Lucas muttered as he walked toward the cabin.

He'd driven up to the Bennett place to do nothing more than deliver a load of firewood and check to see that Sam's granddaughter had everything she needed for her stay at the cabin. Then he'd fully intended to get his butt back to his workshop to finish the wooden toys for the Harmony Falls Christmas party. Instead of doing that, here he was two hours later, fixing to help her decorate for Christmas.

He glanced down at the mistletoe in his gloved hand. What the hell had gotten into him?

After he'd anchored the little tree in the crude stand he'd made out of one of the logs, he'd taken his shotgun from the rack across the rear window of his truck and gone back into the woods. And for what? To shoot down a sprig of mistletoe he'd noticed growing in an oak tree not far from where he'd found the cedar.

Megan had certainly made it clear enough that she'd come to Whisper Mountain to escape the holidays. So why was he being so damned pigheaded about her decorating the cabin?

Normally, he was the last person to meddle in other people's affairs. And if he really believed she meant what she said, he'd walk away and leave her be. But he'd seen something in her eyes that he hadn't been able to ignore. She wasn't trying to escape Christmas, she was blaming it for her loneliness. Unless he missed his guess, she didn't even realize it.

Picking up the cedar tree as he walked by the tailgate of his truck, Lucas wondered why he felt such a compelling need to see that Megan was happy. She didn't want his help. Of course, when his friends had insisted that he celebrate that first Christmas after Sue Ellen died, he'd felt the same way. He'd resented the hell out of their telling him what he had to do. But Sam wouldn't want his granddaughter to be unhappy. And out of respect for the man, Lucas intended to do whatever he could to see that she wasn't.

When he entered the cabin, he tried to sound a lot more cheerful than he felt. "Do you have those cookies ready?"

"I guess they're as ready as they'll ever be," she said, gazing at the platter on the table. "Using a knife instead of a cookie cutter sure didn't do them any favors."

Setting the tree down by the door, he walked over to take a look at her efforts. He pointed to one of the lopsided cookies. "What's that?"

The look she gave him stated in no uncertain terms that she didn't think he was overly bright. "What do you think it is?"

"A star?"

She rolled her eyes and pointed to the top of the cookie. "It's supposed to be a little house. See the chimney?"

"Oh, I see now." He didn't, but he wasn't going to admit it to her.

"They'd probably look a little better if I'd had some food coloring or something to dress them up a bit," she said, frowning.

The disappointment he heard in her voice caused his gut to twist and before he could stop himself, he put his arm around her shoulders to give her a quick hug. "They'll look just fine once we get them hung on the tree, honey."

He'd meant for the hug to be friendly, but the moment he felt her small frame beneath his hand an electric charge shot up his arm and exploded throughout his entire body. He quickly pulled away before he did something stupid like take her in his arms and kiss her senseless.

"Where do you want this?" he asked, walking over to the tree.

"I'm…not sure." She sounded pretty breathless and he knew that she'd felt the jolt of awareness the same as he had.

"It's not very tall," he said, thinking aloud. "Why don't you clear off one of the end tables? I'll move it over in the corner and we can set it on that."

He waited for Megan to remove a lamp and a small figurine of a black bear from the top of the rustic little table at the end of the couch, then moved it into the spot he'd indicated. Setting the Christmas tree on top of it, he asked, "Do you have something to put around the bottom?"

She looked thoughtful for a moment. "I suppose I could use a sheet for a tree skirt. Would that work?"

Megan looked so darned cute standing there nibbling on her lower lip that he needed to put some distance between them in short order. If he didn't, he knew just as sure as he knew his own name he was going to grab her and kiss her right then and there.

Nodding, he started backing toward the door. "While you go get that, I'll see if I can find something in the shed we can use to hang the cookies."

Two hours later, Megan sat cross-legged on the floor in front of the fireplace and ran a needle through the last kernel of popcorn. Tying a knot in the end of the nylon string, she held it out for Lucas's inspection. "I think this is ready."

After he'd finished threading the nylon fishing line through the holes in the tops of the cookies, he'd driven down to his place for a bag of popcorn and a popper she was sure had to be an antique. While she hung the misshapen cookies on the tree, he'd used the long-handled popper to pop corn in the fireplace. She'd tried to tell him that it would be easier to use a kettle on top of the stove, but he wouldn't have it. He'd said that popping corn the old-fashioned way was part of the fun of a country Christmas, and Megan had to admit, it had been an interesting experience.

Looking up from the star he was cutting from a piece of cardboard, he nodded. "You did a great job. Now, put it on the tree."

She eyed the popcorn strand curled around the

hardwood floor between them. "This looks awfully long for such a little tree."

"You'll be lucky if it's long enough," he said, chuckling.

A tiny bolt of electric current ran through every part of her at the deep masculine sound, and she quickly scrambled to her feet to put the string of popcorn on the tree. To her surprise when she began winding it loosely around the branches, she discovered that she came to the end of the garland at the same time she reached the top.

"It worked out perfectly," she said, truly amazed.

"See, I told you it wouldn't be too long." He picked up a roll of aluminum foil and tore off a good-size length, then motioned for her to sit on the stone hearth beside him. When she sat down, he handed it to her. "As soon as you wrap the star with this, you can put it on the top and your tree will be finished."

"Why aren't you doing this?" she asked as she smoothed the foil over the cardboard. "It was all your idea. Remember?"

Laughing, he stood up and started for the door. "While you're working on that, I have something else I need to do."

"Like what?"

He sent her a playful wink that caused her pulse to pound. "You'll see."

When he returned with a piece of grass and a hammer, she frowned. "What's that?"

"Mistletoe," he said, driving a nail into one of the log ceiling beams close to the door.

When he stopped pounding on the nail and hung the scrawny sprig on it, she shook her head. "That looks more like a weed than a piece of mistletoe."

He raised one dark eyebrow. "You've seen a lot of wild mistletoe, have you?"

She couldn't stop her sheepish grin. "Actually, what I've seen is artificial."

"Well, there you have it," he said, walking over to where she sat on the hearth. He held out his hand to help her up. "You can't judge a piece of real mistletoe if you've never seen it."

Her heart stalled at the feel of his fingers closing around her hand and the rough calluses of his palm against her softer skin. "You probably have a point," she said, hating that she sounded like she'd just run a marathon.

When Megan raised her head to look up at him, their gazes met and she felt as if time stood still. She wasn't sure how long they continued to stare at each other, but the sudden pop of a log in the fireplace seemed to break the spell and she quickly pulled her hand from his.

"I, uh, guess I should put this on the tree," she said, shakily. "But I have no idea how I'll attach it."

Seemingly unaffected, Lucas walked over to the coatrack and reaching into his jacket pocket, pulled out a pipe cleaner and a roll of silver tape. Once he'd attached the wire stem to the back of the star with a small strip of tape, he handed it back to her. "This should take care of the problem."

"Duct tape?

"It works."

"Most men think it's the eighth wonder of the world," she said, laughing.

His charming grin made her weak in the knees. "Duct tape holds about half of everything on earth together."

"And what about the other half?" she asked, smiling. "What's holding that together?"

He winked as he held out the star. "The ninth wonder of the world—bailing wire."

As she took the foil-wrapped cardboard from him, her fingers brushed his and caused a tingling sensation to streak up her arm. Quickly turning toward the tree, she raised up on tiptoe to secure it to the top. Unfortunately, she wasn't tall enough.

Shrugging, she started to hand it back to him. "You'll have to do it."

"Nope," he said, stepping behind her. "It's your tree. You have to put the star on top."

When she felt his hands at her waist, she jumped. "What do you think—" The words died in her throat when he picked her up as if she weighed nothing.

"Are you able to reach it now?" His warm breath on the back of her neck sent a shiver straight up her spine.

Unable to think, much less protest, she positioned the star and quickly wound the pipe cleaner around the tip of the tree. "A-all done." Her heart skipped a beat when her backside brushed down his front as he slowly lowered her to the floor.

"It looks real nice," he said, stepping back. They stood in silence for several uneasy seconds before he finally turned and started toward the door. "It's getting late and I need to get home."

Following him, Megan tried to think of something to say. "I, um, appreciate the time you took helping me with the tree."

"Don't fib, honey." He grinned as he pulled on his coat, then placed his hands on her shoulders. "Admit it. You resented the hell out of my insisting you have a tree."

Even though the heat of his touch was doing strange things to her insides, Megan managed to smile. "Well, I might not have wanted a Christmas tree, but it does look kind of nice and it makes the house smell good. Although, I think the cookie ornaments would have turned out a lot better if I'd used cutters instead of a knife."

"You can use them next year."

"Next year?"

He nodded. "Remember? This is the beginning of your own Christmas tradition."

As she stood there looking up at him, his easy expression faded and before she realized what was happening, he slid his palms down her arms to lift her hands to his wide shoulders. "We're under the mistletoe, Megan."

Looking up, she swallowed hard. "I suppose we are."

Easing his arms around her waist, he lowered his head to whisper close to her ear. "Would you mind if I observed another tradition and kissed you?"

"Y-yes."

"Are you sure?"

"No." She shook her head. "I mean, yes."

"Which is it, Megan?" He nipped at her earlobe. "Do you want me to kiss you or not?"

He was teasing her oversensitive skin with his firm lips and she was supposed to form a coherent answer?

"I…think I would like that," she found herself saying.

Drawing back to gaze down at her, he brought his hand up to brush a strand of hair from her cheek with his index finger. "I'm glad because I've spent the entire afternoon fighting the urge to do just that."

"Y-you have?"

He nodded and without another word lowered his mouth to cover hers.

At the first tender touch, Megan's eyes drifted shut and she forgot all about Christmas trees, decorations and lopsided cookies. Every cell in her body tingled to life as Lucas nibbled and teased her lips with his, then slowly increased the pressure of the kiss at the same time he tightened his arms around her and drew her to his hard frame.

The contrast of his solid body against her much softer one sent a shiver of anticipation straight up her spine and caused her heart to skip several beats. But when he used the tip of his tongue to coax her to open for him, she was sure her heart stopped completely. Without a second thought, she parted her lips and allowed him access to the sensitive recesses.

As he explored her with a tenderness that stole her breath, Megan felt as if a thousand butterflies had been released within her soul. She'd been kissed before, but never like this. Lucas seemed to be worshipping her at the same time he demanded that she respond in turn.

Wrapping her arms around his neck, she shamelessly gave into his demands and pressed herself more fully against him. Lost in the feelings he created with each stroke of his tongue on hers, it took a moment for her to realize that he'd moved his hands to cup her bottom. But when he lifted her to him, the feel of his strong arousal pressed firmly to the softness of her lower stomach caused her head to spin and sent a delicious wave of heat flowing through her veins.

Her knees felt as if they were made of rubber and she clung to his soft flannel shirt to keep from melting into a puddle at his big, booted feet. Never had she felt such intense longing, such need. Nor had it ever happened quite so fast.

Frightened by her reaction and lack of control, Megan pushed against his broad chest. "P-please—"

"It's all right, honey." He eased her away from him, but continued to hold her within the circle of his arms. "It was just a kiss."

Shaking her head, she gazed up at him. "No. I don't think so."

"I'd better get going," he said as he released her and reached for the doorknob. "I have some things I need to finish in my workshop."

"Thank you," she said, not sure of what else to say.

"It was my pleasure." His slow smile caused her

insides to feel like they'd been turned to melted butter. "And I hope it was yours."

She knew he thought she was referring to the kiss. "I meant for the firewood and the Christmas tree."

"I know." His grin widened as he opened the door. "Helping you out with those were my pleasure, too." Before she could get her stunned vocal cords to work, he gave her a wink and walked out.

Megan stared at the closed door for several long seconds. What on earth had she gotten herself into by coming to the Smoky Mountains to escape the holidays? She'd not only landed right in the middle of Christmas, she was having to deal with the most frustrating, obstinate man she'd ever met.

Her heart fluttered wildly when she glanced up at the mistletoe. But heaven help her, he sure could kiss.

"Stop it," she chided herself. "You're not interested in Lucas McCabe or any other man."

Walking over to the couch, she curled up in one corner and stared at the logs crackling in the fireplace. She had to put a stop to this nonsense. She wasn't the type to engage in vacation flings, no matter how tempting a man's kiss was or how nice it felt when he held her to him.

Of course, she wasn't any better at long-term relationships either, she thought disgustedly. Any woman who could see a man for over two years and not recognize what a shallow, self-centered little weasel he was had to have less than reliable judgment. And the most enlightening moment about her lack of perception had come when she realized that she hadn't been all that upset about calling a halt to seeing him.

But as she gazed at the glowing embers of the fire, she had to admit that Nathan Kennedy could take lessons from Lucas on meeting a woman's emotional needs. Nathan had disappeared at the first sign she might need his support and comfort, whereas Lucas kept insisting that she needed his help to get through the holidays when she didn't.

She sighed heavily as she pulled the colorful afghan from the back of the couch to cover her legs. It probably wouldn't be an issue, but there wouldn't be any more kisses beneath the mistletoe or days spent decorating the cabin with Lucas. She was here to decide what to do about finding another job and to escape her problems for a bit, not create more.

Around midnight, Lucas turned off the lights in his workshop and stepped out into the quiet night. He'd managed to stain the doll cradles, but the toy trains would have to wait to be assembled until tomorrow. He was bone tired and ready for a good night's sleep.

Glancing up the mountain toward the Bennett cabin, he could see a dim light cutting through the darkness. With the woods between his place and Megan's, he couldn't tell if it was coming from inside the house or if she'd left the porch light on. Either way, it didn't matter. Just knowing she was up there in Sam's cabin had Lucas tied in such a knot, he wondered if he'd ever be the same again.

At first, he'd tried to tell himself that he was only trying to help her get through the first holiday without her grandfather. But somewhere between watching her play in the snow and the fuss she'd made over the misshapen cookie ornaments, he'd admitted to himself there was more to his interest in her than that. That's why he'd done a lot of soul-searching when he'd gone to get the popcorn and come to the conclusion there was no reason they couldn't enjoy each other's company as friends while she was here on Whisper Mountain.

Most likely, she wasn't looking for a lasting commitment and he wasn't either. She was going to be alone for the holidays and he was, too. So why shouldn't they spend the time together and have a few laughs? Then she could go back to Illinois and he'd stay here on Whisper Mountain to work in his shop and remember the good times they'd shared.

But he sure as hell hadn't counted on the intensity of that kiss under the mistletoe. That had more than taken him by surprise. It had damned near shocked his socks off.

He'd only meant for it to be light and playful—a kiss between two friends. But the moment his lips touched hers, he'd felt as if his insides had caught fire. Hell, just the memory of it was making him hard.

Taking a deep breath of the crisp night air, he willed himself to calm down as he tried to figure out why he had such an intense reaction to Megan. He'd courted Sue Ellen for a year, been married to her for five and never experienced the degree of passion he'd felt with Megan in that one kiss. The strangest part of it was, he had a feeling she'd never felt anything like it, either.

As he continued to stare at the light from the cabin, it went out and he figured Megan was probably turning in for the night. The thought of her changing into her gown and crawling under the covers had him wishing he was there to hold her and keep her warm.

His rapidly tightening body had him cursing his own foolishness. No matter how tempting it would be to explore the chemistry between himself and Megan, no matter how bad the burn became to possess her, it wasn't going to happen. Aside from the fact that she was Sam Bennett's granddaughter, Lucas could tell she wasn't the type for a short-term affair. And that was all he was capable of offering.

He and Sue Ellen had had a good marriage. But he wasn't fool enough to think that lightning struck twice in the same place. His chances of finding another woman who would be content with the quiet country life were slim to none.

Climbing his back porch steps, he turned and took one last look toward the cabin on the other side of the woods. He'd do his best to help Megan get through the holidays because Sam would expect that of him. But that was it. There wouldn't be any more tempting kisses under the mistletoe or wishing that he could keep her warm throughout the night.

# Chapter 4

"Go away," Megan mumbled, burrowing deeper under the covers.

When the knocking got louder, she tossed the quilts aside and sat up on the side of the bed. She knew who had to be pounding on the cabin's front door and she had every intention of letting him know just how much she appreciated being awakened at the ungodly hour of—she checked her travel alarm clock on the nightstand—seven in the morning. Never mind the fact that she used to get up every morning at six to get ready for work. She wasn't working, and even if she did have a job, she'd be on vacation now.

Howling at the shock of her bare feet connecting with the frigid hardwood floor, she hopped from one foot to the other as she searched for her slippers. "You are so going to get a piece of my mind when I open that door, Lucas McCabe."

Finally locating the fuzzy purple shoes under the bed, she shoved her feet into them as he knocked yet again. "Megan, are you up yet?"

"You do that one more time and I'm afraid I'll have to hurt you," she grumbled. Hurrying across the living room, she flung the door open and glared up at him. "Do you have any idea what time it is?"

"Good morning to you, too," he said cheerfully. He shifted the evergreen branches and grocery bags in his arms to check his watch. "It's eight o'clock."

She shook her head. "No, it's seven."

"You crossed the time zone, honey." His grin curled her toes inside her fuzzy bunny slippers. "It's an hour later here than it is in Illinois."

"That's a technicality." She shivered from the blast of cold air coming through the open door. "W-why are you here, Lucas?"

He seemed distracted. "What?"

When she followed the direction his gaze had taken, she knew why. In her haste to stop him from pounding the door down, she'd failed to put on her robe. And even though her nightgown was flannel, her nipples had puckered from the cold and were quite visible through the thick fabric.

Her cheeks grew warm and she folded her arms to cover herself. "What are you doing here?"

Apparently she'd broken the spell he was under because his gaze snapped back up to meet hers. "Why don't you get dressed while I get a fire started?"

"I'd rather go back to bed," she said stubbornly.

"You can't." He brushed past her to dump the greenery on the kitchen table and set the sacks of groceries on the counter. "We have too much to do."

"W-what on earth are you talking about…" She shivered uncontrollably. "…and w-what's with the forest on my table?"

"You're freezing." Placing his big hands on her shoulders, he turned her toward the bedroom. "I'll explain after you get dressed and I get a fire going in the fireplace."

Seeing no alternative but to do what he said, Megan went into the bedroom to pull on a shirt, jeans and the thickest socks she could find. When she returned to the living room Lucas was placing the fireplace screen in front of a roaring fire.

"It should start warming up in no time." He rose to his feet. "While you make a pot of coffee, I'll go out to my truck and get the wire."

"Now, hold it right there." She propped her fists on her hips. "Before this goes any farther, you have some explaining to do." Pointing to the greenery, she asked, "What's this all about?"

"You have to have a wreath for your door," he said as if it was the most logical explanation in the world.

"I don't want a wreath."

"You didn't think you wanted a Christmas tree, either." He grinned. "But now that you have it, you like it, don't you?"

She glanced over at the little cookie and popcorn adorned tree in the corner. "Well, it does look nice. But I thought that was as far as this would go."

Shaking his head, he walked over to the door. "After I help you with the wreath, I'm going to hang a few strands of lights along the porch rail while you make the gingerbread."

"I don't have the ingredients for gingerbread," she said, confident that she'd tripped up at least one of his plans.

"Yes, you do." He pointed to the bags on the counter. "I called Margie Lou down at the Harmony Falls General Store and had her gather everything you'll need. She even included her recipe and a diagram for assembling the gingerbread house."

"Now you're enlisting others to help with your crusade?" Megan groaned. "Wasn't letting you coerce me into putting up a Christmas tree enough?"

"Not by a long shot, honey." He winked as he opened the door. "Remember? You're starting your own Christmas traditions. A tree is just part of it."

When he left to get the wire, she eyed the greenery on the table for several seconds before she turned to make coffee. "I think I'm beginning to know where Scrooge was coming from."

Standing beside the kitchen table, Megan frowned at the oval wreath. "Aren't these supposed to be round?"

"I think it looks pretty good for your first attempt." Sitting in a chair beside her, Lucas shrugged as he handed her a roll of wide, red velvet ribbon. "I'm betting you get better every time you make one."

"And how many have you made, Mr. Do-It-Yourselfer?" she asked, measuring out a length of ribbon she hoped would be long enough for a decent bow.

A dull flush spread across his lean cheeks. "Well, to tell the truth…"

When his voice trailed off, she laughed. "In other words, this is a first for you, too."

"Something like that." His charming smile sent her temperature soaring.

She tried to ignore it as she put the ribbon on the table and propped her fists on her hips. "You mean to tell me that you had me worried I wasn't getting this dumb thing put together right, when you don't know any more about making one than I do?"

"You did a great job."

"Do you have a wreath on your door?"

When he nodded, she noticed that he at least had the decency to look sheepish. "I always buy one down in Pigeon Forge or Gatlinburg in November when I take furniture down to some of the shops that sell my work," he said, laughing.

"Oh, you're in big trouble now, mister," she said, trying to sound outraged. But it was hard to do considering she was laughing almost as hard as he was.

"You have a nice laugh," he said, reaching out to pull her onto his lap.

The feel of his solid thighs beneath her bottom and his strong arms encircling her waist, made breathing almost impossible. "Lucas...what are you doing?"

"Damned if I know." His warm breath on the side of her neck sent a shiver of excitement straight through her. "But I can tell you something I do know."

"What's that?"

"I know I want to kiss you again." His southern

drawl wrapped around her like a warm quilt and made her feel as if her bones had been turned to rubber.

"That probably wouldn't be wise."

He shook his head as he ran his index finger along her cheek. "Probably not." His smile caused a delicious fluttering deep in her lower stomach. "But what we want and what's smart aren't always the same, are they, honey?"

"No," she whispered.

"Do you want me to kiss you, Megan?"

She'd told herself that she wouldn't be kissing Lucas again no matter what the circumstances. But the truth of the matter was, that was exactly what she wanted.

"Yes, I'd like that very much."

His brown eyes darkened to deep chocolate as he lowered his head to trace her lips with the tip of his tongue. "So soft, so sweet."

The words vibrating against her mouth sent a thrilling tremor coursing through her and Megan didn't think twice about parting her lips to invite him to deepen the kiss. A thrilling heat filled her veins and caused her heart to thump wildly in her chest when Lucas took advantage of the invitation and slipped his tongue inside to stroke her with infinite care.

Shifting on his lap in an effort to get closer to him, she brought her arms up to circle his neck and tangle her fingers in the hair brushing the back of his collar. Lights flashed behind her closed eyes and her heart skipped a beat when she felt his insistent arousal pressing against her thigh. But when he lifted the tail of her sweatshirt to slide his hand up her abdomen, then covered her breast to tease her hardened nipple through her lace bra, Megan felt as if she'd go into total meltdown.

Wanting to touch him as he touched her, to feel his warm skin beneath her palm, she tried to unbutton his soft flannel shirt. But working buttons free with trembling fingers was beyond her capabilities and she found herself moaning with frustration.

She froze as the sound helped to restore some of her good sense. What on earth was she doing? She'd never acted this wanton in her entire life.

"Easy, baby," Lucas said, apparently sensing her panic. Kissing his way from her lips to the hollow at the base of her throat, he slowly moved his hand away from her breast, then pulled her shirt down. "You don't have to worry. This is as far as it goes."

Confused by her shameless behavior and more than a little embarrassed, she couldn't quite meet his probing gaze. "I…don't normally—"

He cupped her face with his palms and the feel

of his calloused skin on her cheeks had her wondering what it would feel like to have his hands on other parts of her body. Her cheeks heated and had her wishing she could disappear.

"It's all right, Megan." He kissed her so tenderly that it brought tears to her eyes. "Why don't you tie that bow while I drive a nail in the door to hang the wreath?"

She blinked. He was going to act as if nothing had just happened between them?

Deciding that it was probably the best way to handle the situation, she took a deep breath and nodded. "I'm not making any promises about how this bow is going to look, though."

When she started to stand up, his arms tightened around her. "Just so you know, I'm not making any promises, either."

"About the wreath?"

"No." Giving her a quick hug, he set her on her feet and rose from the chair. He grinned as he leaned down to whisper in her ear. "I'm not going to promise you that I won't kiss you again."

Stepping out into the cold air, Lucas took a deep steadying breath. He was playing with fire and he damned well knew it. But where Megan was concerned, he didn't seem to have a choice. He'd told himself to keep things light between them, to be nothing more than her friend. But he could have no more stopped himself from taking her into his arms than he could stop his next breath. And if he'd thought the kiss they shared under the mistletoe last night had done a number on him, he couldn't even begin to imagine the hell he'd suffer tonight when he went to bed.

As he got his hammer, a box of nails and the twinkle lights he'd bought when he stopped by the store to pick up the makings for the gingerbread house, he wondered how long a man could go without sleep. He'd tossed and turned for the past two nights from thinking about the woman who was quickly turning his world upside down. And if he was taking bets on it, he'd wager that he wouldn't have another decent night's rest until Megan left the mountain.

Shaking his head, he made quick work of stringing the lights along the porch rail, then started to drive the nail to hang the wreath. But just as he swung the hammer, Megan started to open the door and he missed the nail head to bring the blow down on his thumb and forefinger.

"I have the bow on the—" Looking horrified, she stopped to cover her mouth with her hands.

"Son-of-a...buck," he said, dropping the nail.

He'd realized what was happening and managed to check the force of his swing, but not in time to keep the hammer from glancing off his knuckles.

"Oh, Lucas, I'm so sorry. Are you hurt badly?" She took his hand in hers. "Let me see."

His knuckles weren't hurting that much, but even if they'd been smashed flat, he didn't think he'd have noticed. How could he? With Megan's soft hands holding his, her fingers feathering over his skin as she looked for damage, he wasn't capable of realizing much of anything beyond the fact that her touch was driving him a little more insane with each passing second.

"It's okay," he finally managed to say around the cotton clogging his throat.

"No, you're not," she insisted, holding up her fingertips to show him a small trace of his own blood.

He shrugged, wondering why she was making such a fuss over a couple of minor scrapes. "I've had a lot worse."

"Let's go inside and I'll see if I can find something to bandage your fingers." Even though his hand was almost twice the size of hers, she still held it as if it were the most fragile thing she'd ever encountered.

Amused, he started to tell her not to bother, but

he held back as she led him into the cabin. "Sit down at the table," she ordered. "I'll be right back. I think there's a first-aid kit in the medicine chest."

Lucas felt a little guilty as he watched her hurry toward the bathroom. She was making a big deal out of it and there wasn't a damned thing wrong with him. But as he stood there thinking about how nice her hands had felt on his, he sat down at the table and waited for her to come back to play nurse.

He hadn't had a woman make a fuss over him in a long time. His mother used to because that's what moms did. But his wife had been too practical to get upset over much of anything.

As he sat there thinking about Sue Ellen's lack of compassion, he had to admit there were times when he'd wanted her attention, wanted to feel as if she was concerned about him. But the realization that he'd never felt all that important to her came as a bit of a shock.

He'd always thought of Sue Ellen as having a placid nature. But had he mistaken his wife's emotional distance and lack of passion for serenity and calm?

"I'm so sorry this happened," Megan said, hurrying back to kneel in front of him.

Snapped out of his disturbing introspection, he shrugged. "Don't worry about it."

"I only meant to ask you if you were ready to hang the wreath," she said. "I didn't mean to hurt you."

"You didn't. I was the one holding the hammer." He couldn't get over how concerned she was.

Lucas watched as she gently dabbed at his scraped skin with an antiseptic wipe, then applied a small amount of antibacterial ointment to the abrasions.

"But if I hadn't opened the door you wouldn't have hit yourself," she continued to argue as she un-wrapped two adhesive bandages, then placed them over the scrapes.

A warmth that he didn't understand and wasn't at all comfortable with, began to fill his chest. Coupled with the overwhelming urge to pick Megan up and hold onto her for dear life, he decided that putting some distance between them would be his best course of action.

"All fixed. Thanks." Rising to his feet, he helped her to hers, then jerked his thumb over his shoulder. "I'm going to drive that nail in the door now. I'll let you know when to bring the wreath out."

Her teasing smile sent his blood pressure up several points and caused a hitch in his breathing. "You mean you don't want my help?"

Oh, he wanted help all right, but not the kind she was offering. "Why don't you start mixing up the gingerbread?" he asked, his voice sounding like a rusty hinge.

"I'm a step ahead of you," she said proudly. "The dough has been chilling in the refrigerator for almost an hour." She glanced at the clock on the stove. "I'll be able to take it out in about ten minutes to start rolling and cutting the shapes."

He edged toward the door. "Sounds like you have it under control."

"I will once you've hung the wreath and come back inside to help." Her smile was one of the sweetest he'd ever seen.

His gut tightened and he felt like he might be drowning. What the hell had he gotten himself into?

"I don't know the first thing about making a gingerbread house."

"This was all your idea, remember? Besides, all I need for you to do is measure the walls the right length and height." She nibbled on her lower lip. "You do have one of those metal wind-up measuring things in your truck, don't you?"

He laughed, releasing some of his tension. "It's called a tape measure. And yes, I have one in my truck."

"Good." Her smile had the tightening in his gut returning tenfold. "You can think of this as a carpentry project."

* * *

An hour later, Lucas decided it was time for him to leave when he caught himself staring at Megan's shapely little bottom like a hound dog eyeing a bone. She'd bent over to remove the pan of gingerbread from the oven and when she stood up, her cheeks were rosy from the heat, and a silky strand of hair had escaped her ponytail to hang over her right eye. She looked so darned cute it took everything he had in him not to grab her and kiss her senseless.

He blew out a frustrated breath and stood up. He was man enough to admit when he'd reached his limit. He'd spent the entire day fighting to keep his hands to himself and failed miserably. Besides, he really did need to get back to work. If he didn't get his butt busy, he wasn't going to get those toys finished in time for tomorrow night's party.

"It looks like you've got everything under way here," he said, reaching for his work vest. "And I have work waiting for me back at the house."

"If you'd like, I could make something for dinner." She smiled as she tossed the oven mitt on the counter. "That is, if you're hungry."

His temperature shot sky-high and he swallowed hard. His hunger had nothing to do with food and everything to do with the woman offering to prepare it.

Shaking his head, he picked up his tape measure. "Thanks for the offer, but I'm fine."

"Before you leave, I have to ask you something," she said, following him to the door.

"What's that?" He hoped she made it quick before he lost every ounce of sense he had and ended up reaching for her again.

"You're not going to wake me up out of a sound sleep again tomorrow morning with another Christmas tradition you think I need to adopt, are you?"

Her green eyes danced merrily and he didn't think he'd ever seen a woman look as sweet, or as desirable as Megan did at that very moment. His resolve to keep his hands to himself went right out the window along with his good sense.

Taking her into his arms, he held her close as he lowered his head to hers. "I think we've just about covered everything, but this."

When he settled his mouth over hers, her soft perfect lips molded to his and Lucas knew he was a goner. He'd tried his best to keep himself in check, but there was only so much a man could take. Megan was a petite bundle of delightful temptation from the top of her pretty blond head to the soles of her little feet, and more enticement than a good old country boy like himself could resist.

Settling her against him, he felt as if liquid fire

flowed through his veins when she wrapped her arms around his neck and pressed her body to his. His heart slammed against his ribs like a jack-hammer at the realization that she was as drawn to him as he was to her. He couldn't have stopped himself from deepening the kiss if his life depended on it.

As he reacquainted himself with her sweetness, the heat coursing through his veins made a beeline to his groin. He groaned from the intensity of his arousal and sliding his hands down her back to cup her delightful little bottom, he lifted her to him.

When she moaned his name, then shivered against him, a shaft of longing shot through him that damned near brought him to his knees. He wanted her more at that moment than he'd ever wanted any woman. And that scared the hell out of him.

Slowly easing the kiss, Lucas kissed her forehead. She looked as dazed as he felt and it took everything he had in him not to take her back into his arms.

"I…" He had to stop to clear the rust from his throat. "…need to get going."

"It would probably be best," Megan said, nodding. He could tell she was as disconcerted by the chemistry between them as he was.

"Take care, honey," he said, opening the door to walk out onto the porch.

"Have a merry Christmas, Lucas."

He stared at her for several long seconds as he memorized every one of her beautiful features. "You have a merry Christmas, too, honey."

Before he had a chance to change his mind, he forced himself to descend the porch steps and get into his truck. But long after he'd driven down the mountain to his place, her parting words continued to echo in his ears. He knew he wouldn't be making another trip up to visit her, and she did, too.

# Chapter 5

Tossing her book onto the couch cushion beside her, Megan felt close to tears. Why did she feel so lonely? Hadn't she come to the Smoky Mountains to be alone?

But as she stared at the little Christmas tree in the corner, then glanced at the lopsided gingerbread house sitting on her mantel, she knew that was the last thing she wanted. Last night when Lucas left, he'd the same as told her he wouldn't be back. And no matter how much she'd like to deny it, she missed him and his interference in her life.

Unlike her former boyfriend, Nathan, who couldn't take the time to be there for her when she needed him most, Lucas had gone out of his way to help when she hadn't even realized that she needed it. He'd seen through her excuses and recognized that she hadn't been running from Christmas, she'd actually been running to it.

Lucas had figured out that she'd come to the Smoky Mountains—a place her grandfather had spoken of so fondly—because she was actually trying to recapture the feelings that she'd had when she'd spent the holidays with him. That's why Lucas had told her she had to stop dwelling on the past and start looking to the future with her own Christmas traditions.

She impatiently wiped a tear from her cheek. The only problem was, the new customs he'd insisted she adopt included him. She sniffed. There wasn't a doubt in her mind that every time she went looking for a tree or tied a big red bow for a wreath, she'd think of him.

But it was for the best that they wouldn't see each other again. The more time they spent together, the more she'd associate him with everything to do with Christmas and it would make it that much harder to observe the holidays without him.

Lost in thought, the sound of someone knocking on the door caused her to jump and as she rose from the couch to cross the living room, she couldn't ignore the anticipation building inside of her. It had to be Lucas. He was the only person she knew on Whisper Mountain. And no matter how much she told herself the less involved they became the better, she couldn't deny that she'd be glad to see him.

Taking a deep breath, she reached for the knob. "Good morning, Lucas." He looked as if he'd rather be anywhere else than standing on her porch. Her smile vanished. "Is something wrong?"

"You could say that."

"Would you like to come in?" she asked, standing back for him to enter the cabin.

Clearly uncomfortable, he shook his head, then ran his hand over the back of his neck in an agitated gesture. "I'm not used to having to do this, but I don't have a choice. I need your help."

"What's wrong?" she asked, taking him by the arm to lead him inside. He looked okay, but that didn't mean he wasn't ill. "Do you feel all right?"

He looked as if he thought she'd lost her mind. "I'm fine. Why do you ask?"

"I thought—" She suddenly felt extremely foolish for jumping to conclusions. "Never mind. Now, what do you need my help with?"

Lucas stared at her for a long moment, then a

slow smile spread across his handsome face. "You were worried about me?"

She quickly shook her head. "No."

He laughed. "Liar."

Miffed that she'd been so transparent, she asked, "Are you going to tell me why you're here or not?"

"How good are you at painting?" he asked, his expression turning serious.

"It depends. I painted my apartment last year and I think it looks pretty nice." She laughed. "But I discovered in my high school art class that I'll never give Rembrandt or Picasso any real competition."

His grin caused her insides to tingle. "Then get your coat. We have a dozen toy trains in my workshop that need to be painted by this afternoon."

Lucas watched Megan tuck a strand of silky blond hair behind her ear, then pick up another caboose and start brushing red acrylic paint over it. He hadn't wanted to ask for help finishing the toys for tonight's party, but when he realized there was no way they'd be ready in time, he'd turned to the person responsible for him running so far behind on the projects.

He'd told himself on the drive up to her place that he was only asking her to paint the trains because it was her fault that he hadn't finished them on time. After all, if he hadn't spent the time taking her out to find a tree or decorate the cabin, he'd have been done with them a couple of days ago.

But he had to admit that was only part of the reason he'd requested her help. The rest of it was a little more complicated and something he wasn't entirely comfortable with. He'd jumped in his truck and hightailed it up the mountain because he just plain missed seeing her.

She set the painted caboose aside, then reached for another one. "How long have you been making toys for the children of Harmony Falls?"

"About twelve years." He dabbed gold paint on the train engine's wheels. "Everyone in town makes something for the party. I give wooden toys to the kids. Margie Lou from the General Store makes homemade jam for the women. Jim Ed over at the gas station gives all the men who smoke new corncob pipes." He shrugged. "No one leaves the party without some sort of gift."

She looked amazed. "I know the population is small—"

"Less than a hundred and fifty," he said, grinning. "That's why we make it such a big deal. For some, it's their whole Christmas."

She stopped painting to look at him. "That's so nice. It sounds more like a family gathering than a community party."

They fell silent for some time before Lucas cleared his throat. "Why don't you join us?" He'd intended to ask her last night, but after that kiss he hadn't been able to remember is own name. "It'll beat spending Christmas Eve alone."

Placing the last painted caboose beside the others, she shook her head. "I appreciate the invitation, but I think I'll pass." Rising to her feet, she walked over to the sink in the corner of his workshop and washed the smudges of acrylic paint from her hands. "I'll probably read for a while, then turn in early."

"If you change your mind—"

"I won't." Megan hurried to take her coat from a peg by the door, then pulled it on. She suddenly needed to be by herself for a while. "Remember? I came here to escape the holidays," she said, trying to sound cheerful. "I can't do that if I attend a community Christmas party. It might ruin my female impersonation of Scrooge."

He hurried to wash up. "Let me get this paint off my hands and I'll drive you home."

"No!" She hadn't meant for the word to come out quite so harsh. At his confused expression, she smiled. "It's only a few hundred yards from here to my cabin and I can use the exercise." Just before she closed the door, she managed to add, "Have a nice time at your party, Lucas."

Hurrying up the path Lucas had pointed out as leading to her cabin, she'd only managed to go a few feet before her eyes filled with tears. Why had his asking her to attend the party made her feel more lonely than she'd ever felt in her life? Shouldn't she welcome the chance to be part of such a heartwarming community event?

As she trudged through the snow, she had to admit that she knew the answers to those questions and the reason for the sadness suddenly filling her soul. He'd asked her to join the party, not go with him. Which she should be thankful for. It had been much easier for her to turn down his invitation that way. And the less time she spent with him was definitely in her best interest.

She wiped her cheeks as she walked out of the woods and up to the cabin. She could easily see why her grandfather had always spoken so highly of Lucas. Strong and capable, thoughtful and caring, he was the type of man who saw someone in need and, without being asked, helped them.

But the very traits that made him special and unlike any man she'd ever known were the things about him that made him dangerous to her peace of mind. Her two-year, dead-end relationship with Nathan had proven she wasn't the best judge of men, so she couldn't rely on her feelings.

"Dumb, dumb, dumb," she chided herself as she stomped up the porch steps of the cabin.

No matter how much she'd fought it, she was starting to fall for the big, interfering, wonderful lug. And there didn't seem to be a thing she could do to stop it.

As he packed boxes in the back of his pickup truck, Lucas decided that if he had sand for brains, he wouldn't have enough to fill a thimble. He was a complete idiot and it was no wonder Megan had turned him down. Instead of asking her to go to the party with him as he'd intended, he'd made it sound as if he didn't care one way or the other whether she went or not. And whether he was comfortable with it or not, he did care.

Slamming the tailgate shut, he walked to the driver's side. But instead of opening the door, he found himself staring at the twinkling lights coming from the little cabin up the mountain.

The idea of Megan spending Christmas Eve by herself made his gut twist into a knot that threatened to bend him double. There was no way he was going to the party without her, he decided as he dug his keys from his jeans pocket and got into the truck.

When the powerful engine growled to life, he put it in gear and steered the truck out of the yard.

At the end of the drive, he didn't even hesitate about turning to go up the mountain instead of down toward town. Come hell or high water, Megan was going to that party tonight.

He stopped the truck in front of the cabin five minutes later, got out and climbed the porch steps to knock on the door. "She'll probably tell you to go to hell," he muttered. He wouldn't blame her if she did.

"What are you doing here?" she asked, opening the door. She looked more than a little confused. "Aren't you supposed to be at the party?"

"I came to get you." Damn, but she looked cute standing there looking at him like she thought he'd lost every ounce of sense he possessed.

"I'm not going."

Lucas guided her into the cabin and closed the door. "Then I'm not, either."

"But you have to." She propped her fists on her shapely little hips. "You made all those toys. The children won't have gifts if you don't go."

He shrugged. "Then I guess they just won't have any this year."

Her frown deepened. "You can't do that to them."

"Then you'd better get your coat."

"Why?"

He almost laughed at her astonished expression.

"Because I'm not going without you," he said, meaning it.

"Don't be ridiculous. Luca-a-a-s!" She elongated his name on a startled cry when he reached down and wrapped his arm around her knees, then picked her up to drape her over his shoulder. "W-what do you think you're doing?"

"You might want to grab your coat," he said, opening the door. "You can put it on in the truck."

"What's wrong with you?" she gasped. "You're acting like some kind of caveman."

"Nope." He waited for her to snag her jacket off the coatrack before he closed the door behind them and walked across the porch and out to his truck. When he lowered her to the truck seat, he waited for her to brush her hair from her eyes. "I'm acting just like a good ol' Tennessee hillbilly, honey."

"A what?"

He laughed at the expression on her pretty face. "Haven't you ever seen those cartoons where a hillbilly has a girl tossed over his shoulder?"

"Sure, but what does that have to do with—"

"You wouldn't go with me on your own, so I had to resort to a little hillbilly persuasion," he said, closing the passenger door.

When he rounded the front of the truck and got

in, she glared at him. "I'm not even dressed appropriately for a party."

Reaching over he took her hand in his. "Honey, this is Harmony Falls. We're not fancy folks. What you're wearing is fine."

"Jeans and a sweatshirt are fine?" He could tell she no more believed him than she believed the moon was made of cheese.

"Yep." He gave her hand a gentle squeeze. "Believe me, you won't feel out of place."

"I'd better not."

He laughed as he started the truck and backed it up. "I'll make a deal with you. If you feel the least bit uncomfortable, I'll bring you back to the cabin. How does that sound?"

Megan breathed a sigh of relief when she walked into the decorated lunchroom of the Harmony Falls grade school and looked around. Everyone was dressed as casually as Lucas had promised.

"Oh, I'm so glad to finally meet you," a middle-aged woman said, rushing up to Megan. Giving her a hug, the woman added, "Your grandpa used to come into the General Store all the time when he was here on fishing trips and I was real sorry to hear he'd passed on."

"Thank you," Megan said, warmed by the woman's sincerity.

"Megan, this is Margie Lou Smith," Lucas said, smiling as he helped her out of her coat. "Why don't you two get acquainted while I carry the toys in from the truck?"

"Go on and do what you have to do," Margie Lou said, waving her hand toward the door. "I'll take Megan around and introduce her to everyone."

Ten minutes after entering the room, Megan stood by the refreshment table, marveling at how wonderful and friendly everyone had been. They'd all shared fond memories of her grandfather, expressed their condolences and told her how happy they were to finally meet her.

"Having a good time?" Lucas asked, walking up to stand beside her.

Smiling, she accepted the paper cup of punch he offered her. "I can't believe I'm going to say this, but I'm glad you insisted that I join the fun."

"Does this mean I don't have to take you back home?" he asked, grinning.

"Not a chance." She looked around the festive room. "The people of Harmony Falls are wonderful."

"Lucas, you want to kick off the party and hand out your gifts to the kids?" a man in a plaid flannel shirt and overalls called across the room.

"Looks like you're being paged," she said, reaching for the cup of punch he was holding. Their fingers touched and a tingling sensation traveled up her arm to spread throughout her body.

He must have felt it, too, because his eyes darkened to deep chocolate and the smile he gave her was so promising her heart skipped several beats. "I'll be back in a couple of minutes."

As she watched him walk over to the large Christmas tree on the other end of the room where a small crowd of children had gathered, her chest tightened. The smile on his face as he passed out the doll cradles and toy trains said louder than words how much he enjoyed what he was doing. He was such a good and decent man there was no doubt in her mind why she was in danger of losing her heart to him.

The world seemed to come to a complete halt as the realization sank in. If she hadn't done so already, she was close to falling in love with him.

"Are you all right, honey?" Lucas asked.

A bit disconcerted to see that he'd finished handing out the toys and walked back over to stand beside her, she nodded slowly as she watched a man handing out pipes to several older gentlemen. "I was just wondering what happens after the gift giving," she said, thinking fast.

He grinned. "That's when the fun really begins."

"Oh, really?" She took a sip of her punch. "And what would that be?"

"Leroy Barker and some of the other guys will set up their band," he explained. "While the kids play with their new toys or go to sleep, the rest of us will dance."

"Do you like to dance?"

"Only the slow ones."

She smiled. "You and most of the rest of the male population."

His rich laughter sent a tremor of excitement straight through her. Then, leaning down close to her ear, his warm breath sent a shiver up her spine. "When we're standing out there in the middle of the floor and I'm holding you close, I'm betting you'll like the slow ones, too."

After the last of the gifts had been handed out, Lucas led her out to the middle of the floor, then took her into his arms, and Megan decided she had to agree with him. She didn't recognize the country song the band played, nor did she pay attention to the words. Slow dancing with Lucas was wonderful and nothing else mattered but having him hold her close. Someone had turned the lights down and with his broad shoulders blocking out everything around them, she felt as if they were the only two people in the room.

As the music wove a sensual spell around them, she brought her hands up to rest on his rock-solid biceps and he laid his cheek against the top of her head. She sighed contentedly. Never in her entire life had she felt such a sense of belonging as she did at that moment in Lucas's arms.

When he pulled her even closer, the feel of his hard thighs brushing hers sent a tiny charge of electric current skipping over every nerve in her body. But her breath caught and her knees turned to rubber when she realized that she wasn't the only one being affected by the intimacy surrounding them. The bulge of his growing arousal against her lower belly had her curling her fingers into his soft flannel shirt and clinging to him for support.

Neither of them spoke as they continued to sway in time to the music and Megan knew they were communicating on a level where words were unnecessary. Lucas was silently letting her know that he wanted her. And she was telling him that she needed him just as much.

## Chapter 6

"Thank you for persuading me to go to the party tonight," Megan said as Lucas parked the truck in front of her cabin.

His low chuckle sent a shiver up her spine. "That's an interesting way to describe how I got you to go."

"Well, I think it sounds better than if I thanked you for kidnapping me," she said, laughing.

She stared down at the small gifts in her hands as she waited for him to get out and come around to open her door. "Seriously, I had a wonderful time, Lucas. And I'm truly touched by everyone's generosity."

"I told you that no one goes away from the party

without a gift of some kind." He guided her up the porch steps. "I'm glad you had a good time, honey."

Megan stared at him for several long seconds before she finally asked, "Would you like to come inside? I could make coffee."

His gaze held hers as he reached out to lightly touch her cheek with his fingertips. "I'd like to come in, Megan. But it's not coffee that I want."

Her breath caught and it felt as if she might never breathe again. He was telling her that if they went inside, he wanted them to make love.

"I...don't think I want coffee, either," she said, wondering if that throaty female voice was really hers.

"Do you still want me to come inside?"

She didn't have to think twice about her answer. "Yes."

He smiled, then taking her into his arms, he asked, "Honey, are you sure? If we go inside this cabin together we're going to—"

Megan placed her finger to his lips to stop him. "I know, Lucas."

Spending the evening dancing with him, being held close to his hard male body, had taken its toll. Right or wrong, she wanted to know what it felt like to be loved by this incredibly wonderful man.

Without a word, he leaned down and gave her a kiss so tender it brought tears to her eyes, then released her to open the cabin door. While Lucas hung up their coats and locked the door, Megan went over to place the gifts she'd been given at the party under the little tree in the corner.

When she turned to face him, he gave her a smile that threatened to buckle her knees and held out his hand. Without hesitation she moved to take it and allowed him to lead her into the bedroom.

He turned on the bedside lamp, then pulled her into his arms. Megan's heart thumped wildly at the hunger she saw in his dark brown eyes, the immense passion.

"Are you nervous, honey?" His deep baritone sent tremors of excitement to every cell in her being and caused her toes to curl.

"A little."

His kiss was featherlight. "I don't want you to be frightened of me." He once again brushed her lips with his. "I swear I'll never hurt you."

"I know."

He claimed her mouth with his and Megan had never experienced anything more tender or poignant in her entire life. But when his tongue swept over her lips, then darted inside to stroke her, she felt as if a flame caught deep within her soul. She savored the taste of him and the intensity of his need.

When Lucas slid his hands beneath the tail of her sweatshirt and up along her ribs to cup her breasts and the heaviness he'd created there, Megan shivered against him from the sultry sensations that seemed to be consuming her. His thumbs chafing her hardened nipples through the fabric of her bra caused a coil of need to form in the pit of her belly and she couldn't have stopped a tiny moan from escaping if her life depended on it.

"Easy, baby." He nibbled kisses along her cheek to the sensitive skin below her ear as he unfastened the front clasp of her bra. "We've got all night and I fully intend to take my time bringing you pleasure."

"All night?" She swallowed hard. "I wasn't aware…I mean, I didn't know…lovemaking could take that long."

His low, intimate chuckle caused her insides to quiver. "Sounds to me like those northern boys could use a lesson or two in how to love a woman."

If Megan could have found her voice, she'd have told him he was right. But he'd parted her bra beneath her shirt and the feel of his calloused palms covering her breasts rendered her speechless.

Wanting to touch him as he touched her, she reached up to unbutton his shirt. Her fingers trembled and as she slowly maneuvered the buttons through the holes in the soft flannel, she pressed kisses to every inch of his newly exposed skin. She was rewarded for her efforts when he shuddered and a low groan rumbled up from deep in his chest.

"Honey, if you keep that up, there's a good possibility you're going to make a liar out of me," he said hoarsely.

Parting his shirt, she ran her hands over the heavy pads of his pectoral muscles. "What do you mean?"

He took her hands in his and lifted them to kiss each one of her fingertips. "We'll be having to wait for me to recover before I can show you what it's like to make love all night."

She let her gaze drift down his body to below his belt buckle. "I, um, think you have a small problem."

"Small?" he asked, grinning.

"Oh, good heavens." Her cheeks felt as if they were on fire. "I meant the problem was small. I didn't mean...well you know...I didn't mean to insult you. I really have no idea—"

He laughed out loud, surprising her. "Honey, do you have any idea how cute you are when you get flustered?"

Too humiliated to respond, she shook her head.

Wrapping his arms around her, he kissed her until her knees gave way and she had to cling to him for support. "I don't want you to be embarrassed or feel like you insulted me." He took hold of her sweatshirt and drew it up over her head. When he tossed it aside, then removed her bra, he held her wrists when she started to cover herself. "I've never been insecure and neither should you." He leaned down to kiss the slopes of her breasts. "You're perfect, honey."

Tiny tingles of excitement skipped through her at the feel of his firm lips on her bare skin. Shivering from the need deep in her feminine core, she reached up and pushed his shirt from his wide shoulders and down his strong arms.

"You're beautiful," she said, running her fingers over his rippling stomach.

"Guys aren't beautiful. We're just a straight line with a few angles thrown in for good measure." He knelt to remove her boots and socks, then took off his as well. When he straightened, the flame of desire in his dark brown eyes caused her pulse to race and her breathing to become shallow. "True beauty is a woman's gently rounded curves." Reaching for the snap at her waist, he released it, then slid the zipper down and eased his hands inside to rest them on the flare of her hips. "Like yours."

His calloused palms caressed her thighs, then her calves, as he pushed her jeans and panties down her legs. She placed her hands on his shoulders to steady herself and by the time she stepped out of them, she wasn't sure how much longer her knees would support her.

When he straightened and reached for the button at the top of his waistband, she shook her head and brushed his fingers aside. "You've spent the last few minutes driving me insane. Now it's my turn to make you a little crazy."

His slow grin made her insides feel as if they'd turned to warm pudding. "Honey, I've been a little crazy since I walked out of the woods a few nights ago and found you screaming your pretty little head off."

Unfastening the button, Megan smiled as she toyed with the tab of his zipper. "You have?"

"Oh, yeah."

When she slowly unzipped his fly, she delighted in the shudder that ran through his big body and the spark of passion she saw in the depths of his eyes. As she ran her finger along the waistband of his white cotton briefs, his stomach muscles contracted and she watched his jaw tighten. But when she trailed her finger down the seam of his briefs toward the open vee of his fly, he groaned and grabbed her hands.

"Remember what I told you about making a liar out of me?" he asked, his eyes blazing with a heat that thrilled her. When she nodded, he shook his head. "It's no longer a possibility, it's an imminent threat."

"Hmm. Sounds like that problem's getting a little bigger," she said, grinning.

"There you go again with references to size," he said, chuckling. He quickly shoved his jeans and briefs down his legs, then kicked them aside.

Laughing, Megan started to remind him that he was supposed to be comfortable with himself, but she sobered instantly at the magnificence of his impressive male body. No wonder insecurity wasn't an issue. The man had absolutely nothing to be insecure about.

"You might not think you're beautiful, but I do," she said breathlessly.

He shook his head as he reached to take her in his arms. "You're the one who's beautiful."

The contrast of his hair-roughened flesh to her softer feminine skin sent her temperature soaring and had her wrapping her arms around his waist for support. "I don't think my legs are going to hold me up much longer."

"Let's lie down," he said, sounding just as short of breath as she was.

He reached out and pulled the colorful quilts back, then, to her surprise, lifted her in his arms and gently placed her in the middle of the big bed. She watched as he retrieved something from his jeans, then sliding it under the pillow, stretched out beside her.

When he pulled her to him, Megan closed her eyes as she reveled in the feel of their bodies pressed together from shoulders to knees. "Mmm. Feels good."

"I promise it's going to feel even better, honey," he said, tangling his fingers in her hair as he cupped the back of her head.

He fused their lips in a kiss that quickly had heat flowing through her at lightning speed. But when Lucas deepened the kiss and she tasted his urgent male hunger and the depth of his passion, it felt as if she might be going up in flames.

Megan drew in a ragged breath when he broke the kiss to nibble his way down to her collarbone, then the slope of her breast to the hardened peak. But at the first touch of his tongue to her sensitive flesh, Megan held his dark head to her breast and wondered if she'd be able to survive the delicious tension arcing between them.

When he took her nipple into his mouth to gently suck on it, he slid his hand down to the nest of curls at the apex of her thighs. He stroked the most tender of her feminine secrets and she thought she would surely burn to ashes from the sensations coursing throughout her body.

Moving restlessly against him, her lower belly tightened to an almost unbearable ache. "Lucas, p-please—"

He raised his head to kiss her. "What do you need, Megan?"

"You."

"Now?"

"Yes!"

"But I wanted to show you what it's like making love all night," he said, even as he moved away from her.

She watched as he tore open the foil packet and arranged their protection. "I'm certain that I'd be a cinder way before dawn."

"I can't let that happen," he said, as he nudged her legs apart with his knee. Settling himself between her thighs, he took her hand in his, then smiling, guided her to him. "Show me where you need me, Megan."

His gaze held hers captive as she helped him make them one and Megan couldn't believe how provocative it was to take such an active role in lovemaking. But all thought ceased as she felt him ease forward and her body stretch to welcome him.

"You're so...tight." She could see the strain on his handsome face and knew the toll it was taking on him as he gave her time to adjust to his presence. "It's been awhile...hasn't it?"

Nodding, she cupped his lean cheek with her palm. "Please make love to me, Lucas."

Without another word, he gathered her in his arms and slowly began to move within her. Megan couldn't believe how rapidly her body responded. Spiraling ribbons of desire seemed to thread their way through every part of her, then twine together to form a tight coil of need in her lower body.

She wrapped her arms around his broad back and held him close in an effort to prolong the feeling of being one with Lucas. But all too soon she reached the summit, then shattered into a million glittering shards of intense sensations a moment before she heard him call her name, then join her as they became one body, one heart, one soul.

As the dark of night faded into the pearl-gray light of dawn, Megan gazed at the handsome man beside her. His arm lay possessively across her stomach and she smiled when he mumbled her name in his sleep, then pulled her a bit closer.

Throughout the night, Lucas had taken great care to make her feel cherished, encouraged her to take all that he had to give. And never in all of her twenty-six years had she ever felt as complete as she did when he held her in his strong arms.

Tears filled her eyes as she continued to watch

him sleep. She might have only known him a few days, but that didn't matter. She loved him with all of her heart and soul.

Gently touching his cheek with her fingertips, she thought about all that he'd done for her in the past few days. He'd shown her there was more to Christmas than going on a vacation or giving expensive gifts. Whether it was walking through the woods to find a tree or sitting in front of a fireplace stringing popcorn and wrapping a cardboard star with foil, it was the time they spent together that really mattered.

As she thought back on all that Lucas had given her, Megan was ashamed to discover that she'd done very little for him in return. But what could she do? How could she possibly make him feel as cherished and special as he'd done for her?

She slipped from beneath his arm, got out of bed and putting on her slippers and robe, wandered out into the living room. While she started a fire in the fireplace to chase away the chill, she tried to think of something—anything—that she could do for him.

When her gaze strayed to the kitchen, a smile began to tug at the corners of her mouth. Making Lucas breakfast and serving it to him in bed was such a small thing, but it was something she was sure he'd enjoy.

Hoping she could get everything prepared before he woke up, she set to work and within no time she walked into the bedroom holding a tray with two cups of coffee and two plates full of food. "Merry Christmas, sleepyhead."

"Merry Christmas, honey." Lucas patted the mattress beside him, then realizing she wasn't in bed, rolled to his back and stretched. "What time is it?"

When he started to get up, she shook her head. "Stay there. I'm serving you breakfast in bed."

"You didn't have to go to all this trouble, honey," he said, sitting up to take the tray from her. He waited for her to sit down beside him. "I've never had anyone serve me a meal in bed before."

"Good." She smiled happily and handed him a fork. "I hope you like your eggs scrambled."

Careful not to spill the tray of food, he leaned over to kiss her. "Scrambled is fine. But I don't understand what this is all about."

She picked up a slice of toast. "You've done so much for me in the past few days. I wanted to do something to let you know how special I think you are."

Her sweet smile just about sent him into orbit and he could tell his reaction meant everything to her. "Thank you, honey."

Lucas didn't know what else to say. To the best

of his recollection, he'd never in all of his thirty-two years had anyone make him feel as cared for as Megan did at that very moment. His chest filled with an emotion that he refused to put a name to, and had been trying to ignore from the moment he met her. The only trouble was, it was growing with each passing second and there didn't seem to be anything he could do to stop it.

Not at all comfortable with what he suspected, he decided a change of subject was in order. "When will your parents get back from Costa Rica?"

"Not until mid-January." She looked wistful. "Even though I accept that my parents are anything but conventional and I love them very much for their uniqueness, when I have a family, I want to spend every moment of the holidays with my husband and children. I want them to know that they're the most important part of my life and that the most precious gift of all is the time we share together." Smiling, she kissed his cheek. "And I have you to thank for teaching me that, Lucas."

He almost choked on a bite of crisp bacon. "Me?"

"Yes, you." She gave him that little grin that made his heart pound and sent the blood racing through his veins. "You took the time to show me what Christmas is all about."

The feeling in Lucas's chest expanded to overwhelming proportions. And it scared the living hell out of him.

Suddenly needing to put distance between them, he tried to think of a way to leave without hurting her feelings. Deciding on a half truth, he glanced at the travel clock on the bedside table. "Damn! I need to get home. I was supposed to call my mom and wish her a Merry Christmas fifteen minutes ago."

"Where does she live?" Megan asked, taking the tray with their empty plates and placing it on the dresser.

"She moved to Florida to be close to her sister shortly after Dad died," he said, rising from the bed.

Reaching for his clothes still lying on the floor where he'd discarded them the night before, he tried not to feel too guilty. His mom did live with his aunt in Orlando and he was supposed to call to wish her a Merry Christmas. Just not at a specified time.

But when he turned toward the door, the sight of Megan stopped him cold. She looked utterly lost as she watched him prepare to leave. Unfortunately, as much as he wanted to stay, he needed time to think.

Taking a deep breath, he walked over to her and gave her a kiss that had him wishing he could throw her over his shoulder and take her back to bed. Instead, he touched her satin cheek with his fingertips.

"Thank you for last night and this morning. It was all very special to me."

"I'm glad," she whispered.

If he didn't force himself to leave now, he never would. "I'm sorry, honey, but I have to go."

"I understand," she said quietly. He could tell she didn't from the hurt expression on her pretty face, but she was putting up one hell of a brave front.

As he walked across the living room and out the door without a backward glance, his guilt increased tenfold and he felt like the biggest jerk alive. But that couldn't be helped. He needed time to come to grips with the feelings that were threatening to consume him.

There was no longer any need to deny what the emotion was and there was no way in hell he could ignore its existence. He'd tried to fight it, but he knew now that he'd been waging a losing battle. He'd fallen in love with Megan.

Now, all he had to do was figure out what he was going to do about it.

# Chapter 7

Lucas leaned against one of the support posts on his back porch gazing up the mountain at the lights coming from the Bennett cabin. After running out of Megan's place this morning like a tail-tucked dog, he'd spent the entire day in his workshop, thinking of nothing but the fact that he'd fallen in love with her.

But what was he going to do about it? What *could* he do about it?

He wasn't even sure how she felt about him. He knew she cared about him. That much he knew for certain. Megan wasn't the type to make love with him if she didn't. But did she love him?

Lucas was pretty sure she did. Of course, he'd thought his late wife loved him as much as he'd loved her, too. In hindsight, he wasn't sure that had been the case.

Oh, he was sure Sue Ellen loved him as much as she was capable of loving. But he knew now that their marriage had been far from perfect.

As he continued to stare at the little cabin up the mountain, something Megan had told him this morning kept coming back to haunt him. Even though her parents loved her, they'd still put their vacation plans ahead of her during the holidays. That's why she'd said she intended to spend every Christmas making sure her husband and kids knew they were the most important things in her life.

His gut tightened. It was crazy, considering the short time they'd known each other. But he wanted to be that man and he wanted those kids to be theirs.

Unfortunately, there were other things to consider besides the issue of loving each other. Her life was in Illinois and his was here on Whisper Mountain. She seemed to like it here, but she was only visiting. Could she be happy living here all the time?

Lucas shook his head. He didn't have any more answers now than he had when he'd left her cabin this morning. But there was one thing for certain. He had to see her again. Even if it was only to tell her goodbye.

* * *

Giving up all pretense of reading, Megan turned off the lamp beside the couch and drew her knees up to wrap her arms around them. Staring at the burning logs in the fireplace, she decided it was time to face facts. Lucas wasn't going to return today or any other.

Tears threatened for at least the hundredth time since he'd walked out this morning. Apparently her judgment where men were concerned was just as faulty as it had been six months ago. She'd been wrong about Nathan Kennedy, and now, it appeared she'd been wrong about Lucas as well.

Megan impatiently wiped her eyes. She'd spent the entire day wondering if Lucas had left because of something she'd said or if he'd decided that last night was a mistake and he just wanted to distance himself from the situation entirely. He certainly hadn't been able to get out of the cabin fast enough this morning. And it hadn't been lost on her that he failed to say he'd be back.

Her heart felt as if it was breaking into a thousand pieces as she realized how much Lucas had come to mean to her in such a short time. She'd never felt this way about any other man and she knew for certain that she would never, as long as she lived, get over loving him.

It would definitely be in her best interest to leave Whisper Mountain first thing tomorrow morning. That way she wouldn't run the risk of seeing him again and end up torturing herself over things that could never be.

"Megan? Are you awake?"

She jumped at the sudden knocking on the door. "Go away, Lucas," she called.

Even though she loved him with all her heart, at the moment, he was the last person she wanted to see. He'd take one look at her and know that she'd fallen in love with him. And she had more pride than to let him see how foolish she'd been.

"Megan, what's wrong?"

"Nothing. Just go away."

"Like hell," he shouted. "You've got two choices, honey. You either open this door or I kick it in."

"You wouldn't dare."

"Watch me." From the sound of his voice, she had no doubt he meant what he said.

Walking over, she threw the door open. "What do you want, Lucas?"

"Are you all right?" He walked past her without being asked to come inside. "Why didn't you want to see me?"

"I just didn't," she said, closing the door before all the heat inside the cabin escaped. She took a deep breath before she turned to face him. "Was there a reason you stopped by?"

"We need to talk," he said, removing his coat as if he intended to stay a while. He took something from the pocket, then hung the jacket on the coatrack.

She shook her head. "Maybe tomorrow. I'm really tired and—"

"You've been crying," he said, walking over to her. Before she could stop him, he wrapped his arms around her and held her close. "What's wrong, honey?"

"N-nothing." She tried to escape his warm embrace before she made a fool of herself by sobbing uncontrollably.

"Yes, there is." He led her over to the couch, sat down, then pulled her onto his lap. When she tried to get up, he held her firmly against him. "Come on, Megan. Talk to me."

She searched for something to tell him other than the truth. "I've been thinking…about Grandpa."

"I don't think so," he said, shaking his head. He wiped a tear from her cheek with the pad of his thumb and his gentle touch was almost her undoing. "You want to know what I think?"

"No."

"I think you've been crying because of me," he

said gently. "I think you were hurt by the way I acted this morning."

His low voice sent tremors coursing through her, but she tried her best to ignore them. "Not even... close," she lied. Holding back her tears was becoming increasingly more difficult with each passing second.

"That's debatable, honey." Another tear made its way down her cheek. He kissed it away. "I'm going to tell you a story, Megan. And I want you to promise that you'll hear me out before you say anything."

"Whatever." Maybe if he had his say, he'd leave and she could fall apart in private.

"A few days ago, I was working late in my woodshop and noticed smoke coming from my old friend, Sam Bennett's cabin. When I went to investigate what was going on, I walked out of the woods to find the most beautiful blonde I'd ever seen screaming her head off." He chuckled. "Once I got her to quit trying to wake up every bear on Whisper Mountain, I found out she was Sam's granddaughter."

He thought she was beautiful?

She bit her lower lip to keep it from trembling. It probably didn't mean anything more than he was trying to make her feel better. "Will you please get on with it so you can leave?"

"Don't rush me, honey," he said, kissing her forehead. "Anyway, I decided that Sam would want me to watch out for his granddaughter while she stayed at the cabin."

He'd only been seeing her out of respect for her grandfather. Her heart felt as if it shattered all over again.

"Please…I'd rather not…hear anymore," she said, hating that her voice trembled uncontrollably.

"But this is the best part, honey." He smoothed his large hand over her back in a soothing manner. "When I discovered how much she missed Sam, and that she'd come to the mountains because it was a way she could feel close to him, I decided to help her through her first holidays without him."

"I…didn't even realize until yesterday…that's the reason I came here," she admitted.

"I know, honey." He pulled her closer. "But something happened between helping her find a Christmas tree and taking her to the Harmony Falls party." When she remained silent, he asked, "Do you want to know what happened?"

"I—I'm not sure," she said, wishing he would

hurry and get this over with before she broke down completely.

"Look at me, Megan."

"No." If she did, she wasn't certain she'd be able to keep her composure intact. It was slipping terribly as it was.

He tilted her chin with his thumb until her gaze met his and her heart skipped a beat at the emotion she saw in the depths of his dark brown eyes. "I fell in love with Sam's wonderful granddaughter."

Megan was sure her heart stopped completely. "You did?"

His smile took her breath away. "I sure did."

"Oh, Lucas, I love you, too," she said, throwing her arms around his shoulders. "So very much."

He kissed her with a tenderness that made her head spin. "But the story doesn't end there, honey."

Smiling through her tears, she asked, "What happens next?"

"That depends on Sam's granddaughter." He handed her the object he'd removed from his coat pocket. It was a small burlap wrapped box. "But first, I'd like for her to open this."

Megan's fingers trembled as she slipped the red ribbon from the burlap, then unwrapped it. When she opened the lid, she removed a tiny cradle. "Oh, Lucas, it's precious. Did you make it?"

He nodded. "After I left here this morning, I spent the rest of the day in my workshop. It's where I do my best thinking."

"But what is it's significance to the rest of your story," she asked as she ran her fingers over the tiny ornament.

"I'm hoping Sam's granddaughter will agree to be my wife," he said, his voice hoarse. "And if she does, I intend to build her a full-size cradle to rock our babies to sleep."

Tears flowed down Megan's cheeks and she couldn't have found her voice if her life depended on it.

He dug a bandana handkerchief from his hip pocket and wiped the moisture from her face. "I'm hoping those tears are happy." When she nodded, he gave her a grin that curled her toes. "I didn't expect to find you, honey. But now that I have you, I don't ever intend to let you go. Will you marry me, Megan, and let me make a cradle to rock our babies in?"

"Y-yes," she said, happier than she'd ever been in her entire life. "I love you more than you'll ever know, Lucas McCabe."

"And I love you, honey."

As he held her close, she asked, "Are we going to live in your cabin or mine?"

"Do you think you'll be happy living here in the mountains, Megan?"

She sat up to cup his lean cheeks in her hands. "I love it here. I don't want to live anywhere else. I'll try to find a job in Pigeon Forge or Gatlinburg. But if I can't, I'll be more than content to stay at home and rock babies in that cradle you're going to make me."

His smile warmed the darkest corners of her soul. "Do you want to wait to get married until after your folks get back from Central America?"

Nodding, she smiled. "Maybe it will inspire them to do the same."

"Honey, I must have missed something," he said, looking extremely confused. "You want your parents to renew their vows?"

She couldn't help it, she laughed out loud. "If you'll remember, I told you my parents are pretty unconventional." When he nodded, she shrugged. "They've been completely committed to each other for almost thirty years, but they never felt the need to get married."

He looked a little surprised and she was sure that as traditional as he was about everything else, he'd naturally assume that everyone's parents were married. "But you're okay with us getting married?" he asked.

"Absolutely." She almost laughed at the relieved expression on his handsome face. "I'll have to go back to Springfield to close my apartment and pack, but as soon as I return, we'll start making plans for our wedding." A sudden thought caused her to smile. "I can't wait to see the look on Greta's and Kayla's faces when I meet them in Chicago next week."

"Are they your friends?" he asked, nibbling tiny kisses along the side of her neck.

A shiver coursed up her spine from the delicious sensations racing through her. "We became friends a few days ago when our outgoing flights from O'Hare Airport were cancelled because of a blizzard." His lips on her sensitive skin was making it extremely hard to concentrate. "When we discovered that our returning flights were scheduled to arrive around the same time, we made plans to meet and share our Christmas experiences."

"That's nice." He sounded as if he was more interested in the hollow behind her ear than about her new friends. "But I have a plan of my own."

"Y-you do?" she asked as a tremor of need ran through her.

Cradling her to his wide chest, Lucas stood up and carried her toward the bedroom. "I plan on loving you tonight like I intend to do every night for the rest of our lives."

"I like your plan, big boy," she said, putting her arms around his shoulders.

And to Megan's delight, he put his plan into action and did just that.

# *Epilogue*

Scanning the crowded Admiral's Lounge at O'Hare International Airport, Megan spotted Kayla, Greta and Lilly sitting in an alcove not far from the entrance. "Had you given up on me?" she asked, walking over to join them.

"We were beginning to wonder if you'd missed your flight," Kayla said, smiling.

"Or cut your trip short and flown home earlier than planned," Greta added.

"I don't know what it is about me, flying and the weather," Megan said, laughing as she seated herself at the table across from them. "My flight out of Knoxville was delayed because of a winter storm."

Both women laughed and Megan couldn't help but notice that the overall mood was considerably lighter than it had been when they were stranded over a week ago. "So tell me about your holidays. Did you enjoy your reunion with your friend in St. Croix, Kayla? And how was your visit to Houston, Greta?"

"Uncle Brodie is going to be my new daddy," Lilly announced. Yawning she crawled up on Greta's lap. "We're going to live in a real fort."

"You are?" Megan and Kayla asked in unison. They glanced from the little girl to her mother.

"Is there something you'd like to tell us, Greta?" Kayla asked, grinning.

Positively beaming, Greta nodded as she cradled her sleepy daughter. "My late husband's brother, Brodie, taught me that love is a gift too precious to turn down. We're going to be married as soon as Lilly and I can pack everything and join him in Louisiana. He's a captain in the army and has been assigned to train soldiers at Fort Polk."

"Congratulations," Kayla said, smiling.

Megan nodded. "I'm really happy for you and Lilly." When she noticed that Kayla wore the same radiant expression, she asked, "Is there something *you'd* like to share about your trip to St. Croix,

Kayla? You look like the cat that swallowed the canary."

"Actually, there is," Kayla said, laughing. "My friend didn't even show up. She sent her brother instead." She shook her head. "I didn't realize it, but Karyn must have known I was in love with her brother, Mark, when we were younger and decided to play matchmaker. And it worked. Mark and I are getting married in June after I finish my first year of law school in Oregon. Since he works in D.C., I'm applying to Georgetown for the fall semester."

"Now your best friend will also be your sister-in-law," Megan said. "That's wonderful."

Greta nodded. "I wish you and Mark every happiness." Turning to Megan, she asked, "What about you? Were your holidays happier than you expected?"

"As a matter of fact, they were." Megan couldn't seem to stop grinning.

"Don't keep us in suspense," Greta said, laughing. "Tell us what happened."

"You've met someone, too," Kayla guessed.

Nodding, Megan grinned. "I met this wonderfully pushy man named Lucas who refused to let me feel sorry for myself. He insisted that I had to have a traditional country Christmas and somewhere between tromping through the woods to find a tree and my lopsided attempt at a gingerbread house, we fell in love."

"Are you moving to Tennessee, or is he moving to Illinois?" Greta asked.

"I'm going back to Tennessee as soon as I make arrangements to have my things moved and turn the keys in to my landlord," Megan said happily. "Lucas and I are planning to be married as soon as my parents return from their trip to Costa Rica."

"I'm happy to hear things worked out for you, too, Megan," Kayla said with a smile.

"I'm thrilled for both of you," Greta added. She glanced at her watch. "I'm really sorry that Lilly and I can't stay longer, but it's almost time for our flight."

"Mine, too," Megan said, gathering her purse and carry-on bag.

"I've really enjoyed sharing our Christmas experiences," Kayla said.

"I have, too," Megan agreed wholeheartedly.

"Why don't we exchange addresses?" Greta suggested. "I'd love to stay in touch with both of you."

"That's a marvelous idea." Megan dug through her purse for a pad of paper and pen. "I'll give you the address in Tennessee."

After trading the information and promising to stay in touch, they hugged each other and proceeded to their departure gates. The holidays had turned out better than any of the three women could have possibly imagined. They'd found love, happiness and two very dear friends. And all because they'd each decided to go on a Christmas getaway.

* * * * *

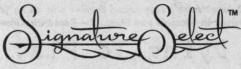
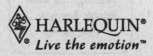

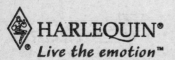

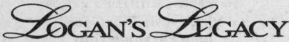

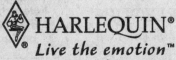

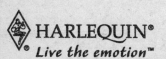

If you enjoyed what you just read,
then we've got an offer you can't resist!

# Take 2 bestselling love stories FREE!

# Plus get a FREE surprise gift!

Clip this page and mail it to Silhouette Reader Service™

**IN U.S.A.**
3010 Walden Ave.
P.O. Box 1867
Buffalo, N.Y. 14240-1867

**IN CANADA**
P.O. Box 609
Fort Erie, Ontario
L2A 5X3

**YES!** Please send me 2 free Silhouette Special Edition® novels and my free
surprise gift. After receiving them, if I don't wish to receive anymore, I can return the
shipping statement marked cancel. If I don't cancel, I will receive 6 brand-new novels
every month, before they're available in stores! In the U.S.A., bill me at the bargain
price of $4.24 plus 25¢ shipping and handling per book and applicable sales tax, if
any*. In Canada, bill me at the bargain price of $4.99 plus 25¢ shipping and handling
per book and applicable taxes**. That's the complete price and a savings of at least
10% off the cover prices—what a great deal! I understand that accepting the 2 free
books and gift places me under no obligation ever to buy any books. I can always
return a shipment and cancel at any time. Even if I never buy another book from
Silhouette, the 2 free books and gift are mine to keep forever.

235 SDN DZ9D
335 SDN DZ9E

| | |
|---|---|
| Name | (PLEASE PRINT) |
| Address | Apt.# |
| City | State/Prov. | Zip/Postal Code |

*Not valid to current Silhouette Special Edition® subscribers.*

*Want to try two free books from another series?*
*Call 1-800-873-8635 or visit www.morefreebooks.com.*

\* Terms and prices subject to change without notice. Sales tax applicable in N.Y.
\*\* Canadian residents will be charged applicable provincial taxes and GST.
All orders subject to approval. Offer limited to one per household.
® are registered trademarks owned and used by the trademark owner and or its licensee.

SPED04R                                    ©2004 Harlequin Enterprises Limited